A Wounded Tigress

MRIDULA MITRA VYAS

KRONOS BOOKS | *Bayeux Arts* INCORPORATED

A wounded tigress
Vyas, Mridula Mitra
© Copyright 1996 Bayeux Arts Incorporated

Published by

Kronos Books/Bayeux Arts Inc.

119 Stratton Cres. S.W.
Calgary, Alberta, Canada T3H 1T7

Spantech House
Lagham Road, South Godstone,
Surrey RH9 8HB, U.K.

P.O. Box 586
1 Holway Point,
Machias, Maine 04654, U.S.A.

Canadian Cataloguing in Publication Data

Vyas, Mridula Mitra.
A wounded tigress

ISBN 1-896209-42-4
I. Title
PS3572.Y37W68 1996   813'.54   C96-910761-7

Price US$ 14.95

Printed in Great Britain by The Ipswich Book Company, Suffolk.

To my parents,
Indu Bhushan Mitra and Shubha Mitra,
for giving me life, unconditional love
and the liberty to express myself.

ACKNOWLEDGEMENTS

My heartfelt thanks to my parents, my sister, Mamata Roy and my brother-in-law, Ranen Roy of Bombay, and my very dear friend, Irma Chatterjee Thakkar of Washington, D.C., whose relentless help and encouragement gave me the energy and inspiration to make this book a reality.

Special thanks to Dr. Kana Mitra, a teacher of philosophy; to my friend and former colleague, Ray Fowler, and his wife Sue Fowler.

I owe my gratitude to all of them for taking the time to read my manuscript and offer me their unbiased comments. Lastly, I must thank my friend and colleague, Allen Kann, who took time off his busy schedule to proof read the entire manuscript and offer me some valuable suggestions.

Mridula Mitra Vyas

Contents

The Infidel Sleeps in the Casket — 7

The Owl, Raven and the New Moon — 35

Yours Truly — 65

In The Silence of the Night — 104

Grandpa's Legacies — 134

The Philosopher and the Philanderer — 168

Glossary — 209

THE INFIDEL
SLEEPS IN THE
CASKET

As our white bulky Ambassador jostled along the bend of the river Tapti, we caught our first glimpse of the huge dome shaped green canopy that looked gorgeous from a distance. The cool Tapti breeze carrying soft melody of shehnai approached us like a messenger, saying — you are not too far from your destination. As we drove nearer, the image of the green canopy, built for the occasion on the neatly landscaped lawn of Shaha's palatial bungalow, gradually magnified and the sound of shehnai resonated profoundly in the summer sky. After five hours of an uninterrupted, and needless to say, an exhausting drive through the Ahmedabad-Bombay Highway, I felt suddenly quite zesty at the inviting sights and the sounds from the bridal canopy.

Our greatly relieved chauffeur, after parking the Ambassador outside the canopy, dragged himself out and stretched out his dark, lanky limbs with a few lazy, loud yawns. While the rest of us quickly tidied our dishevelled hair, then glancing in the mirror, hoping it would assure us of a presentable appearance, we followed the groom in a procession. Along with two other cars that followed us, also both Ambassadors, were about to burst from the seams as we were in all twenty of us. I was with the groom and his immediate family who decided to travel by road. The rest of the wedding guests from the groom's side took the train. They actually reserved a whole compartment that left

Viramgam early in the morning and reached Surat around noon via Ahmedabad.

The green canopy, heavily decorated with garlands of fresh yellow and orange marigold, made an impressive entrance through a tall make-shift gate. The gate was elegantly arched at the top wherein sat the maestro with his accompanist at tabla. From a distance, I could see the bride's father, terribly preoccupied, probably sharing some last minute thoughts with the caterer. As soon as he saw us afar, he left the caterer with his mouth half open as he was just about to offer his valuable suggestions to the bride's father. I watched the bride's father hastening towards us and then smiling ear-to-ear, he cordially escorted us through the make-shift gate into the canopy. In a corner, a makeshift parlor of chintz and chenille was especially arranged for the groom and his entourage. Not too far from the parlor was the nuptial altar, where the religious rituals of the ceremony were to take place that evening. Upon discovering the pomp and grandeur with which the bride's family greeted us into the parlor, it left me spellbound. Forgetting all my etiquette, I must have gawked with awe at all the young ladies delicately draped in pure silk and glittering with precious jewels. They stood meticulously on either side of the long corridor, forming a perfect array, blowing conch shells and sprinkling rose water from a bronze decanter and strewing our path with fresh petals of red roses. Such a majestic gesture of welcome befits only the gods — as though Lord Indra himself had descended from heaven and made pious the ground he treaded on — and not any mortals, certainly not our Naveen. I had never seen a wedding like this one.

"What would you like to drink? May I get you something cold like fruit juice, mango shake, thandai, thumps up, or would you prefer almond sharbat with a dash of saffron... or are you in the mood for something hot... tea or coffee... perhaps? Please, give me the opportunity to serve you," begged the bride's father, as he humbled before Naveen, rubbing his palms together in submission, his eyes glistening with gratitude, for here was in flesh and blood — the perfect match for his little girl, the most suitable boy for his daughter, a charming prince for his princess. After all, Naveen was his savior, the one and only, who could salvage him by unburdening his most crucial of all worldly onus — a daughter of marriageable age. I could see his face lit up a thousand watts at the fulfillment of his moral obligation.

"A glass of water will do," said the groom softly.

"No, no, no! how can that be? I can't offer you plain water. Well, how about a glass of nariel pani then and may I also suggest some sweetmeats to go with it?" the bride's father coaxed. Naveen smiled in affirmation, embarrassed by his would be father-in-law's overly genteel mannerisms. How very flattering! I thought to myself.

The clean shaven, shampooed and mildly perfumed groom, dressed in tasar silk with a row of diamond buttons glittering at the front top opening of his kurta, a fine, white, calico dhoti and footwear of white suede to go with it, our Naveen was groomed to perfection, glowing with youth and vigor. It was hard for me to tell what exactly was going through his mind at the time, but, as I recall, I sensed some nervousness in his voice, "how long do I have to keep this on my head?" Naveen mumbled to one of his entourage, slightly irritated, as he held on to his white nuptial headdress made of Indian cork and tried to prevent it from falling off his head. Just then, I heard the famous maestro from his nahabat pouring his heart into his instrument. Being a student of classical music myself, I quickly recognized the raag which I believe was Basant Bahaar — the raag that creates the mood for vernal jubilation. The maestro was especially invited from Agra to grace the occasion. I heard whispers among some of Shaha's elite guests.

"Did you know you are listening to Khan in the nahabat? Mr.

Shaha must have a refined taste to appreciate such classical music," said one.

"Well, he has money. He can afford to have a refined taste," said another as the gold buttons on his silk kurta sparkled ostentatiously.

"Not necessarily," argued the former, as he took a deep puff of his cigarette through a slim ivory holder, and then as he blew rings of smoke into the air, he continued, "I have seen some moneyed men with such gaudy and glitzy taste, you wouldn't believe."

They chuckled snobbishly.

Poornima looked pristine in her bridal attire that day. She was wearing a red Banarasi with gold border. She had a matching red blouse trimmed with gold paisleys on her sleeves. That morning before bathing, Poornima had applied turmeric paste all over her body as part of the wedding ritual, the paste made from the freshly ground turmeric roots. As the evening glow of the setting sun lavished on Poornima's honey glistened complexion, her face gleamed beneath a veil of vermillion crepe chiffon. Minatee, her favorite cousin, a year older and recently married, like an artist at her best, one who was impeccable with a paint brush between her fingers and deep concentration, adorned Poornima with an exotic makeup of intricate designs drawn on her cheeks and her chin with red and white sandalwood paste. And all that, she did with the flower-like end of a clove picked out of a spice jar from the kitchen. Fine lines of kohl accentuated her almond-like eyes. Her long black wavy hair was tied into a bun with a gajra of fresh jasmine buds encircling it. Ornaments of diamonds, pearls, rubies and jades studded in gold hung exquisitely from her pint sized physique.

The dowry, of course, was given in cash, an amount close to a hundred thousand rupees. The actual transaction of the dowry preceded the wedding ceremony. Then followed the rituals which must have seemed tedious to the young impatient couple.

The old Brahmin priest, with the sacred thread around his shoulder and wrapped in silk shawl, zestfully chanted Sanskrit verses. As he did so, he sprinkled milk, honey, ghee, curd and lord knows what else into the blazing fire of the yajna. The ritual could not have meant much to the bride who had just turned sixteen. The groom sitting across from her looked stealthily at his bride. "Is this my dream-come-true or what?" Naveen murmured to himself. Poornima's grace and beauty stunned Naveen for they were far beyond his imagination, let alone his expectation. As for the bride — it was love at first sight. The Sanskrit mantras, which the old Brahmin priest chanted, pronouncing them as wedded partners for life, reverberated in and around the nuptial canopy. But the bride paid no heed to it, for she was quietly avowing to remain faithfully his, not just in this life alone, but for many lives to come.

They never met before. They were not supposed to meet until the first night after their wedding. Of course, it is a little different today. With the passage of time a lot of the social customs have changed, but by no means are they allowed to have any sort of intimacy before the wedding. Is it necessary that they should? Within the Hindu convention, there is no scope for falling in love before marriage and out after. On close scrutiny, one feels, it almost transcends love. The argument that favors such a concept is a pragmatic one, that, as beautiful as love is, it can also be very fragile and frivolous. Therefore, a sentiment as delicate as love can neither be the ultimate base nor sound enough a beginning for a sacred institution as marriage. It can only stand on the lofty foundation of a moral stricture.

Poornima, like the rest, learned to believe that marriage was a commitment for life here, and after. Over the years she heard the elders in the family talk about marriage as one that began with a sanctimonious and an unsurpassable sense of commitment that was conceptually and deeply embedded into the relationship. A girl such as Poornima, from her early childhood learned that impeccable lesson from the world around her, that a virtuous nurturing of trust, loyalty, and respect gradually perpetuated a sense of understanding, adjustments and appreciations out of which grew love and affection. So, although a Hindu bride and a groom do not necessarily enter into this sacred relationship with a preconceived notion of love, they do realize it in their union and live through it until death do them part.

Just as Poornima knew that the basic elements, like air and fire, have a natural tendency to rise above, and earth and water flow below, she knew that it was just as natural for her to enter into this marriage with as deep a veneration for the commitment itself as for the person she would be committed to. On the other hand, a marriage prospect such as this one engulfed her heart with an aura of romance as pristine and enigmatic as the rainbow at the other end of the sky. Particularly, with the utmost restriction imposed against any sort of romantic involvement or association prior to her marriage, the anticipation grew all the more intense and the longing deepened for a pleasing relationship to blossom on their first night.

"This is one match that is definitely made in heaven as you can see," Shivnath chuckled gleefully as he could not say enough about the match, while chewing on his mouth full of paan. Poornima's parents anxiously listened as Shivnath elaborated on all the minute details of their prospective son-in-law. It was the parents of Poornima and Naveen, burdened with the arduous task of first scanning through the gamut of proposals brought by a professional match maker, Shivnath Chakrabarty. The scanning of the proposals, usually based upon caste, class, family background, education, career, health and appearance of the prospective bride and the groom, also weighed heavily on their character references. So after the two families had sieved out the most favourable proposal through a process of elimination, this was the match that survived the rigors of the scanning and then after crossing one last hurdle of an astrological scrutiny, the two families negotiated on more mundane matters like dowry, jewelry, clothing, dining, entertaining and other miscellaneous expenses.

"One would be foolish to turn down such a match," Shivnath reiterated, eager to earn his fee for all the time and effort put into it, and then get on with some more match making for the sons and daughters of many other anxious parents. It had been a busy season for Shivnath. So busy that he had no time to even buy himself a new pair of sandals. Ever since the beginning of the summer, he had been dragging his feet in these worn out leather sandals, his cotton dhoti of coarse fabric getting tangled between the torn straps of the sandals every now and then. It irritated Shivnath to no end, specially when he had to walk at least a couple of miles every day, if not more, baked in the sweltering heat and the dust of ruthless summer afternoons, with his only shelter provided by his black, old umbrella. But there was not a moment to waste.

Many anxious parents in town looked forward to seeing Shivnath and so he was always welcome, at all odd hours, with dozens of interesting prospects and proposals, all put down in tiny scribbles, some of them complete with horoscopes to match with, rolled up like a scroll in his cotton bag that hung from his shoulder. Anguished parents whimpered as their daughters reached their late teens, for their chances for a suitable boy decreased as the years added to their age. Then, they were left with no alternative but to make do with whatever was available — I mean, compromise. Poornima's parents were rather fortunate for Shivnath, with his expertise in the business of matchmaking had fetched them the perfect match for their daughter.

Poornima's large eyes reddened from the smoke emitting from the blazing fire of the yajna. She fasted all day, while the guests feasted on a scrumptious dinner of pilaf made of the finest Dehradun rice cooked in pure ghee and garnished with saffron and shredded almonds, poorees also fried in pure ghee, curried cauliflower with potato and peas, prawn cutlet, fish korma, paneer kofta, mutton curry, sweet and sour mango chutney with lots of raisins, followed by a deliciously sweet and creamy curd and a variety of homemade sweet delectables for desserts — quite typically a Bengali wedding dinner.

That night Shivnath, a Brahmin by caste, shamelessly gluttoned in a manner one would think it was his last meal. Shivnath voraciously ate a hearty meal at all his clients' wedding and then faithfully carried home some for his family. His family of wife and four children, who lived off a modest means always looked forward to such occasions to satisfy their equally ravenous appetites as Shivnath's. The youngest one, of course, always fell asleep without eating anything, while the older children, determined to stay awake with their mother, dozed off momentarily and woke up with a startle to the sudden bark of a stray dog or at the slightest sound of footsteps outside their window. Until Shivnath finally arrived, soaking from sweat and paan stained mouth, carrying a pile of food packed in large banana leaves and earthen pots. Instantly, their two and a half room flat filled with the exotic aroma of the kind of food that only the very wealthy could afford. The older children would wake up, then slouching from a sudden pang of hunger, sleepily drag themselves to the kitchen, while the wife poured a cold glass of water from an earthen jug for her husband. Shivnath's throat parched from the long walk, the balmy heat and the rich food he ate that night. She would then carry the youngest one still half asleep to the kitchen and serve everyone a brass plate filled with mounds of food. The wife, as usual, helped herself with large morsels from the leftovers in the banana leaves and earthen pots after the children had eaten.

"Now, eat all you can until you can't lift yourself up," Shivnath chuckled heartily, "I brought plenty for all of you, should have seen the look on that cook's face, kept giving me those mean looks, as if I was a beggar, luckily Shaha sahib dropped in right then, held my hands and thanked me for finding him such a jewel of a boy for his daughter and then yelled at one of the servants and ordered him to pack me some food. Had it not been for him you all would be starving tonight. Now, here's one who has the heart of a king. May God bless him with many grandsons."

It pleased Shivnath immensely to see his family gobbling up huge morsels of rice pilaf and mutton curry to their heart's content.

"Did you eat enough or should I bring you two rasgullas?" asked the wife.

"Oh, no, I stuffed myself," Shivnath, stretched out like a log of wood on a charpoi in their veranda assured his wife, gently stroking his ugly, hairy, potbelly with the palm of his right hand as he kept on belching offensively, "you know me, when I sit down to eat, there's no tomorrow." True, Shivnath lived to eat.

Anyway, all Poornima was allowed to have that day was some of that sweet and creamy curd and some fresh summer fruits like mangoes, chikoos and bananas.

By the time Poornima joined her husband in their bridal room, it was past midnight. She was too exhausted to even keep herself from dozing off over his shoulder. The hustle and bustle of the marriage ceremony took its toll on the petite little girl all bundled up in silk and gold and mild perfume. They sat on a large bed of black mahogany carved with interesting gargoyles on the head board and on the bed posts. The bed shimmered from the peacock blue velvet bedspread and embellished with strings of rajani gandha delicately trimmed along the frame of the bed. At the moment, all Poornima could care for was a soft downy pillow to rest her head.

Poornima was the only child of a wealthy diamond merchant and grand daughter of a Bengali immigrant who had domiciled in Surat and had started his career early in life as a diamond cutter. Surat lay along the west coast of India, where the art of cutting diamonds has thrived for ages. The city is almost equidistant between Bombay and Ahmedabad. Poornima's parents had rejected many proposals in the past until this one came along, which seemed just right for their princess. That is what they called her affectionately. Naveen was no ordinary suitor for any princess, either. He was the only son and the youngest of eight siblings. His father was a well established textile merchant in Ahmedabad, a city known for its textile industry, also situated along the west, about three hundred miles north of Bombay. Naveen's father had inherited the business from his father who migrated from Calcutta in the late eighteen hundreds. Unlike his father, Naveen never wanted to join in their family business and made no bones about it. Right from his childhood he had a dream of going to England to study law and become a barrister. He was bright and ambitious. The dowry he had received from the marriage would adequately pay for his passage fare and other miscellaneous expenses that go with it. Naveen was like the shining star in the sky any girl's parents would like to reach for in their dreams.

In the recent past, when Minatee shared with Poornima the amorous experience of her first night, the colour of Poornima's cheeks burst out like a pair of ripe peaches.
"Stop it, I don't want to hear any more."
"Well then, maybe you should become a sadhu," Minatee ridiculed her. Later on, as she would quietly ruminate on all those embarrassing details that Minatee had secretly shared with her, Poornima's face would slowly begin to blush with subdued passion. But tonight she could not care less. She never stayed awake this late ever. As for Naveen, the night was still quite young and thirsty for love. In the still of the night, as the jasmine buds quietly seduced the air with its fragrance and the heart wrenching nahabat mellowed to raag Darbari Kanhara — the raag that befits the mood for deep and solemn love on a quiet moonlit night, Naveen looked at his bride hidden behind her

chiffon veil and felt justly inspired to a night of pure romance. The maestro, a true genius at creating such a spellbinding mood with his enchanting melody, greatly complimented an unforgettable moment as this.

"Poonam!" said Naveen, gently lifting the veil off her face, "tonight, I salute your creator, the one I feel most indebted to. Oh! I can't imagine all that time and patience and artistry lavished on you." It was as if he was exalting an ivory sculpture displayed in a museum.

"I didn't know you were a poet?" Poornima responded.

"I certainly am tonight. The presence of such rare beauty makes me feel like a poet tonight." Then, as he lovingly freed her from the clutches of all her jewelry one by one, he whispered again, "I notice that even the full moon in the sky is envious of my Poonam tonight." Those magic words had their wondrous effect on the bride. The young virgin slowly awakened and wondered if all those words he uttered were a prelude to something very special that she had been yearning for quite some time now. Naveen caged her with his robust arms around her neck, that squashed her cheek like an overripe nectarine against his bare chest and said, "Poonam, can I ask you a question?" The bride trembled like the wings of a hummingbird. Never before was she embraced by a man. Then, as he tenderly let her hair down and put the sweet scented jasmine gajra beside her, he continued, "have I lived up to your expectation or would you have rather married someone else? Tell me, please, and don't toy with my patience tonight." Poornima's voice choked with passion. Naveen cajoled, "don't be so cruel to me. Your silence is torturing me, Poonam! Please, tell me, or should I just assume that I have shattered your dreams?"

She loved the way he called her Poonam. It made her feel so close to him already. Every time she heard her name on his lips, an unbridled desire drove her to belong to him and yet the night had just begun. The shy little girl whispered, "you are my God, how can I judge you?" The rest of the night went by like a fleeting moment woven into a lovers' unforgettable fantasy.

Naveen's parents wanted them to have a son before he left the country. But Poornima was unable to conceive.

"Hope you aren't barren," the mother-in-law pungently poked at her daughter-in-law every now and then. The days swiftly rolled into weeks and months and before long it was time for Naveen to leave his family behind for further education abroad.

The night before Naveen left for England Poornima could not sleep a wink. She tossed and turned and finally woke him up to drag a promise out of him, that upon his graduation, he should return home immediately.

"By leaving me like this," she said, "I feel, as if you are running away with my soul, leaving behind only my corpse! What am I to do with it? Why don't you instead give me some poison and put me to sleep forever."

Naveen's bare chest moistened from Poornima's tears. She wept and pleaded like a child for she dreaded the very thought of being left behind with her in-laws.

"You want me to give you some poison so I can be put away behind bars instead of becoming a bar-at-law from England!" smirked Naveen with his eyes closed, still half asleep. Naveen was her god of love and life — the traditional concept of a husband.

"I rather die as a bride than live to be an old unhappy wife whose tears never dry. Don't you see, what I mean?"

"Yes, I know exactly what you mean, but your ghost will haunt me wherever I am." Naveen delighted in making a mockery of her sentiments.

"Never, even my spirit will never wish you ill. Oh! Naveen, only if you knew how much I care for you." Poornima's breasts heaved with a heavy sigh.

"Let suppose, I do as you tell me to and then I get married and bring home a beautiful bride," Naveen turned towards her with a sudden zest, "you mean to tell me your ghost will never haunt us? not even her! come on now, that's a little too hard to believe." Amused by his own callous humour at Poornima's expense, Naveen chuckled and then rolled over on the other side and began snoring once again. Poornima's eyes slowly brimmed with tears as she pondered in remorse — whatever happened to my Naveen, the one that could not take his eyes off me all night long and would not let me fall asleep until dawn.

I vividly recall that afternoon when Naveen was taking leave of his family before boarding the plane. Poornima hurled herself on the white marble floor in their veranda, tossing and turning as she beat her breast mercilessly.
"Please don't leave me like this. Something tells me you'll never come back." Poornima begged him not to go as she sobbed bitterly. I was dumbfounded. I had never seen any one in such excruciating pain before. My mother rushed to her comfort when our landlady, Poornima's mother-in-law retorted, "what do you have to offer to my son that he should come back to you? You couldn't even bear him a son."

Thus, started Poornima's relentless journey of waiting and yearning for her husband's return. In the meanwhile, Poornima and I became good friends, though our family background varied distinctly. Being the daughter of a wealthy businessman, Poornima grew up in the lap of luxury, but totally devoid of literacy. She came from a conservative background that taught her to cling to all her traditions blindly. I came from a family that worshipped erudition. My family would vehemently oppose any belief borne out of ignorance and hence the disparity between us.

Since, I was not related to her in any way and only a year older than her, she found a companion in me that she could comfortably confide in. In the summer holidays, during the long drawn afternoons when all the elders in the house retired for an afternoon nap right after a heavy meal, Poornima and I impishly disappeared for hours together. We would be on the terrace of our bungalow sharing our innermost thoughts and feelings. As Poornima was still quite innocent and her heart filled with an insatiable love for her husband, I could see how all her hopes entwined with the thought of her one and only — Naveen. Her love, though vibrant with energy, found little or no expression at all that could touch Naveen's heart. As young as I was, I could not yet tolerate this handicap in her that muted their relationship, a relationship already distanced by his ambition.

So I volunteered to write on her behalf long and passionate love letters to Naveen. We picked the terrace of our bungalow, a part of which fell under a cool and shady jamun tree as the most favorable venue for our newfound venture. One afternoon Poornima showed up with a fountain pen, a bottle of ink, and a rose scented letter pad. I rushed in moments later with a bottle of pickled mangoes to snack on and a novel. Poornima curiously pointed at the writings on the jacket of the book and asked me to read it to her.

"Letter from Peking, by Pearl Buck", I hurried through and then quietly murmured to her, "Listen, I've a clever plan for you. We'll copy some of the most romantic pages from the novel and post it to Naveen. He won't know the difference. That ought to entice him back to you in no time. But you must promise me you'll never tell my parents."

"Tell what?" She asked.

"That I stole the book from their library."

"Why not," Poornima looked puzzled.

"Oh! you don't know my father. If he ever finds out that I've started reading novels, he would get so worried that he would start looking for a doctor or an engineer or some I.A.S. officer and marry me off right away."

"Why, what is so bad about a novel?" Poornima still looked puzzled.

"You don't know, there are some fascinating passages in every novel that are almost out of this world. I don't quite know how to say it or what it does to you, but as you read them you feel like falling in love."

"Oh! now I can see why they are forbidden." The newlywed's face suddenly sparkled with a hidden delight, but then her brows quivered and her eyes slowly dimmed as if in doubt, as she continued, "I don't really know how good of a writer your Pearl Buck is, but I don't think that any writer really knows enough how a wife feels when she is in the arms of her husband. If I were to choose between Lord Krishna and my husband, I would choose my husband without question and you know I am a very religious person."

"Really!!" What could be more convincing than this? I was amazed at what love could do to a girl, when all of a sudden, there appeared from behind like an apparition — my mother, the disciplinarian. That abruptly and quite unpleasantly terminated our venture that afternoon. Nonetheless, that incident prompted my mother to take an action which later became a very significant milestone in Poornima's life, a true blessing in disguise.

Weeks later, after much persuasion, when our landlady was finally convinced that her daughter-in-law does need some schooling to enable her to communicate with her husband, my mother enrolled Poornima in her elementary school. The only reason my mother had to first get her mother-in-law's approval, prior to initiating any such move, was strictly a matter of protocol. There is an unwritten yet rigidly structured hierarchical order within every Indian family, where the mother-in-law plays an extremely vital role in making most of the decisions for the entire family. Interestingly enough, the same woman who plays a subservient role as a daughter-in-law, emerges as the omnipotent and quite often as incorrigibly dominating as a mother-in-law.

I guess, Poornima was well aware of the fact that it was a belated start in her life. So, she started burning the midnight oil. She was just as intelligent as assiduous. Several months later, one evening, I found this special student of my mother ecstatic with joy as she was finally able to scribble down a whole page of her first and much awaited love letter to her husband. To Poornima, it was a mission well accomplished. A couple of days later one evening I saw Poornima presenting my mother with an expensive gold fountain pen along with a handwritten note that said:

GOLD GLITTERS BUT NOT NEARLY
AS BRILLIANTLY AS LITERACY

I found Poornima's eyes oozing with a deep sense of gratitude for my mother. That day, perhaps, for the first time, I felt a great sense of pride in being my mother's daughter.

With one giant stride, Poornima entered into a world enriched with expression. She could now read, write and give vent to all her subdued thoughts. It was as if she finally unshackled a prisoner from within her. Zealously, she wrote to her husband everyday, but before posting her letters, she always wanted me to proofread them. For a novice like her still trying to grapple with the art of writing, I was quite impressed to find how well she expressed herself. They were meant to kindle a husband's desolate heart eloigned from his wife. But, Naveen, unfortunately, seemed absolutely cold towards her for he hardly ever wrote to her. Yet, Poornima neither lost the zeal nor the fervor, nothing could hold her from writing to him. At times, she even condoned his callousness by calling him merely 'a lazy bone'. To this day, I wonder if she really meant it, or was it just a cover-up to the world outside. Then, one winter afternoon, as we were both on the terrace jumping rope and eating spicy, pickled tamarind, one of our favorite midday snacks, the postman walked into the veranda holding out an envelope from overseas. It was a letter from England. Naveen wrote:

My dearest Poonam:
I am coming home. I am coming home to be with you. It's been

such a long time since I held you in my arms. You must think it's cruel of me for not writing to you. I don't blame you. But, I also want you to know that to me you are just a thought away. I have been dreaming of holding you in my arms and watch you blossom with passion. Believe me, at night I close my eyes just to see that sweet dream. I am coming home to hold that dream in my arms. Stay well and take good care of yourself for me. Will you, please?

Your everloving husband.

Naveen

Poornima's god finally listened to her prayers. She was exultant. Tears of joy streamed down her cheeks, like warm drops of rain on a parched desert. Like a little girl ecstatic with joy, she hugged me and kissed me, "I knew my Naveen couldn't live without me." She repeated over and over again. It was such a thrill to watch her, as she let loose her rein that had always held in check all her emotions. For a few precious moments her spirits lit up and I wondered if all her inhibitions and her fears of her in-laws had taken leave of her.

Servants in the Mullick Villa slogged from predawn to well after dusk. They had less than a week to paint, clean and redecorate the entire bungalow. They dusted and rearranged most of the massive old furniture of classic designs that were made of Burma Teak and spread out all the brilliantly colored Indian carpets in every room that had been put away in the storage. They polished all the antiquated silver, bronze and copper accessories and displayed them immaculately in every room. They made several trips to the bazaar bringing home wicker baskets loaded with fresh vegetables, fruits, some fresh water shads, carps, large prawns and a variety of sweetmeats. Naveen's mother carefully prepared the list, for she could not wait to pamper her son with all his favorite food. Finally, the day before Naveen arrived, the servants had a few moments to themselves, so they squatted down under the same jamun tree that hung over their terrace, a part of which spread a canopy of cool shade in their compound, but the quiet afternoon was ruptured by the harsh and repetitious cawing of a raven perched on a high bough. The servants rested awhile smoking bidis and chatting about the soon-to-arrive 'barrister sahib from foren'. With all the hullabaloo in the rest of the Mullick Villa, it was almost like a wedding in the family.

The evening before Naveen arrived, the mother-in-law took Poornima to shopping. As she pointed out to the most expensive sari for her daughter-in-law, she bragged to the shopkeeper, "my barrister son is coming home from foren, you know". Then, pointing to Poornima with an askance, "as you can see my daughter-in-law looks so dark and haggard with crows feet under her eyes, almost pitiful to look at, god forbid, if one of those white mem from foren should turn my son's head giddy, I'll not be able to show my face to the world, we don't yet have an heir to carry on our family name, you know." Poornima felt terribly embarrassed. Only if there was a way she could escape this humiliation. But the mother-in-law took great delight in making her feel just that way.

As the Boeing 707 jumbo jet carrying Naveen in its womb, finally came to a screeching halt through the runway at Santa Cruz Airport, one could probably feel its thunderous vibration in Poornima's heart. It was the most exhilarating moment in her life. Three lingering summers had painfully dragged by. The bitter pangs of separation began soothing its way from the day she received his letter to its final recovery at his arrival today. Tonight, she was not to be the sleepy young girl any more that she was on their first night, all bundled up in six yards of silk and heavy jewelry. At the wake of her adolescence, she had quietly blossomed into a vivacious woman and tonight was to be her night of triumph both as a wife and a lover.

A WOUNDED TIGRESS

That night Naveen seemed a little preoccupied at first which did not go unnoticed. Poornima just finished taking her evening bath. She was still smelling of sandalwood soap. Drops of water trickling down her neck and her bare shoulder glittered like jewels on her soft fair skin. While Naveen lay back in their bed as if lost in reverie, Poornima quickly draped herself in a passion pink voile sari and a low-neck blouse of pink delicate lace to match with it, then snuggled into his arms, unabashed, pining to make love and to be loved. Then as she unbuttoned his silk kurta and fondly slithered her fingers over his wide chest, his broad masculine chin and his fine lips, Poornima seductively drew his attention, "why are you so quiet tonight?"

"You don't want us to be loud and noisy, do you?" Naveen tried to evade her attention.

"I am dying to hear my name on your lips". Poornima flirted leaning over his chest.

"I think you are being a little too dramatic". Naveen griped.

"Why are you so unromantic tonight? Is there anything wrong with me. Am I not sensuous enough for you any more?" She caressed him.

"You are definitely more talkative now, than you ever were." Groaned Naveen.

"Well, I was then a girl, now, I'm a woman as you can see me."

"Yes, I can see that. Your breasts are much fuller and your buttocks more shapely." Naveen's palms clasped against her bare breasts. "Tell me, have you ever set your eyes on any man behind my back?" If there was one thing he would not tolerate in his wife was infidelity.

"Why do you ask this?"

"Because you do look very coquettish."

"Ever since you left, any man I look at, seems to me like a shadow, you're the only one in flesh and blood." Then after a moment's pause she carefully put it to him, "do you know what your mother sometimes calls me, a eunuch, and that hurts me, you know."

"I don't find anything lacking in you", said Naveen, gently rubbing his cheeks against her warm neck.

"Yes, there is... I haven't given you a son, yet."

"Well, in that case, she won't have anything to complain after tonight." Naveen suddenly sparked up with new vigor for procreation, when Poornima stopped him right there and said,

"Not yet, not until you tell me something and tell me honestly, have you been sleeping with another woman there? With one of those white mem, have you? Is it true, that they can mesmerize any man to make love with them? Tell me, is it true?" Poornima intended on being direct. Something stirred inside Naveen as if he was caught off guard. Just like an earth quake — transient yet tangible. But, just as quickly he wiped it off his countenance and painted it with a smile. Then, stealthily he sneaked the question on Poornima, "but, why do you ask that?"

"Because," warned Poornima, "I'll not have any bitch steal my husband from me, and if that ever happens, believe me, I'll turn into a tigress and chew her alive".

"I don't have time to think about such things. I've been studying very hard to earn my degree. I still have a year to go," murmured Naveen as he tried to brush aside any aftermath of the tremor.

"Does that mean you're here only for a while?"

"Well, I'll be here for a couple of months."

"You must take me with you then this time."

"I can't. Not until I finish my studies."

"Then, when can I join you?"

"I'll be back next year."

"What if you don't?"

"You must trust me."

Trust. Just the word she wanted to hear from him. With that one very crucial word, Naveen instantly dispelled any suspicion that might have crept up in Poornima's mind. From then on, the days and the nights of the briefly reunited couple seemed to race against Poornima's will. Then came the final moment once again

— the moment she dreaded most. To say good-bye to Naveen was the most harrowing experience for Poornima. Leaving her parents behind the day after her wedding, was not nearly as painful as this. In fact, the day she joined her husband in Mullick Villa, a sense of bitter-sweet feeling of some sort had overpowered her, which she could not quite understand herself, much less explain it to anyone. It was, perhaps, like a cup, half empty with sorrow for leaving behind her family and yet half filled with joyous anticipation of belonging to that special someone that every girl dreams of.

As Naveen headed for the airport, Poornima stood there in their veranda with a vacant look in her eyes like a hollow sculpture carved in rock. She was determined not to spill her emotions this time and make a spectacle of herself. I had never seen her so placid before. Perhaps, this time she was not as lonesome for she was now sharing and nurturing a part of him. Poornima was carrying Naveen's child. As if he was leaving behind for her an epitome of their love... until next time. This time even the mother-in-law was exceptionally sweet and compassionate to her, since she was now bearing her family heir. Poornima glowed with all the love and attention her mother-in-law generously poured over her although it only lasted briefly. That was again when the two of us stole every opportunity we could get to escape from the eyes of the adults. Quietly, racing on tiptoes to the terrace of our bungalow, we sat ourselves down under a full moon and then I listened with awe as Poornima relived those moments, that she and Naveen had just luxuriated together. It was as lovely as a fairy tale, and I, for one in my raw, impressionable age, just could not help falling in love with the very idea of love.

"Poornima is in labour", I heard my mother whispering to my father. The reason my mother whispered was because I was in the next room. For a young unmarried girl, it is only proper to remain oblivious of such facts of life as marital conjugation. In

fact, had I been ignorant about it, I would be all the more praise-
worthy for being "so pure and innocent" for it is commonly
believed that sheer knowledge to a great extent can and do rob
one of its innocence. Premarital sex is a taboo that pervades our
entire society irrespective of its caste or class. Indians, in general,
hold an aristocratic view about sex which takes the color of piety
in wedlock, and otherwise, an indulgence that behooves only
lower forms of animals. Although, a nonconformist to such a
value is by no means unheard of but such an act is certainly
scorned at as a disgrace to the society.

Anyway, Poornima writhed in labor for eighteen hours before
she gave birth to a girl. In an auspicious moment on the sixth day
of her birth, as Vidhata invisibly inscribed her fate on her forehead — as is commonly believed — Poornima's mother-in-law,
to the contrary, as virulent as she was, turned the occasion into
an inauspicious one. Such a day is usually marked by celebration,
so mother and I decided to visit the family with some gifts for
the baby and the new mother. But, no sooner we set foot in their
drawing room, our landlady came charging in from her puja
room retorting with unabated anger.
"What is it with you all? How can you think of celebrating when
my son is still without an heir?"
"How can you be so prejudiced against your own kind? Besides,
tell me, can there can be any procreation with just either one?"
my mother argued.
"You may talk all you want but what good is it, when it doesn't
do anything to keep up our family name," rebuked our landlady.
"Well! not having a grandson is not the end of the world. Is it?"
my mother tried to reason with her.
"Surely it is for my family." That afternoon there was nothing
that could convince our landlady that a woman's life can be at all
worthwhile if she could not give birth to a son. So, once again
she became quite belligerent with Poornima. But, who could
reason with her that a woman should not in the least be victim-

ized for giving birth to a girl, plus the obvious fact that neither of them have a choice in the matter to which our landlady was not willing to listen. Even if it was plausible enough, why give in to such arguments when there was a sacrificial goat she could hack away as a mother-in-law.

Consequently, the new motherhood brought little comfort, much less any joy to Poornima. Yet, she tenaciously carried on with the drudgeries of life while fervidly nurturing a sweet hope that one day there would be a knock at the door and there he would be standing at the threshold, her barrister husband from England. Her hopes and her dreams kept her alive and well. In those alone, she found her strength and her reason to live.

One afternoon there was a knock at the door. It was the postman. He was carrying a parcel in his hand. It was a beautiful doll with strawberry red hair and sea green eyes. A gift from Papa to little Shubha on her first birthday. The doll was almost as tall as Shubha, as if it was her sibling from across the ocean. Along with it there was also something for Poornima, a letter from Naveen. Her eyes welled up with tears as she read the letter:

My dearest Poonam:
Please don't be disappointed with me for not being able to keep my word. As much as I would like to come home and spend the rest of my life with you and our daughter, I am not able to do so at the moment as I have not been keeping well lately. Nevertheless, I want you to know that you both are always on my mind. I am still planning to come home as soon as I get well. In the meanwhile, take care of our little doll — Shubha and yourself. With tons of love.
Naveen

It broke her heart to know that he was ill. She wished she could be there day and night, by his side, nursing him until he came back to health. Since she could not, she felt so helpless that she had to resort to something, something beyond all temporal or terrestrial power that could impact her husband's health and well being. She had known all her life that, when all else fails, one can always count on the mystical power of the celestial bodies. So, she resorted to vrat. Poornima avowed to fast every Tuesday and Saturday until Naveen recovered from his illness. It was to appease Mars and Saturn, each representing the day respectively, the very same planets that are notoriously known to cause havoc on human lives when enraged.

Despite her steadfast belief in life, Poornima's fate conspired against her. Naveen never recovered from his ailment. A week or so later, one autumn afternoon the family received a telegram from an anonymous, saying that Naveen had suffered from pneumonia and passed away. They were bringing him home. A couple of days later Naveen arrived in a rosewood casket, blissful as ever at his journey's end. Right beside his casket stood his English widow Pamela. Naveen had fallen in love with Pamela and had secretly married her while attending law school in England. They had a three year old son named Charles.

In the eerie light of an autumnal gloam, the two young widows looked pale and ghastly like spirits. As if the sting of their husband's unfaithfulness had its venom suck the very life out of them. It was truly one of life's irony that the stark revelation of Naveen's infidelity and his death thundered simultaneously on both his widows? Perhaps, one will never be able to fully grasp the intensity of the trauma the two women endured then. While seeing little Charles quietly standing beside his father's casket, our landlady lamented, "this must be the fruit of my own karma, I see the burden of all my past sins today, how very strange, today I have a grandson and yet I wish I did not have one."

Many years had elapsed in the meanwhile. It was one October

afternoon, I was passing through an overly crowded downtown area of Calcutta, when purely by chance my eyes fell on a woman. Her face seemed extremely familiar to me. She was standing on a wooden platform with a microphone in her hand speaking to a crowd of no less than a couple of thousands. They were mostly women from all walks of life. For a while, as my car schlepped through the crowd, I kept taxing my memory, when suddenly it all flashed before me. It was like an old painting that I had long lost, and then as if out of the blue it surfaced from under a pile of knickknacks when I was not even looking for it; that was when it also dawned on me that the impression of that picture had really never lost its mark on my mind. I asked my chauffeur to take me back to the spot where the rally was being held.

To be in the streets of Calcutta — a hive that hums with life and energy of its own, to be able to witness the nerve and sinew slit open through which flows the lifeblood of an urban culture — is a breathtaking experience. Amidst the filth and squalor, the choking crowd and the clamour, you could actually feel the heartbeat of the city throbbing palpably in the streets. The public meetings and the public speeches, the processions and the picketing, and then the celebrations of anniversaries of great men and great events spread all over the labyrinthine feature of the city like measles, were all a part of the daily scenario, which offered a constant reminder to an observer such as myself, (of course, only after I had recovered from an initial numbness caused by the shock), that despite the physical decadence, the city was not brain dead. On the contrary, every faculty of the human mind was seen and felt at its sharpest in the otherwise wretched and despicable state of affair. They were the twentieth century coliseum where one could witness the spontaneous and heroic battles of political, social, cultural and artistic awareness and upheavals fought vehemently and at all cost. The book fares on the streets, the roadside artists, and the open-air concerts drew the attention of the multitudes. Not to mention, its subway, probably the only one in the world that has its walls come alive with large and exotic paintings, which at a sweeping glance, give the onlooker an impression of a gallery of fine arts. Haggard looking little tea shops by the wayside, steaming with heated dialogues and debates over any and every topic under the sun ranging from antiquity to medieval to contemporary issues — like the Athenians of the ancient — are ever vigilant to every human cause. Then, there was this spectacular conglomeration of traffic, one of the widest varieties of vehicles that could rarely be seen elsewhere. As my white Maruti approached the rally at a snail's pace, I instantly became a part of that faceless crowd.

That day, Poornima's presence formed the nucleus of that crowd. She had aged quite gracefully. I believe she was speaking on the ROLE OF MODERN WOMAN — her plea to the modern woman was to find her own identity. To be aware of her rights and her duties; and to be cognizant of her strength and her weaknesses and so on and so forth. I asked my chauffeur if he knew what her name was. He answered me with a question, "are you asking about Poornima Mullick? She could be our next mayor. Madam, you must have come from abroad, there's hardly anyone who doesn't know her name today." Quite embarrassingly, I murmured to myself, "yes, I've been away from home for too long, maybe that's why I don't know the woman that everybody knows. I only knew the girl she was." Unlike the rest of her audience, I could hardly pay any attention to what she was saying. Just the sheer power in her voice had mesmerized me. Is she the same girl years ago who knew only how to love and yearn and beg and weep? What transpired her to rise to this stature today? My mind was caught in a puzzle. As she finished speaking, I rushed out of my car and made my way through the crowd to get as close to her as I could. A couple of times I saw her eyes meet mine and yet went unnoticed. For a moment I wondered if I could ever gain her attention and take her back to the past we both shared together once. She seemed so distant from that past. Then, as she was unmindfully passing me by, I could not hold myself any longer. I stopped her abruptly and asked her, "Poornima, do you remember me? I am Nupur, years ago we lived upstairs in your Mullick Villa. If you remember, you came to Mullick Villa as a bride and then we became friends." I watched while Poornima's mind went fleeting back twenty five years and then as she gazed at me, I saw her eyes suddenly beam with wonder. She screamed excitedly, "Nipu!" (That was my nickname and I was thrilled to see her still remember it). "Oh! How can I forget you? Where have you been all these years? We have been out of touch almost a life time, haven't we?" Then she quickly turned to her side and pointed to a young lady who was standing right next to her. She was tall like her father. Poornima asked me, "do you recognize her, my daughter, Shubha?" and then with great pride she continued, "Shubha graduated from the National School of Law at Bangalore. She's soon leaving for England for further studies." Just then I felt a sharp pang of a bitter memory that was tucked away somewhere come alive. And yet, at the same time I was deeply moved by an overpowering sense of joy and pride for the two women. It was as if the two of them had rebelled against all odds in life and triumphed so marvelously.

That afternoon Poornima insisted that I should join her over tea. I found the invitation too tempting to resist. So we sat under a palm tree outside her suburban home and spent all evening picking up the fragments of our lives and sharing it with each other. Poornima gloomily reminisced as I listened. After Naveen's funeral she took little Shubha, and went to live with her parents. There was a lot of pain, she said, but she had also unearthed a reservoir of strength which she had never known before. From then on she refused to turn back on her life. For the first time, she realized, she knew precisely what she wanted to make of her life. So she went back to school and continued until she completed her Masters in Social Welfare. Then she moved to Calcutta, home of her ancestors, where she began her career by visiting the orphanages and the shelters, the homes of the destitute and the downtrodden. Seeing them in pain, she realized, she was not alone. From there on she just moved on dedicated to her cause.

"Oh! life is such an irony," she said with a sigh, "if you know what I mean. It's simply inconceivable, that sheer pain and misery that you might think would break you, can really bring about such herculean energy and faith in you. I've come to realize, that a hedonistic approach towards life, in fact, can be very detrimental to your inner growth." She continued as her eyes tried to grapple with something from far beyond. "I'll tell you this Nipu, life has taught me some valuable lessons. You know, there's a lot of myth and illusion in our mind about security," she paused, looked me in the eye and then with added emphasis, continued, "security lies in your own strength and faith in yourself and that is what keeps you alive and going." I could have listened to her all night.

While she did most of the talking, my mind occasionally meandered through those dark avenues far behind in her life. It amazed me, that she carried no trace of that young girl in her who used to be so gullible and so very pitiable. "Oh! I must tell you", Poornima distracted me, the tone in her voice suddenly changed, "the day I heard in the news that Pearl Buck passed away, believe it or not, I had you on my mind all day long, just reminiscing." Soon, her eyes flooded with old memories. I could see them in her tears. I wanted to ask her, "Poornima! tell me, how does it feel today to be envied and not pitied?" Instead, I just reached for her hands and held them tightly in my hands. I suppose, I was speechless with adoration.

THE
OWL, RAVEN
AND THE
NEW MOON

An owl perched atop a neem tree in their backyard hooted all night long. Right then the old aunt had a hunch. She just knew that Megha had to be the bearer of some ill omen. As if that was not enough, the next day at the crack of dawn as she opened her eyes, the first thing she saw was a raven sitting on their fence and cawing. "Shanti Shanti," the eighty five year old widow mumbled to herself as she tried to chase the inauspicious bird away. Its presence had defiled the atmosphere in and around the house, so, Girija had to sprinkle gangajal all over the house, and as she did so, she mumbled again, "shanti shanti". Ganga flows pure and pristine and according to Hindu mythology that delineates the birth of the river, she is the mother of all rivers and is one of the greatest expiators since the beginning of time.

The story goes that the ancestors of King Bhagirath, who, once enraged Kapil muni, were consequently turned to ashes by his curse. When King Bhagirath learned about it, he began to meditate and it was later revealed to him that if he could bring river Mandakini from heaven, then, by her very touch, from the ashes of the cursed would resurrect his ancestors. So, upon King Bhagirath's request, river Mandakini descended to earth and acquired the name of Ganga. Today Ganga emerges from Gomukhi in the Himalayas and flows across north to east of India through cities like Badrinath, Rishikesh, Hardwar,

Farrukhabad, Kannauj, Kanpur, Allahabad, Banaras, Patna, Bhagalpur and then enters into Bangladesh, merges with Brahmaputra where it acquires the name of Padma and finally merges into the Bay of Bengal.

Girija had her gangajal bottled and stored next to the alter where she placed all her icons of the Hindu deities.

"I know, I should not open my mouth," the disgruntled widow had to yet open her mouth before it was too late, "after all, you both are from big cities, and in these modern days nobody likes to listen to an old, illiterate, village woman like myself, but let me tell you, I have seen a lot more in my days than you can ever imagine..." "Oh! Girija aunty, will you stop beating around the bush and get to the point," Milan had to raise his voice. He was no stranger to her idiosyncrasies. She loved to dwell on her puny stories and petty details and according to Milan they were of poor taste and showed little interest in them, whatsoever.

"You always catch me at the wrong time, anyway, go on, what's bothering you now?" Said Milan, somewhat irritated as he was rushing to get his luggage together. Megha had packed too many pieces of luggage. If it were up to her, she would have probably carried her bridal cupboard along with her. They were on their way to the Temple of Khajuraho, a haven for honeymooners. If they missed that train, there was not another one until the next day.

"Where's everyone?" Milan yelled at the servants. "A bunch of idlers, absolutely good for nothing. I can't get any help around here when I need it. They must be killing flies at the paan shop, chewing paan, and puffing away bidis."

"Now, now, don't be impatient," the old widow scolded her nephew, "you've always been that way, ever since you were a lit-tle boy. I want you to sit down and listen to me calmly."

"Listen to what?" Milan looked at his aunt with annoyance.

"The owl!" the octogenarian had a strange way with words.

"What are you talking about, what about the owl?" Milan's

patience was wearing thin. His bashful bride stood behind the door quietly smiling as she listened to the two of them trying to communicate, rather, at the lack of it. The two of them were worlds apart in their beliefs and never understood one another. Yet, Megha thought to herself, there was so much love and affection between them and most of all tolerance which is so important in any relationship.

Milan had lost both his parents in a car accident while they were on their way to Mt. Abu to spend their summer holidays. Three year old Milan, sleeping on the back seat of their car survived miraculously. Ever since then Girija parented him like her very own. Her attachment for Milan had always been so strong that it had been very hard for her to let go of him, even to this day, as Milan and Megha were on their way to their honeymoon.

"Didn't you hear the owl hooting all night long?"

Milan was about to hit the roof but managed to keep his composure. "No, I didn't, I was too tired to keep awake and listen to your owl hooting." Milan lied.

They were wide awake and for a pretty good reason too. It was not even a week they were married. Though Milan seemed a little piqued, he was actually quite amused by her remark. He thought to himself as he hastily fastened the zipper and buckled his last piece of luggage: the old woman must be really out of her mind to think we had nothing better to do than to lie quietly and listen to the owl hooting.

"Anyway, are you finished?" Milan hurriedly glanced at his gold wristwatch, a wedding gift from his well to do father-in-law.

"No" She replied.

"Now, what?" he snapped.

"Well, this morning as I opened my eyes, the first thing I see is... guess, what!"

"Please, don't waste my time any more, Girija aunty. Tell me, what is it?" Milan still determined to keep his composure.

"A raven sitting on our fence, facing our house and cawing!!"

She gave the final touch to her scenario.

"So?" Milan looked exasperated.

"Don't you get it? Besides, tonight is amavash. No one in their right mind will travel today, especially newly weds like you both. You should not be starting a new life with an ill omen following you like a dark shadow."

The old widow from the nineteenth century just could not fathom how her nephew could be so blind about it. She had just depicted a perfect scenario with all the signs and signals of an ill omen that was about to befall them. After all, how modern can one be? "Girija aunty, you know very well, you can't make me believe in all those old wives' tales of yours. Still, you don't quit. You go on and on and on. We'll be just fine. Trust me." Milan, without paying any heed to Girija's premonitions, hastily ran through a list of last-minute instructions. "Oh! and that reminds me; don't worry about us if we're a day or two late. We might just fall in love with the place and decide to stay a little longer than we plan to right now. Anyway, one of us will call you if there's a change in our plan. Now, I've told the servants to take good care of you and do exactly as you tell them. Kaloo will bring you fresh fruits and vegetables from the market every morning and Raanu will grind all your masalas for you." Milan was always very attentive to all her likes and dislikes. He turned to Megha as he spoke, "you know, my Girija aunty doesn't like to refrigerate her food or use any sort of processed and packaged spices in her cooking. She has to have everything absolutely fresh. Now, is there anything else I need to take care of while I am here?" Milan looked preoccupied. A brief silence followed. "Well, in that case, may we ask for your blessings before we leave?" The newlyweds bowed down and touched Girija's feet, the traditional gesture of paying reverence to the elderly. The widow murmured, "Shiva, Shiva" as she blessed them, and then as she wiped the haze of her bifocals and her bleary eyes with the corner of her white cotton sari, she advised the bride whom she treated like her own daughter-in-law, "Now, I want you to take

A WOUNDED TIGRESS

good care of my nephew, do you hear me? He's all I have."
Megha obediently nodded her head, and then as the chauffeur
sped away for the railway station, the couple waved at their
Girija aunty from the back seat of their little Fiat. The lonesome
widow waved back at them from the veranda until the black Fiat
slowly diminished into the distance and then disappeared beyond
her sight.

Girija, now, had the whole house to herself and all those long
hours that dragged through the day. She felt restless. So, she
busied herself bossing around, over petty matters, with each and
everyone that crossed her path. She squabbled with all the servants in the house. One afternoon, she ordered the gardener to
come and see her immediately and then told him off — that the
garden looked pitiful with all sorts of English flowers and none
of the ones that she needed for her puja everyday. "Not a single
marigold to offer to my gods! Do you want me to do my puja
with ashes and mud?" Then, one early morning, she charged the
milkmaid, "you've been adding more and more water to the milk
lately; soon it'll be all water and very little milk. Your mother,
unlike you, was always very faithful to her customers, you know."
Another day, after scrutinizing through a bundle of laundered
clothes which the launderer had just delivered, Girija hurled it
back at his face and told him to get lost. "Don't show your face
ever again until you learn to remove the paan stains from my
white saris." Believe it or not, she even yelled at the chauffeur,
one afternoon, who was always such a gentleman, and had
slammed the door on his face for no apparent reason. She spared
none, not even the neighbor's children for being loud and noisy
while playing in the street as she took her afternoon nap.

Girija never had any children of her own. She had three miscar-
riages and, of course, according to her they were all because of a
jealous old witch who lived in the same village. The witch was
supposedly jealous of Girija's beauty and had cast a spell that
would disable her from bearing any heir to her husband. Then,

at twenty-one she lost her husband. She could never remember her wedding night. She dozed off in her father's lap right in the middle of the wedding ceremony which took place in the middle of the night. The lagna muhrat for Girija's wedding happened to fall at an odd hour — the auspicious moment, that is. For Hindus, the time for performing religious ceremonies are not picked at random merely to one's convenience, but strictly according to the Hindu calendar, normally referred to and suggested by the priest. Quite understandably, the bride who fell asleep in her father's lap was nine years old then. It was three quarters of a century ago. Ever since she lost her husband, Girija lived the life of an ideal Hindu widow adhering to every stringent norm of widowhood, including shaving off her head, restricting herself to one vegetarian meal a day and, of course, chastity for the rest of her life. In her days, total abstinence used to be the golden motto of Hindu widowhood, so, the question of remarriage simply never arose.

At the other end of the spectrum were the young honeymooners. Milan and Megha found the Hindu classical pantheon of Khajuraho a breathtaking experience. Together, they marvelled at the epics of love and war so eloquently depicted in stone. There were carvings vibrant with virile Gods in cosmic evolution, demons in revolt, and mortals engrossed in ardent love and consummate passion.

A myth recalls that Chandra, the legendary father of the Chandella dynasty, once saw a daughter of a priest of Banaras named Hemavati of unrivalled beauty, bathing in the moonlit lake of Rati and so he descended to earth and embraced her. Before leaving, Chandra told Hemavati that she had just conceived and would in due course give birth to the founder of a valiant dynasty. A son was born, and one of his descendants performed a sacrifice in the town of Khajuravahaka. History records that around 925 A.D., a reigning prince of the Chandella dynasty decided to build a temple of Vishnu in his capital at Khajuravahaka. This was the beginning of a period marked by a marvelous architectural feat built in three segments, eastern, western and southern in the central plains of India. To pay homage to the Gods, Surya, Shiva and Vishnu, a total of eighty-five temples were raised, stretching across an area of eight square miles, between the tenth and eleventh century, the golden period of the Chandella dynasty, of which only twenty-two have survived destructions. A few of the temples are dedicated to Buddhism and Jainism as well — bearing testimony to the religious eclecticism of the Chandella kings. The largest of the Jain temples in the eastern segment was dedicated to Parsvanath, one of the twenty-four Tirthankars, fabulously sculpted, including the renowned one of the apsara removing a thorn from her foot.

As they reveled at the panels of cosmic drama in the temples of Khajuraho, they wondered — with what magic could they have chiselled such grace and fluidity into those formidable rocks that emitted with various moods of voluptuous women — reflective, pensive, playful, amorous. Such erotic postures of couples exquisitely sculptured on the exterior of the temples, symbolizing the worldly pleasures that belong only to the outer core of human life and therefore should be renounced once you step into the interior. Another school of thought expounds the historical theory, that during the tenth century in India, an excess of spiritual motivation among people caused a significant decline in the population and therefore to arouse them sensually, shrines of such erotic nature were built. As Milan and Megha quietly walked to the temples, whether through the soft morning glow of a rising sun or through the flamboyantly ruddy sunset, the silhouette of the minarets rising majestically like the Himalayan peaks against a crimson sky held the newlyweds in absolute awe for several days together.

Megha could not have asked for more from life. As a husband

and a lover, Milan, like the gods, had surpassed every dream of Megha. She vividly recalled one rainy afternoon as the two of them were in the mood for a siesta, she lay quietly cuddled into his arms, like a pussycat drowned in thoughts when Milan remarked, "what's the matter? You've something on your mind."

"I was just thinking about us." She sounded blissful, content with life. She threw her arms around Milan, "I was just thinking, if for some reason, Brahma, Vishnu or Shiva from the Heavens descended on earth and offered me three boons of my choice, do you know what I would ask for?"

"Let me think, humm... do they have to be in a certain order?" asked Milan.

"Yes, absolutely."

"Alright then, the first thing you'd ask for is a trip to Switzerland... now, while enjoying the sights and scenes of the Alps... you'd want to conceive a son gifted with his father's charm, naturally", said Milan with a smirk, "and last but not the least, you'd want to write your first novel. I remember, when I first met you, I wanted to know what your greatest wish was. You said you wanted to be a writer some day."

"I'd love to have all of those, but I'm sorry to say... you're wrong." Megha could not wait to tell him what they were.

"What!!! what more... I mean... what better things could you ask for?" Milan exclaimed.

"I'd only ask for my Milan, my Milan and my Milan as my husband for as many lives as I'll ever live," she said.

"Well! in that case, I too will never ask for anyone else as my wife but you," said Milan, mimicking Megha and then with a spark of mischief piercing through his eyes, "lover... may be one or two... here and there... every now and then... but wife... only you."

Megha threw a tantrum like a little girl, ranting and raving, while Milan took the pleasure of appeasing her with kisses and vows of love, one better than the other.

Together, they had seen such beautiful dreams. Whatever happened to those dreams? It was not until years later, one day while Megha was cleaning the dust off her bookshelf when her eyes caught sight of an old album. Within moments, she fleeted into a misty past. As she glanced through those pictures of their honeymoon at Khajuraho, her heart quietly slipped away into reminiscence. All afternoon she sat in her recliner without batting an eyelid, holding on to her dreams lest they should escape again. Mesmerized by those pictures, Megha began to revisit all those bygone days over and over again. With a withered and vacant look on her face that said — everything is lost but not forgotten — Megha recalled all those times when they felt insecure, jealous and possessive of each other's love. They talked nonsense, called each other names, fussed over petty matters, and then ended up having heated arguments over nothing. Until they stopped talking to each other, but, only momentarily. Come bedtime, Milan sweet talked his way into her heart, made love, then exhausted, the two drifted into a sleep. When they woke up, they were ready to mate again like a pair of love birds in the springtime. One of their favorite pastimes was to tease one another over silly matters and laugh over it until tears rolled down their cheeks. On weekends, they would drive to the nearest hill station which was only a few hours away, and then from the top of a hill, call out each other's name and listen to the multiple echoes that resonated the sky. They felt as if they were listening to a voice from far beyond, whispering their names time and again with an eerie charm, in an attempt to endorse their names forever together in the vast expanse. One would think they were worse than children. They were, in all reality, like any other newlyweds, simply feverishly in love with life and youth.

Today, there were no echoes heard. No more laughters rang in the air, not even a call or a whisper stirred the silence, only her heavy sighs and the soft sounds of his footsteps come and go in the dead of night. Love, that she once thought would spring forth immutable joys in their life, now, buried into a distant past. As she wondered how all those delightful days of love and romance froze into the remote, and filled her heart instead with a chilling void, her eyes gradually turned liquid. All those years that she had carefully shelved them in her memories, as if they were each a leaf in a book of poetry. Every time she turned a leaf off her memories, it left her with an inexplicable sense of love and hatred for Milan, both woven so intricately that she could never separate one from the other.

Ever since Milan confessed his infidelity, Megha's life became disenchanted. It had been almost ten years now that she had been spending her nights like a nocturnal creature, just like the one that hooted all night long during the first week of their marriage. She sat by the window and watched inch by inch, moment by moment, the death, that slowly crept into their twelve years of loving, caring and sharing, and then over its carcass, she sat and mourned relentlessly. Milan's extramarital affair ruptured Megha's emotions so ruefully, that it took leave of all her rationality. She ceased to live and merely existed like an old piece of raft that drifted away aimlessly in a sea of time. At times, as grotesque as it may sound, she even doubted her own existence, as if her very sense of being was gradually and perniciously dwindling into a thick haze of unconsciousness. Had it not been for Zohra, her one and only true friend, Megha would not have had her sanity today.

"I want you to do something more worthwhile with your life, Megha. Don't let it waste away on someone who's not worth a moment's thought or a drop of tear." Zohra's anger compounded as she saw her friend each day fall deeper into an abyss of remorse and resignation.
"Had you been married to a man for as long as I have been, you would know how much it hurts," Megha would react.
"True. I never married. But, nonetheless I was madly in love

with someone who turned out to be very much like Milan. You remember him, don't you?" Zohra's voice mellowed. "To this day he is the reason why I can never dream of settling down with anyone else. Let me tell you something," continued Zohra, "though I don't suggest for a moment, that you should simply walk away from this marriage and put it all behind, because I know it's easier said than done, but having lived through pain myself, I also realized that there can be a lot more to life than just pining and lamenting."

"But, don't you think you're trying to escape from something?" Megha questioned.

"Well, Maybe, I am," said Zohra, "but, all I'm saying is one must have a passion in life for something... something other than one where there's always a question of reciprocity, that can give a new direction, a whole new meaning to our existence. If you see what I mean," Zohra cleared her voice again, "any relationship can be fragile because there's always an element of reciprocity — at any level, whether it's social, emotional, platonic or marital, there has to be an absolute synchronization like the trapeze in the circus, which looks smooth on the surface, yet you can't refute its intrinsic element of risk." Zohra spoke like a philosopher, her smooth and sophisticated flow of words leaving a trail of profound thoughts on the listener's mind. She sighed, her eyes still drowned in reflection, "as you know, my sitar is not only my joy and pride but also my greatest solace." She paused again for a moment, looked Megha in the eye and continued, "let me tell you something, the other day at my sitar recital at the National Academy of Music, guess who was in the audience?"

"Must be the Governor or the Prime Minister... the President maybe?" Megha replied.

"No, Yusuf," Zohra's eyes gleamed as she uttered his name. "That evening at the end of my performance there was a standing ovation that lasted for about five minutes. I felt very honored but I felt even greater honor when suddenly out of the blue I saw Yusuf walking towards me to congratulate me personally. I was deeply moved by his gesture. He called me Shama-e-bazm. Just from the way I felt, I knew I could never stop loving him. But then again, that night lying in bed I pondered over life, love and relationship and realized that he was not my only love anymore, since my passion for sitar had rivalled over him. Anyway, enough about me." Zohra was rather abrupt.

"I admire your strength and wisdom, Zohra. Please, find me something that can also make me forget my woes," Megha begged.

"You have to find it within yourself, Megha," Zohra suggested, "only that which you'll find from within yourself will give you the ultimate joy. I know you've always had a passion for writing. Have you given any thought to it?"

"What is there to write? Tell me, what will I write about?" Megha's voice sounded empty.

"Write about yourself, I mean... your innermost thoughts... your feelings... your experience... all that pain you've been enduring for so long... let them seek expression in your words."

"Ha! There's no language that can express even an iota of my pain, Zohra." Once again Megha drooped in self pity.

"That's not true," there was firmness in Zohra's voice, "bitter pain and sufferings have given birth to the finest and the most intense of all human thoughts and emotions. Those are the fountainheads from which sprang the most profound expressions in various forms of art. Take, for example, some of the most fascinating poems, paintings, music, sculptures... it can be anything... a novel or a play. Megha, I want you to stop crying and start living and I know you can do it, and you can do it through your writings. Don't you remember, you were the editor of our school magazine! Also, in our interstate college competition, you were the one who came home with the Best Essayist Award and the other time, remember, The Author of the Year Award from our university! What's the matter with you, Megha, don't they mean anything to you anymore?"

"Not any more," Megha's voice echoed from a deep and despairing hollow within her. It was as if someone had fled with Megha's spirits, leaving behind the burden of her meaningless existence. She was no more the feisty, intelligent and ambitious girl that she used to be during her college and university days.

There was a time when such discourses between the two friends were not so infrequent, for Zohra felt a compelling need to remind Megha of those times, hoping that perhaps some day she would be able to rejuvenate her spirits. But lately Zohra had been so involved with musical tours all over Asia and Europe that she hardly had any time to herself or for Megha. But, every now and then a picture postcard with a few kind words from Venice or Milan or Petersburg or London would stir Megha's emotions, though momentarily. For a while she gazed at those pictures and wondered if she could ever untie the emotional bond of her unhappy marriage and aspire to a new life. Only if she could leave behind forever the ghosts of her past memories and old wounds. The haunting memories of Milan's infidelity, Girija aunty's psychic predictions, the birth of her stillborn baby — all of which have left her with nothing but countless nights of pain and agony.

Zohra's words always had a soothing effect on Megha's wounds. Besides, Zohra was always very eloquent. She had a well of emotions that she could dig in and vent through words that echoed with both energy and sensitivity. Megha tried to recall those thoughts and loved to ruminate over them whenever she felt lonesome. Especially, an account of Zohra's love affair with her music which she enjoyed mulling over from time to time.
"Do you know, Megha, in the dead of night," said Zohra one day, "during monsoon, when it's pouring heavily out there, I'd open my window to let the rain drenched wind play in my room, while I'd hold my sitar close to me and soon I'd be immersed in playing raag Megh-Malhar, (the raag that lends the mood for rain) and then, there I would be in a state of mind, when I'm no

longer fragmented by stray thoughts or feelings or inhibitions of any sort. For once, I'm not numerous fractions of myself chased in different directions by unbridled whims and desires, but one whole entity. As if I've finally attained that pyrrhic victory over my mind, the most unruly part of oneself. At that point, playing that particular raag as best as I can, becomes the nucleus of my very being." She would pause to take a deep breath and then continue, "that's the only time I feel as if I've reached a new height... more like... being on a different plateau, altogether."

Megha, in awe with Zohra's love for music, her transcendental experience with the instrument, as if, waking up from a sweet dream, her voice chimed with serenity, "no wonder, Yusuf plays second fiddle in your life, Zohra. For that matter, who needs a man, when you can reach such a crescendo with your music? I envy you Zohra, I really do, believe me."

"You can do it, too. That was the point I was trying to make the other day when I talked about having a passion for something... if you remember?" Zohra's large pair of eyes lit up with new hope for Megha.

Megha had just dozed off while reading Tagore's collection of short stories. She enjoyed reading them from time to time, as if to quell her thirst from the fountain of inspiration, when life seemed so arid with hopelessness and despair. His writings, so luminous and vibrant with inner power and yet so warm and tender with sensitivity and compassion for women. Megha, like many other women of Bengal, always found solace in reading Tagore.

The loud commotion in the servant's quarter woke her up with a startle. She looked at the clock. It was past midnight. Milan was not home yet. Lately, he had been coming home at all odd hours, sometimes it would be dawn before he got home. These days his goings and comings were all at the fancy of his mistress. The loud screaming of the gardener's wife distracted her again. Megha lay there quietly feeling sorry for her and her children.

The gardener's wife had four little ones with one more on the way. These days the gardener would come home every night dead drunk, then wake his wife up to serve him dinner and then as he would be halfway done with eating, in a sudden fit of rage, he would hurl his dish of rice and curry at her and beat her up until she turned black and blue all over. Every night he found new ground for torturing her. One night it might be for using too much chili powder in the curry, the next night it could be under a false pretext of her infidelity with the cook — a figment of his imagination, of course. Another night it could be something else. To the contrary, it was he who frequented the whorehouse routinely.

Megha lazily rolled on her side, pondered over her own self for a while, as her eyes unmindfully welled up and then a tear or two trickled down quietly. Her thoughts, like a grasshopper hopped on all those lives that touched her life. First Milan, then Esha his mistress, then back to the gardener's wife again, and then her thoughts suddenly took to its wings to the land of the Greeks where Zohra was to perform that weekend. Megha had just received another postcard from Athens that afternoon. Zohra had written to her in Urdu:

> Liye rababko seenese guzarne lagay hai sham-o-sahar jabsay
>   honay lagee hai charcha hamari dur dur tak
> Kuch you samjho rabt hamari iss kadar ki rakeeban kya
>   cheeze ashiq bhi khaak ho jai jalkar.

(Ever since I've started spending my days and nights, holding my stringed instrument close to my heart, people from far away have started talking about us. Our relationship is such that let alone the rivals, it has made even a sweetheart burn to ashes with envy.)

Megha pulled out another postcard, now used as a page mark for another book that she had left off half read. Zohra had written from Petersburg:

> Mai hun be-nawaa be-niyaaz, mera na koi iman, na koi
>   imtiyaz

Nahi maangti duaye Allhasay, na padhti fajrko yaa to zuhr,
Aasar, magreb yaa Ishaaki Namaz, khaak Musalmaan
    hun mai,
Na hun maghrib yaa mashriki, sirf ek fankar, itnahi kafi.
(I have no belongings, no desires, neither any belief nor any discrimination. I don't ask for Allah's blessings nor do I read the
namaz [prayer] of fajr [predawn], zuhr [midday], aasar [predusk],
magreb [twilight] and Ishaa [midnight]. I am not a Muslim. I am
neither from the west nor from the east, just an artist and that's
all about me.)

Megha read those Urdu verses over and over again to see how it
feels, even if it was only for a fleeting moment, to take a flight on
the wings of Zohra's lovely rubaeeyat, to the very edge of her
world where every human thought and spirit, unmasked,
unshackled and laid bare of all its premordial bias and fears,
purged under the fountain of sweet liberation — a true daughter
of nature indeed who had the courage to negate all forms of
indoctrination, of preachings and dogmas that caused people to
judge people by their faith and distanced them from one another
had lost its appeal to her. Instead, Zohra was deeply inspired by
the writings of the nineteenth century transcendentalists, the
Boston Brahmins as they were called, particularly Ralph Waldo
Emerson and Henry David Thoreauu whose philosophy enlightened her. She embraced their idea of true religion as one that
dwells within oneself. Zohra's music had brought her closer to
the human soul full of love and compassion. Megha tried to envision her before a large audience, meditating on her stringed
instrument that would elevate her inner being to another plateau.
Often, when the subject of religion came up, Zohra would gladly
quote Emerson who could not have said more simply than,
'Nothing is at last sacred but the integrity of your own mind.'

She remembered Zohra from her childhood days in Calcutta
where they were neighbors and playmates. Zohra's family had

moved from Lukhnow to Calcutta right after her birth. As Zohra and Megha grew up together, they became such bosom friends that people sometimes mistook them for twins. They even looked alike in many ways and shared all their thoughts and feelings. As they approached adolescence their curiosity grew larger by the day. The two things that fascinated them most were, one — their physical changes that they had begun to experience gradually, and the other — boys. Those were also subjects of immense embarrassment to them. It was as if only they had quietly discovered and were never to be shared with anyone else.

Megha vividly recalled, one early November during the Diwali holidays Zohra rushed into her study and screamed with joy, "Khudaki kasam (swear on God) Megha, you won't tell anyone?"
"Magar, baat kya hai?" (But, what is it?)
Though both Megha and Zohra studied in the convent where the medium of education was English, but quite often, when excited or overjoyed over boys or some such thing, they unpremeditatively spoke in Urdu or Bengali. In their own home each spoke a different language, but as part of their mutual admiration they had decided to learn each other's language. So, Megha learned Urdu and Zohra Bengali.
"No, no, pahele kasam kha" (first swear). Zohra was impatient.
"Thhik hai, thhik hai (ok, ok) kasam." Megha swore.
"I heard khalajan mention my name to ammijan, so I eavesdropped and guess what I heard?"
"What! tell me, tell me." Megha couldn't wait.
"Yusuf is coming home for the holidays....and guess what?"
"Will you stop it... and just tell me what you heard?" Megha had to scold her for trying her patience like this.
"Khalajaan was talking about our betrothal!" Zohra whispered.
"You mean...engagement!" Megha exclaimed.
"Yes, stupid! And then after he gets his degree in Engineering... which is next year... phir hamari shaadi hogi (then we'll get married). Of course, you know, we've been dreaming of this day for

a long time." Zohra and Yusuf fell in love at her sister, Nadiyaa's wedding, when she was eleven and Yusuf sixteen. He said he had never met a girl as beautiful as her. In the last five years they must have written at least a thousand letters to each other and she had saved every single one of his. "Hope this year goes by fast," added Zohra.

"Its only a year, it'll go by just like that." Megha attempted to ease her agony.

"So you think, but not if you look at it as twelve lingering months. Besides, how would you know, you've never fallen in love." Megha thought to herself, if love makes one so impatient then she really doesn't care for it.

"He calls me Zohra-jabeen in his letters," Zohra blushed.

"And what do you call him?" Megha couldn't wait to hear her speak, as she noticed her cheeks suddenly break into two halves of a pomegranate.

"I like to call him my Shahar Yaar. Of course, lately he hasn't written much." The color in her cheeks flushed out as she murmured, "khalajaan was saying these days he's very busy with his college studies."

That day Zohra, in her sweet sixteen, like a mountain brook, light hearted and spontaneous, dancing on her toes as she spoke about her Yusuf, with rainbow in her eyes and radiant with dreams, babbled on. But those dreams disappeared as soon as Yusuf came home with his bride Neesha. Zohra's khalajan seething with rage, humiliation, and disappointment called Yusuf, her only son nang-e-khandan for he had brought home a Hindu girl. Yusuf eloped with Neesha, got married in court and then in fear of being chased by Neesha's parents took shelter in his own home. Alarmed by her daughter-in-law's unorthodox ways, khalajaan griped and groaned to Zohra, "Behaya! na purdah karti hai na kuch (shameless! no veil over her head, nothing of the sort). Zohra, tu dekh lena, iss nafsaaneeko mai gharse nikaalkar hi rahungi (Zohra, you just watch, I'll chase this sensuous coquette out of my house and then rest)."

But, Zohra had totally withdrawn herself and responded to her khalajaan's constant whining rather nonchalantly, "Khalajan, aap mujhe mere haalpe chhor dey to achha. (aunty, it'll be better if you just leave me to myself)."

That was when it first dawned on Zohra that classical music was something that she could dive into and remain immersed as long as she wanted to. She always had a penchant for music, but could never confine herself to long hours of practice behind closed doors. But now her life, like a river, took a different course and she found herself obsessively drawn towards it. Absorbed in the complexity and the richness of those various modes of Indian classical music, she found her reasons to live and live well. In the process, two things happened simultaneously which transformed her inner self. One, her love for music grew enormously and the other, it unlocked before her a new paradigm to life beyond all the sham and the trivia of her every day world.

For the first time she found herself into its depth, practicing for hours together, sometimes late into the night, utterly oblivious to the fact, that it was the same wound inflicted by her beloved, which had quietly settled deep within her, like a sleeping volcano and left her numb on the exterior, veered towards music and then gradually emerging as the medium of her passion that erupted with a vigorous release of emotions.

Thus, she continued for about fifteen or so years under the guidance of her grandfather Ustad Fayyaz Ali Khan, a renowned musician, also settled in Calcutta. Once she mastered all the rigorous norms and the grammer of strumming the instrument from her guru, she became one with it. Her audience felt no dearth of fiery passion that sprang from deep within her, through the vibrant chords of her instrument, and straight into the hearts of millions. In the process, though the pain of her disillusionment left behind scarred memories, but in the meanwhile something else happened to her — she found her solace. In lightening the burden of her heart through her music, she was able to share a sense of exhilaration with her audience. At the same time, if there could be a state of mind between the intensities of love and hate, between smiles and tears, it was in her immersion into the realm of music, where she nestled in absolute bliss. While devoted to classical music, she also finished her masters in linguistics, a year after Megha received her degree in physics.

From early on, Megha was a bright student and did brilliantly in all her academic curriculum. After completing her high school, when it came to selecting her major for her bachelor's degree, it turned into a family predicament. Her parents demanded that she take up science, so she could have a lucrative career and not waste her effort in meddling with literature or arts.

"That sentimental stuff won't get you anywhere, listen to what I say and you'll never regret." Advised Megha's father.

"What's wrong with literature? I've always enjoyed writing and some day I might even become a writer."

"Listen to her," Megha's father had a hearty laugh before he turned to his wife, "are you listening? our daughter is on her way to becoming a writer now." Father's sarcastic pinch hurt Megha's pride.

"Yes, I heard it," replied the mother, as she tilled a moist patch of soil in the middle of her garden with a trowel before she planted the rose bush. Father sat at the other end of the garden under a palm tree in their front lawn, while Megha sat across from him on the steps of their veranda. Then turning to her daughter, "don't be so stubborn, and like your father said if you listen to your parents now, you'll never regret." Mother tried to coax her.

"That's all fine, but tell me why I can't be a writer?" Megha was willing to listen to them, but it would take a lot to convince her for they would have to come up with a sound reasoning.

"Because everybody is not as fortunate as Tagore, Tolstoy or Shakespeare." Argued Dr. Mitra, a graduate from Delhi School of Economics and a especial advisor in the Indian Foreign Service.

"But who said I want to be one of them?" Was her counter argument. "O! I see, so you want to be like one of those thousands of starved and frustrated poets who live their entire lives hoping they will make it one day." Spoke the realist in her father.

"Leave her alone, I say," Megha's mother had a sudden change of heart, "after all, a girl's fate is written in her husband's prospects, if she's fortunate enough, she'll live like a queen."

"Don't be silly," The sheer dullness in her complacence and her ridiculously old fashioned ways of thinking at a time like this annoyed her husband. "As her father, I want to see her do well, especially, when I know she has the brain."

"Well, I don't see much use in all that career business of yours, unless you plan to keep her unmarried all her life." Megha's mother spoke her mind as she saw fit.

"Maybe you should stay out of it and leave this up to me." Dr. Mitra tried not to lose his patience although he found himself getting no where in his pursuit. While he tried to determine what was best for their daughter, neither of the women understood him. "Alright, alright I'll take up science, but I still want to be a writer one day." Megha did not want her parents to quarrel over her. So she yielded to her father without giving up her dream.

"I have no objection to your becoming a writer, but at this point, all I'm saying is, it's much easier to make it in the field of science, mathematics or economics than as a writer."

They met at the University library where Milan was preparing for the I A S examination — a tough challenge for even the most meritorious students. It was in the spring of 1955, a week after the world had lost one of its intellectual giants, Albert Einstein. The famed British physicist Stephen Hawking was a mere boy of thirteen then and the astrophysicist S. Chandrashekhar had not won his nobel prize yet. Megha had completed her B.Sc. in physics and had just enrolled for her masters program when she met him. That afternoon she had just checked out Einstein's The Meaning of Relativity and had hardly gone past the first few words of the book which ran thus: 'The theory of relativity is intimately connected with the theory of space and time,' when Milan got up from the next table, came forward and introduced himself to her. He told her that he had seen her on several occasions and wanted to meet her but never had the opportunity to do so. That he was so impressed with her eulogy on Einstein which she had delivered before a packed auditorium last week, that he was not sure what intrigued him more, whether it was her or the theory of general relativity that she talked about. That day, Megha was so taken with Milan's way with words, his refineness and the culture that exuded in his disposition, that she could not wait for her parents to meet him. It was as though, she had finally emerged from behind a pile of mathematical equations and theories and found something that was even more enigmatic. After that it was only a matter of months, before Megha's parents could meet with Girija aunty and finalize the wedding date, the amount of dowry and other major demands that the girl's parents would have to generally meet with. They were married the following year right after their final exams.

Here, in the Khan household, contrary to orthodox Muslim tradition, where a girl from an elite family should never be seen in public, Zohra went against all odds to do away with the purdah and signed up for public recitals. Under severe pressure from her family who considered every woman as primarily a genetrix, that she should now leave her ego aside and marry Yusuf who was now ready and willing for a second wife. The idea was further pursued by the fact that Neesha had not given birth to a son yet. Driven by fusty family views, Zohra decided to leave home and started for Bombay.

In the meanwhile, right after their honeymoon, Megha joined her husband in Bombay and settled down quite comfortably in a large fashionable bungalow in Santa Cruz. As Megha and Zohra, like two siblings, always stayed in touch, Megha knew that for Zohra a move was in the offing and so when Zohra took that ultimate step, it delighted Megha more than anyone else. Zohra is such a great artist, she could have been anything — a painter, a poet, Megha thought to herself, as she found another postcard written from Paris:

> Merey shahr-yarko yaadkar pee hai mainay saile-ashk
> Magar aajka nasha kuch aur hai, gulpham kuch aur
> Merey chhalay jaaneke baad na rulana merey jigarko
> Sham'a-e-mazaarkay badle chhor aanaa merey rababko

(I've drunk a flood of tears, in remembrance of my prince,but today I am drunk with another kind of intoxication. After I am gone, please don't let my heart weep. Leave my sitar in place of the lamp on my grave.)

Megha heard their little Fiat driving through the main gate. Milan just got home. The noise in the servant's quarter subsided. Megha feigned to be asleep. Milan sheepishly entered into their bedroom, lest he might wake her up, and then quietly lay down next to her. Suddenly the room started smelling of a strong perfume. It was the perfume his mistress wore. I suppose he couldn't be left alone, Megha thought to herself. When his mistress was not there with him, it was the strong odor of her perfume that he brought home. Megha found it despicable. It made her sick to her stomach. She felt like vomiting, so she grabbed her pillow and stormed through their bedroom door out in the hallway and into their guest room. The rest of the night, she lay there cold and still, listening to the owl hooting all night long. She could not see it in the dark, only a faint silhouette of it. It was Amavash.

She must not have had her forty winks when a raven perched outside her window pane, cawing harshly, woke her up, shrouding her mind and her memories with dark thoughts. It reminded her of Girija aunty. She used to say that ravens and certain other animals have the instincts of an extra sensory perception, that lay dormant in us because we do not care to cultivate it. As she lay there thinking of her, she recalled the day when Girija tried to blame Megha when she learned that Milan was being unfaithful to his wife. "I knew it was bound to happen," Girija kept mumbling to herself.

"What did you know, Girija aunty?" Asked Megha.

"That a bad omen was following you like a shadow. Right from the day you came to this house as a bride, I knew it." Girija said it in a matter-of-fact tone, as if it was only expected that she would be unhappy, but what really alarmed Girija was Megha's attitude towards this whole state of affair. So, she lectured Megha in a lengthy soliloquy.

"We women from the old world may not be literate like you folks but we're no dummies as you may think, anyway," she interrogated Megha sternly, "what's this I hear about you, that you want to leave your husband, just because of another woman? An ideal wife will never give up her husband and her home that easily. I've never heard of such a thing in my entire life, and as you can see I've lived a long life. Let me tell you something, it's the wife's responsibility to either make or break a home, not man's. Men are like birds who love to roam around under an open sky, but, come dusk, they are all homebound. When they are young, they like to do such things, but if you learn to be patient with your man, you'll see how soon he realizes that there's no place like home. In today's world the problem lies with those women who have no tolerance. Besides, you've not been able to bear him a son yet, so, how do you expect him to feel the bondage between you both?" Girija sprinkled salt on Megha's wound.

Out of sheer reverence for the elderly, which is of great significance to the eastern culture, Megha was not about to start a

A WOUNDED TIGRESS

rebuttal with her, but she certainly wanted to speak her mind and get it off her chest.

"Girija aunty, let me ask you this. Just suppose, you were in my situation, what would you have done?" Megha looked her in the eye.

"Shiva Shiva," she mumbled, as she turned her face away from Megha, "what could I have done? Nothing. After all, how can you go against your own destiny? And destiny is determined by the karma of your previous birth. Haven't you read our Hindu scriptures?"

In fact, Megha was well versed in the Gita, the summum bonum of all Hindu scriptures. Indubitably, karma is the principal word in the Gita, but nowhere in the Book does it preach such inertia. To the contrary, the Book preaches you to be wholly responsible for all your actions. Though Megha could never agree with her in principle, still she would never belittle the old woman by questioning her wisdom. It would be very unbecoming of her. So, their dialogue on marriage and infidelity hit a dead end that day and forever.

As she lay in bed ruminating over her bygone days, a loud bang at the door startled Megha. Hastily, she got up still half asleep and then as she strained her eyes, she saw the gardener's wife with her face all puffed up and her children behind her all lined up at the other end of the hallway.

"What is it, Pushpa, what did he do now, did he throw you out again?" Megha asked her.

"No, but I leaving him this time." There was fire in her eyes. Megha was not about to dissuade her from making that move. Those low class men are so savage, they don't even deserve to have a wife and a home, Megha mumbled to herself in contempt and wished Pushpa could teach him a lesson this time by not coming back to him ever. It happened in the past when he would throw her out in a fit of rage and then later he would beg her to return, and then get her pregnant almost immediately upon her return, which would invariably follow with another episode of brutal torture. Over the years Megha observed a certain pattern to Pushpa's plight. From seeing Pushpa live through her ordeal time and again, Megha unfortunately developed a certain amount of insensitivity and so looked at it as just another fiasco.

Besides, Megha herself, a prey to not a very dissimilar situation, endured severe emotional torture herself. Milan's secret courtship with an air hostess left Megha totally devastated when she found out about it. It was during one of his international flights when Milan first met Esha. Milan was a marketing director of a multinational tea company that exported tea from both Darjeeling and Assam to all over Europe and North America. His profession demanded much of his time overseas and away from Megha. It was not until late one night when she happened to answer the phone, that she had learned of Esha, his secret paramour. Megha's instant reaction was to divorce him, but as time went by, she dreaded the very thought of its social repercussions that might eventually drag her to utter degradation. The stigma attached to such social taboos in Indian culture could be very intimidating, especially for a woman, for she would be the one to bear its brunt.

Today, Megha was happy that there was someone who had the audacity to defy her own destiny.

"So, where are you going from here, Pushpa?" Asked Megha.

"This is why I come to you. One day remember you said, women like me work and they pay money so you live happy, husband not allowed there to jump on you when he like and beat you till blood come out, you happy, your children happy, is like heaven to me. O mem sahib, take me there today." Pushpa could not hold herself together any longer, she burst into tears, "see my face." Her lower lip was split open and still bleeding. The gardener had beaten her with an iron spatula. "See my back." She removed her sari off her shoulder to show her those raw scars. They were deep and bloody. "You tell me, mem sahib, what I done wrong? All day I work like animal. I given him four son. Now, tell me, mem sahib, why he go to those whores and throw money and when I ask for rupees to buy some wheat and lentils for our children, you know, what he say? He tell me to go sell my body and bring food for our children. Sometime, I pray to god, they born in a whorehouse. At least, there they eat three meal one day. Here, I not have even one piece dry rotee, or one bowl daal to put in their mouth. What kind mother I, you tell me, mem sahib, what I done wrong?"

"No, no, don't say that, you have done nothing wrong." Megha could hardly hold her tears back, "in fact, they're very fortunate to have a mother like you. You have no reason to blame yourself for all this." Megha tried to offer her some courage so she would not break down and make hopeless of her bad situation. But courage she had plenty.

"I know god punish me for I say this, but take me and my children from that shaitan. I not take this anymore. Mem sahib, please, you save my children and god give you many son." Pushpa threw herself at Megha's feet begging for help. That's one blessing I can do without, Megha mumbled to herself in bitter scorn. Ever since she found out about Esha, she refused to even let Milan touch her, let alone have a child by him, who, for all she knew must have already sired a bastard to that whore by now. Megha was just as vexed and hurt that morning as Pushpa was, but Pushpa had the courage that Megha did not have. Megha, too, endured many scars but she hid them well all within herself and for too long now.

With four innocent, frightened and hungry children and seven months pregnant herself, with sores and bruises all over her body, and all five of them in rags and bare footed, they were on their way to start a new life. Megha readily drove them to the women's shelter. Then, at the shelter, as she filled out enrollment forms for Pushpa, she also found out that, had Pushpa not been so far advanced in her pregnancy, she could have opted for abortion. Megha looked at the person who sat across from her at the other end of the table, the head of the supervisory board and requested him to kindly expound on the matter to her.

"Yes madam," the man was gentle and precise, "I will be more than happy to explain it to you. We give every mother a chance to exercise her own free will. We provide them with ample information, but do not in any way impose or even influence our personal feelings on them. It would be undemocratic and definitely very uncharacteristic for all that we stand."

"Do you have a lot of pregnant women who come to you for shelter." Megha was curious.

"In the hundreds, every year." The supervisor stated in a matter-of-fact tone. His response astounded Megha, to say the least.

"Our study shows that battered women are most vulnerable during their pregnancy," the supervisor continued with the same tone in his voice, "as there is a gross misconception among men, who habitually batter their wives, that the women are somewhat incapacitated by their condition, so they are bound to be at their husband's mercy and therefore more tolerant to torture."

Right then Megha knew Pushpa was at the right place, at the right time, and for the right cause. The supervisor also informed Megha that this shelter, aided by the State Government, and in collaboration with the cottage industry, provided various skills and occupations to all the homeless and destitute like Pushpa herself who could now earn a modest living with dignity and self respect. Megha could clearly envision that day, not too far away, when all five of Pushpa's children growing up both physically and emotionally healthy, and Pushpa herself an independent, able and a proud woman who had the strength to take charge of her own life and prepare her young ones for a better future.

Megha drove home that day from the women's shelter feeling extremely pusillanimous about herself. A host of thoughts paraded through her mind — what good was the university degree? How am I any different from Girija aunty? Am I really a modern woman? Why am I then a captive of my own fears and inhibitions? What does it take to be liberated from within? The more she introspected, the lesser she thought of herself.

Zohra just returned last night from her trip to the mediterranean. She had not seen or heard from Megha in a while. She was just thinking of her when the doorbell to her modestly kept suburban flat overlooking the Arabian Sea, chimed melodiously.

"What a surprise, I was just thinking of you!" Zohra was thrilled to see Megha.

"There's more to follow," said Megha calmly.

"How do you mean?" Zohra looked a little puzzled.

"I left Milan for good. Moved into a ladies' hostel temporarily. Once I have a job, I'll have my own little place, my very own, just like you." With a vacant look in her eyes Megha uttered those words and then with a deep sigh she looked at Zohra, as if to say —it's all over now between us, but, I'm ready to live my life all over again. Zohra stood there absolutely flabbergasted. This is the Megha she had never seen before and yet this is the woman she wanted to see in her.

"When did all this happen? How did you do it? All these years we have been talking about it and you never seemed inclined to take any such step. Then, one week I am gone and next week you emerge like a heroine out of a page of a novel." Zohra was ecstatic with joy and pride for her dear friend who had finally triumphed. Megha had after all pulled herself out of the quagmire.

"I'm not the heroine, it's Pushpa. I can't take credit for something I don't deserve," Megha's voice rigged with confidence.

"Who's Pushpa, what are you talking about, do I know her?" Zohra looked more puzzled than ever.

"My gardener's wife, Pushpa, you might have seen her, she lived in our servant's quarter. She was the one who was actually in the driver's seat. I just followed her."

Zohra noticed how Megha's disposition had changed remarkably.

Today, after almost a decade, Megha can stoically look back and see it all as one perilous journey, but, not without a destination. It was right around the time when she walked out of Milan's life that she began to weep through words. The pain she swallowed for years together, slowly veered into a fountainhead of inspiration which poured through her wealth of writing. To her, writing became synonymous to catching a glimpse of the sky from the prison window. It was both very personal and exhilarating. In her writings, she often fantasized herself as a lonely spirit wailing in the dark ruins of a magnificent castle. In the backdrop of her mind, the magnificent castle stood as the emblem of her once glorious past — a past which is irretrievable like the dark ruins. Soon letters began to pour in from all her readers saying they have wept with her too. The applause she won as a writer became the opium of her life. But that was in the beginning when her own writing offered her the catharsis she needed. Since then, she had been passionately creating a prolific and a purely cerebral world around her. When Megha is not busy writing, she devotes her time to SAHELI, the women's organization she and Zohra together have founded to provide shelter for women like Pushpa, and help them realize their potential.

YOURS TRULY

The funeral pyre at Manikarnika's ghat is ablaze. A few men in white cluttered around the pyre, some in groups of four or five chatting quietly and others all by themselves sitting by the ghat staring at the Ganga and waiting for the last flame in the pyre to extinguish. Arundhuti is sauntering along the ghat intoxicated by the cool, crisp breeze of the Ganga — nectar of dawn. As she gazes at those spiraling flames, afar in the pyre, rising towards the heaven, like a child with its arms stretched, reaching for its parent, the sun, she begins to contemplate on the soul unshackled today from its earthly bondage, just when the twenty second verse of the Shankhya Yoga (Yoga of Knowledge) from the Gita comes to her mind:

> *'vasangsi jirnani yatha vihay*
> *navani gruhnati naroparani*
> *tatha sharirani vihay jirnani*
> *Anyani sanyati navani dehi'*

'As a person puts on new garments, giving up old ones, similarly, the soul accepts new material bodies, giving up the old and the useless ones.'

The dark silhouette of a person sitting at the step of the ghat catches her attention. Arundhuti's feet tremble. Had the ghat been a woman, it would be able to read her mind today, as to why after all these years, Arundhuti's steps should suddenly falter. Is he who I think he is... no, no, it can't be true... or am I hallucinating? she wonders. The lonesome man, startled by the rustle of those dry leaves crushed under her feet, now turns around and stands face-to-face from Arundhuti. The nebulous light of an autumnal dawn is enough to reveal that face, whom Arundhuti had long forgotten or at least she thought she had.

"Is that... I mean are you... is your name... Oh god!... you look so much like my... Arundhuti... is that you?" The man stutters.

Freshly bathed and clad in saffron, with her long black hair almost touching her knees still dripping wet from the bath, wearing a bindiya of white sandalwood paste that looks like the full moon between her finely arched brows and above her delicately shaped nose, looking mysteriously beautiful, she appears like an apparition to him. How can I ever believe this? A sudden spur of thoughts lashes her mind riotously while the steely look in her eyes runs a chill through his spine. After all these years!... how could he recognize me?... is this true what I see?... has he married since?... is he happy with his wife?... do they have children?... did he ever miss me?... does he love his wife?... did I ever cross his mind, even momentarily?... let see, how long has it been?... I can't count any more!... could he ever forget me?... does he love his wife?... or did he ever want me back? The sheer unexpectedness of the moment which made it so tumultuous descended upon them like a lightning leaving them both speechless.

Today, after all these years, their unforeseen meeting began to rather scourge her emotions violently. She feels light headed and breathless, the back of her neck and behind her ears feel warm. Beads of perspiration moisten the tip of her nose and her forehead. Perhaps, she needs Malay to rescue her from collapsing again, just like that day eighteen years ago, when she needed him most to save her from being dragged to shame and degradation. That day she wanted him to hold her in his arms. She even begged for his mercy but that day Malay stood there without uttering a word, unyielding to her ceaseless begging.

"Don't you remember me? I'm your... I am... Malay." His voice only caused a mere ripple in the air before it drowned into deeper silence. He only wished Arundhuti would speak up and say something but that day all that was left in her was her gaze with an eerie void that made him terribly uncomfortable. There was something so intimidating about her that it almost numbed all his senses. While every moment seemed timeless as the two silently confronted, Arundhuti impetuously slipped into a sentimental corner of her mind which she had kept aloof and locked for a long time from the rest of herself, just when she realized something. Certainly, it was not becoming of her, she thought to herself. She does not need him today, or for that matter neither his love nor his sympathy. If anything, he should have had faith in her that day. Perhaps, then, he could have done justice to her and that was all she needed from him at the time — justice, absolute justice. The last thing she should have ever asked of him was mercy, after all, it was not of her making for which she should be punished. But that was all she could think of that day. She was on her knees, clinging on to his feet, sobbing bitterly, her tears streaming down her face and trickling down on his feet drop by drop. Malay stood there like a rock. That day Arundhuti called him her god, her savior but he stood there simmering with rage, nothing could move him, not even her relentless stream of tears could evoke a drop of mercy in him.

Arundhuti looked at the burning pyre, violently in flames.

"My mother," Malay answered to the look in her eyes, "it was her last wish to be cremated at Manikarnika's ghat," he continued, "you know what they say..."

Yes, Arundhuti knew that it was a common belief among Hindus that if the mortal remains of the dead are cremated at Manikarnika's ghat in Banaras, then the soul attains instant moksha. A smirk quivers around her lips but the look in her eyes still remain unaffected by her thoughts. Then, what about karma? Doesn't karma play a cardinal role in attaining moksha? True to her indisputable conviction, that it was karma and not the ghat that should affect moksha, Arundhuti remained unfettered to those age-old beliefs. But it was neither her position nor an appropriate time to question it, much less defy. What good would it serve to anyone in anyway?

"So, how have you been...?" Malay attempted again to strike a conversation, though with little response from her. Yet, he persisted. "It's amazing that after all these years fate should bring us together, I had never expected to see you again, I see you wearing saffron... you have not taken sanyasa, have you?"

Such questions from him seemed so pointless to her today. She had given up this worldly life in search of something greater, something more meaningful.

"I'm doing well and that's all I can say. How are things with you?" She was vigilant.

"Now that mother is gone I feel lonesome again... just like the time when you left me. I have no one now." Malay lamented.

"Didn't your mother find you another wife?" She looked at him stoically.

"Mother tried, but I couldn't... you still dwell in my heart. It wouldn't be fair to her, of course, I wasn't fair to you either but anyway, when I realized that it was a little too late, I went to your house to bring you back home but your mother told me, you had left for good and couldn't tell me where you were."

"Did you see my father?" asked Arundhuti.

"Your father!... don't you know about him?" Her enquiry about her father caught him off guard.

"Know what?" Arundhuti looked slightly perturbed.

"I thought you knew... he passed away soon after you left home." At first, the news hit her with a dizzy whir. Then, she gradually immersed into contemplation — when one embraces sanyasa, one is supposed to remain detached to pain, pleasure, greed, lust, envy, anger, fear and hatred — the enemies within ones ownself. Just then the twenty seventh verse of Shankhya Yoga from the Gita illumined her thoughts... 'Jatasya hi Dhruvo
mrutyurdhruvam janma mrutasya cha

Tasmadpariharyathey na
tvam shochitumaharsi'

'Indeed, certain is death for the born, and certain is birth for the dead; therefore, over the inevitable, you should not grieve.'

"I am sorry to be the bearer of this bad news," Malay's voice mellowed in condolence. But one who has grasped the true essence of the Gita requires no condolence. Once again the stolid expression on her face arrested Malay's attention.

"Anyway, you didn't answer my question," asked Malay.

"And what is that question?" She looked at him unhesitatingly.

"Have you taken sanyasa?" Malay anxiously awaited an answer as if his life depended on it. Against the backdrop of the Ganga, she stood there looking pristine.

"I have to go." Arundhuti looked at him with unflickering flames in her eyes. He wondered, what is it within her? What is it that ignites such fire in her? Malay's heart fluttered like a little moth intrigued by those flames. He could not let her go today, not without retaliating to her move that had trampled his ego once before.

"If you don't want to answer my question, just say so, but don't try to run away from something that you can't face. After all, you're still young, how can you possibly survive with dignity without a husband?"

Those words sounded so vacuous today, especially, since they came from him and after so many years. Wouldn't it be better, she thought, had they remained unspoken. She walked away in a daze towards the ashram which has been her home for the last several years or at least she thought it was until this day.

"Listen to me Aurndhuti, please, listen to me," pleaded Malay as he tried to follow her, "don't run away from me like this, I never meant to hurt you ever, will you at least listen to what I have to say? don't let your pride come in our way, it will only ruin you, believe me."

As those words of admonishment gonged in her ears over and over again, the thought behind those words slowly began to creep in through a heap of doubts, like worms feeding on rubbish, as if soiling her mind and eating through the core of her spiritual being. Am I really running away... why?... after all, what is it that I'm running away from?... why did I not answer his question?... am I not a true sanyasini?... if I could walk past a storm these several years, then, why should a small gust of wind suddenly ruffle my heart today? By now she had left the ghat far behind and the voice grew fainter until she could hear him no more. But she couldn't stop running as she encountered a herculean wave of questions churning through those newfound doubts in her. She quickly turned around to the corner of the Shiva temple, gasping for breath, as if she was chased by a deadly stranger. Then she entered into the compound of the ashram and sat underneath the wood-apple tree, still gasping for more air. It was as if the brave face she was wearing all these years had suddenly fallen off her head.

At the ghat, Malay, battered by a sudden desire to reconcile with his long lost wife, wanted to hold her hand just to stop her from walking away from him this time. He wanted to talk to her for a while or at least find out if she would be willing to see him another time, somewhere else, not at the ghat. The eventuality of life, rather morbidly inevitable, glares at you at the ghat. It turns you into a hopeless cynic. A boat ride in the Ganga instead would be fitting. The Ganga, by the twilight, could perhaps lend them both a more romantic setting, the two torn apart by a ghastly ill-fated event that hurled them each into a separate orbit of life. Maybe today the holy Ganga can act as the gravitational force between them and miraculously draw them closer. Now that mother is gone, Arundhuti might be even willing to give up sanyasa and reunite with him. All that could be possible only if she would give him another chance. But Arundhuti's life had changed its course like the river, and now it could only move on and on until it flows to something greater and grander, like the ocean, to which it will ultimately surrender.

She has walked this path for quite some time now, but today after all these years how did she arrive at this juncture? Why these sudden uncertainties and chasms in her thoughts? Perhaps, she had not realized until now, that there could still be a mountain of desires submerged within her, and today they are struggling to resurface, causing her an insurmountable amount of doubts and trepidations about her own self, her faith, and her strength of character. Her peace of mind disrupted, she unmindfully slipped away into a distant past.

"You better listen to me now or else you'll regret later, I've prepared her horoscope, believe me, doesn't look good at all." Devangshu Mitra had cautioned his son, "your daughter's marriage line breaks very abruptly." His prognostications never failed him. For once, he wished his knowledge of astrology would prove him wrong. Arundhuti was born with mangal overshadowing her fate causing a stumbling block in her marriage. The dark thoughts cast a gloom on Devangshu Mitra's face.

"A well educated boy from a well-to-do family, same caste as ours, what more can one ask for? He looks alright, nothing princely about him, but that's alright, our Rini (everyone at home called Arundhuti Rini) is not an apsara either." Biplav was quite excited about the proposal and was confident that his father would also agree with him, but Devangshu Mitra adamantly nodded his head from side to side, negating the whole idea of getting his granddaughter married, at least, not for awhile.
"She is going to be a sanyasini, mark my word, you can write it on the wall if you wish." Devangshu Mitra pronounced those words distinctly and continued, "as you know, at the time of ones birth, the pattern set by the conjugation of the celestial bodies impacts every individual which eventually determines one's fate.

In our Rini's case it is the mangal" Engulfed in sadness, he continues, "very disturbing, very disturbing, indeed, this particular period of her life as I see it clearly, is extremely hazardous to her." Saying so, he became suddenly very quiet as if his mind wandered off into the distance. Biplav listened to his father quietly but unaffectedly.

Devangshu Mitra was known as The Astrologer in town. People revered him like a prophet and graciously accepted his words as oracles, with the exception of his youngest son, Biplav. Biplav, to the contrary, found no plausible explanation in such theories and discarded them wholeheartedly. How can any one in his right mind elucidate the correlation between those planets millions of miles away and us puny little creatures on earth... haa! must be one of the grandest fantasies of a mind gone mad. Biplav thought of his father in derision. Certainly, he could not be a party to it. Biplav was an avid believer of Charbak philosophy — the ancient Hindu philosophy based on pure materialism which in some ways resembles the Epicurean philosophy of the Greeks. Biplav's philosophy towards life, based on bone-dry pragmatism held him in his own esteem as highly rational. His analysis, analogies and arguments, based within the confines of pure physics and mathematics were pivotal to all his rationale and his intellectual investigations towards the existence of life in this universe.

But after Devangshu Mitra had given his son a patient ear all he had to say was, "it's a vast subject my son, requires years of concentrated effort and enormous study, but it never interested you, anyway, you'll remember me when the time comes." The astrologer had nothing further to say to his son.

"My Rini a sanyasini!!" laughed Biplav, the old man must be approaching senility, the son thought to himself and then spoke his mind that sounded more like a threat than anything else, "well then, in that case I'll have to pursue this matter without your blessings. Your granddaughter will be married, no matter what."

"God forbid if I should wish her ill, but just you see," rumbled the astrologer. Each one unwilling to cross the threshold of their intellectual domain ridiculed the other as fanatic. Thus, father and son, both left the conflicting premise in subdued anger.

Biplav had gone to see his father to discuss about a suitable boy for his daughter. The young man had just completed his Ph.D. in Pharmacy. He planned to take up some lectureship at the University and also look after their family business. His family owned three pharmaceutical shops in town. As a father of a marriageable
daughter, Biplav just could not let this offer slip by. Lately Biplav had noticed some bizarre attitude in Rini's disposition which prompted him to look for a match rather urgently.
"Rini's ma, do you notice anything different about our daughter? I have a feeling, she's trying to throw dust in our eyes," Biplav's suspicion was growing larger everyday, "make sure she's not involved with any loafer in the neighborhood? I suggest you keep a strict eye on her." Biplav advised his wife gingerly for he certainly had his dart right on the bull's eye. But Savitri was too naive to sense anything at all. She was always very trusting and trustworthy, as those virtues usually go together. Arundhuti felt very dearly towards her mother, but she also knew that if need be, she could pull the wool over her mother's eyes any day, but not so with her father. Biplav remained disconcerted for quite some time. Nothing ever escaped his eyes. That made her all the more judicious of her father's hawk-like presence and therefore, of late, she tried to evade his attention whenever she could. Of course, Arundhuti was not involved with any loafer, not in the least, but rather much worse in a way.

It all started during the Puja holidays. Devangshu Mitra, desirous of a grand celebration of Durga Puja, decided to have one at his residence in South Calcutta, an old but massive four-storied brick building with several large rooms, low, narrow windows with shutters forever closed that gave a dim, conservative look to the interior, small square ventilators cut through the upper regions of the wall where flocks of pigeons customarily roosted, high ceiling, a spacious terrace, and an equally spacious compound built by Devangshu Mitra's father, also an astrologer by profession. The puja was to be performed in the compound. The astrologer, generally conservative in his outlook towards life, turned into quite a wastrel, when it came to religious matters. He had invited everyone to attend the celebration, even those who were remotely related to him. At one point, it felt as though the roof of this lofty, nineteenth century house would collapse over the entire household with all the relatives that gathered from all over — Delhi, Agra, Bombay, Poona, Madras — each one arriving at some odd hours through the night and into the day prior to the festival.

Devangshu Mitra's only sister, Krishnamani, with her son, Dhruva, arrived ten days prior to the celebration. He had trunk called his sister and personally urged her to leave for Calcutta at their earliest, so that she could help her brother with the preparation, things that he would not trust anyone else with, not even his own wife, Swarnalata, or his daughters-in-law, none of whom were half as ingenious as Krishnamani, especially when it came to monitoring large finances during a family gathering of this magnitude.

That morning the train from the west coast lazily entered into Howrah Station bringing in Krishnamoni and Dhruva, almost an hour late as usual, amidst an avalanche of passengers pouring out from every compartment and flooding the platform with a stream of travellers. Led by coolies in bright red turbans, carrying luggage over their head, around their shoulders and in their hands, making strange gutteral sounds as they meandered along swiftly, cutting through the crowd in an almost acrobatic manner, Krishnamani boisterously moved along with the current, while whining about everything and everyone around her.

"I say, you keep an eye on the coolie Dhruva and make sure he doesn't disappear, they can outsmart us, you can never trust these thugs, I don't know how people can live all their lives in a city like this." Krishnamoni mumbled to herself nervously.

"Alright ma, can't you keep your voice down a little? He can hear us, you know," Dhruva whispered, embarrassed by his mother's volatile ways and her verbal abuse of the poor man.

"Let him hear, so what, do you think I'm afraid of him? You don't know what these people can do." Krishnamoni refused to be intimidated.

It was midday by the time Krishnamoni and Dhruva arrived at south Calacutta and as expected Devangshu Mitra was quite relieved to see his sister come home. Although, it had been awhile they had seen each other, with Krishnamani there was never a right time to sit around and exchange niceties, so, she quickly unpacked, bathed, changed and then after having declined from taking anything other than milk and fruits for lunch, since it was ekadashi, upon Swarnalata's request, she wasted no time in changing her mind and ended up relishing on half a dozen poorees fried in pure ghee with a variety of vegetarian dishes, chutney and sweetmeats. Then, retired to her room for a quick snooze. Now, having had a brief rest, there was only one thing left that could shake off the exhaustion of her journey, so she yelled from her room for one of the servants to make her a strong cup of tea. After that she meant nothing but business, as she left her bed and plunged into her mission with her usual vigour and self confidence. Devangshu Mitra had asked her to take charge of the kitchen and in charge she was.

In the meanwhile, the word got around in his neighbourhood that since this year was to be his last puja celebrations, Devangshu Mitra contemplated on cutting down his expenses towards the cultural functions which he sponsored every year during the puja holidays and instead would deliver hot meals to a number of neighbourhood shelters and homes of the poor and the destitute for all five days. Everyone hearkened with delight including Biplav, except one person and she was none other than his own sister Krishnamoni. Not that she would rather be entertained by the local artists than feed the hungry but to her the very idea of feeding them for five days was absolutely pointless.

"Who will feed them the remaining three hundred and sixty days, you can't remove poverty from this world by putting food in the mouths of a few thousands for five days, can you?" Krishnamoni argued.

"No, although, I wish I could, but nevertheless each one of us must do what little we can. I'll say if you can feed even one hungry mouth for one day, you have done your share for that day." Devangshu Mitra's response would make her quiet but not yet convinced, so, he would continue,"look at it this way, Krishna, you may not be able to make the problem go away, but if you can lessen it even by a fraction, why not do it? Just look him in the eye and you will find a world of contentment in his heart and do you know why because you cared enough to feed him that day."

"Yes, of course, if you put it that way, it does make sense." Until now, Krishnamoni, like many others had learnt to look at it as one huge faceless problem for which there was no easy solution so, why even question it. In essence, as long as it does not affect our lives than why make it our business? But that day Devangshu Mitra made it his business to get the point across her. Though Krishnamoni could now appreciate her brother's noble gesture from an ideological point of view, yet, it did not make her task any lighter or easier. Now she had to account for thousands of mouths in the neighbourhood to one meal a day for five days, over and above the entire 'battalion' of Devangshu Mitra's joint family that have descended upon his house that she had to cater to with at least three meals a day for about five to ten days. So, she launched into her mission by chalking out a few vegetarian menus that would be served for the week. Favoured by a general consensus within the family, Krishnamoni managed to keep the menu to a staple meal subject to some variations from day to day of rice and lentil cooked together to a spicy hotchpotch along with a variety of pakodas, a mixed vegetable curry (which is usually a seasonal treat), spicy shredded cabbage curry with potatoes and fresh peas, tomato chutney and rice porridge with raisins, or poories served with fried eggplant, chana daal, paneer kofta curry with potatoes and peas, papaya chutney and once again rice porridge for desert. Next, she discussed the budget with her brother and made a note of the items that needed to be paid in advance to the local grocer. After that, for the next five or so days she remained absolutely bogged down accounting balances, lending and receiving credits for some additional errands where she saw fit, exacting a thorough calculation of every rupee spent against every item, scrutinizing every item delivered to the storage, delegating authorities to those whom she could rely, and demanding absolute responsibility from all those who at first volunteered their services and later regretted for being so foolishly zealous of such arduous tasks. But her tasks did not end there. She hired some professional cooks and explained them their chores for the week. She even walked up to the local grocer to caution him that if he were to disappoint her delivering second rate products then she would look elsewhere for another grocer. She spared no one, not even her own sister-in-law, Swarnalata. She found everyone inefficient and their services ineffective. None according to her or her brother was half as competent as herself.

Arundhuti and her parents had also arrived that same evening from Lake Road where Biplav had purchased a flat. Unlike rest of his brothers, Biplav had to move out of his father's house for he could not take the stress of living in a joint family, the kind of stress that stemmed from constant squabbles or vice versa, for he had not been able to determine yet, which of the two precedes the other. Almost every week, one or the other member of the family quarreled about something or the other, which invariably and sometimes unwittingly dragged in a few other members of the family until it took the shape of another ugly wrangle. So, when Arundhuti was born, Biplav used it as a pretext to get out of this precarious situation. He told everyone that he needed to move out so that he could provide his daughter with a more civil upbringing. As outspoken and callous as he was, he shocked everyone in the family with his radical and irreverent comment about his own family members, after which each one of them formed a different opinion about him — some found him too bold, some arrogant and still some others selfish, but the general consensus was unanimous and univocal — an eyesore to everyone concerned. But then again with time as things cooled off, as they eventually do, no matter how infuriated they were at the time, later on they all greeted the estranged Biplav amiably when he brought his wife Savitri and little Rini over to his father's house for an occasional visit.

That evening when Arundhuti, along with her parents, arrived at South Calcutta for the puja holidays and saw Krishnamani and Dhruva, she could hardly remember seeing them, though, she had met them once before during one summer holidays. Krishnamani and her husband had just adopted Dhruva that year. Since the couple never had any child of their own, they always wanted to adopt one of the several nephews of Krishnamani's husband. Dhruva was the youngest of them all and they took an instant liking to him soon after he was born. But the couple had to wait awhile before Dhruva could join them. It was the happiest time of their lives. That summer, Krishnamani invited her nephew Biplav and his wife Savitri with their daughter to visit them, none of which Arundhuti remembered very clearly except the train ride from Bombay to Poona. She carried a vivid image of the entire journey blotting everything else from her mind. To this day she could see the train slithering its way upward through the narrow winding rocky path above the Western Ghats, as the panorama of mountains and numerous waterfalls provided a breathtaking sight. Frequently, as their train brush passed a natural water falls, splashes of mountain cool water showered little Rini through the open window and her heart leaped with delight. Whenever the train entered into a tunnel, she shuddered, as though the darkness inside the bowel of the mountains would swallow her alive. It was an unforgettable experience in her life. Though she carried some verbatim recollections of that train ride, yet, she could hardly associate any recollections of Dhruva with it. So it was virtually their first meeting and it could not have been a happier occasion. They both met someone who evoked some special interests in them and that held them bewitched for hours together every day. It was Shambhu, the potter and a wonderful story teller who had arrived before everyone else.

Amidst scattered stacks of hay, lay heaps of soft and moist clay with bamboo sticks piled up high and ropes coiled up all over in Devangshu Mitra's compound and Shambhu in the middle of his buttress sat deeply engrossed in his craft. That is how the two teenagers had first seen Shambhu.

"Shambhuda, how long does it take to make the pratima?" asked curious Rini.

"Aaaa... should be done in another week or so," said Shambhu, without taking his eyes off from the six-foot tall skeleton framed in bamboo and stuffed with hay and then tied together at the joints with rope, which he now slapped with hunks of clay and then carefully molded while puffing his half-burnt bidi.

"Shambhuda how did you learn to make these?" asked Dhruva.

"Aaaa... from my father... the best sculptor that ever lived. Long time ago, let me tell you, my father made a twelve-foot tall Durga pratima, and believe it or not, he won the best prize that year in Calcutta. Since then he's regarded as the royal sculptor of Baagbaazar, you see raja, maharajas and the zamindars know the value of a true artist." Shambhu quickly took a puff off his bidi as if to refuel his spent energy, "believe it or not, they are the ones who kept us alive for so many generations and of course your grandfather and your great grandfather too. Your great-grandfather was a cherished customer of my grandfather for many years and do you know who my grandfather was?" The young listeners curiously exchanged glances and nodded their head from side to side.

"He was the royal sculptor of Rupnagar, yes, my grandfather. Before my grandfather's time we were simply known as potters in our little village, but ever since my grandfather won the title of a royal sculptor of Rupnagar, we don't call ourselves potters any more, you see. Yes, as I was saying, today there's nothing left of Rupnagar, it is just a stretch of sand with water all around it and a mermaid, I believe, is seen occasionally, a beautiful mermaid."

"What happened to Rupnagar?" Dhruva looked puzzled.

"And where did the mermaid come from?" The thought of such fantastic creatures intrigued Arundhuti.

"You see, what happened was on the night of Dashera, the night you are supposed to immerse Durgama in the river after the puja, the raja of Rupnagar found the pratima so beautiful that he refused to let go of her and instead kept her in his palace, believe it or not, it was the pratima my grandfather made, you see," said Shambhu boastfully, reiterating the fact since it was pertinent that the two ardent listeners be reminded here that it was none other than his grandfather, who was the creator of such a work of art and also the source of a legend. "So, as I was saying, when the raja of Rupnagar went against the sacred tradition, Durgama decided to teach him a lesson with one deadly curse. During monsoon, before the next Durga Puja, river Bhairavi spread her arms and washed away the entire kingdom of Rupnagar which was situated on its bank. Since then nobody has ever dared to set foot on that cursed land. But fishermen from nearby villages, who sail across Bhairavi for large carp that spawn during mon-soon, have seen a mermaid sitting on the sand dunes of Rupnagar on a special night every year, on the night of Dashera, believe it or not, they say, she's Durga."

Shambhu's story of Rupnagar flabbergasted the two listeners

beyond words. They remained firmly planted next to Shambhu for quite a while, as if mesmerized by the fantastic picture of the 'beautiful mermaid on the sand dunes of Rupnagar' drawn by Shambhu. Dhruva did not know when or how he began walking through a reverie on the sand dunes in the middle of nowhere with Rini, beautiful Rini sitting on it, until Shambhu opened his mouth again, "now, tell me something, do you all know the story of how Durga was born?"

"The story of Durga!... yes!... we do." They looked at each other with newfound interest and quickly added, "but we could hear it again from you. Nobody can tell a story like you do," said Arundhuti to which Dhruva quickly agreed. Shambhu chuckled with pride and seemed pleasantly in agreement with both of them.

"Alright then listen to this, remember though this is no fable, it actually happened, but before I start the story I want you to do something for me, go tell your maid to bring me a cup of tea." Shambhu took a long puff off his bidi and looked refreshed. Arundhuti was off to the kitchen and back in a flash. She could not wait to hear the story of Durga yet another time.

"So this is how it all began," said Shambhu, "the demons and the gods fought a battle for a hundred years until one day the demons kicked the gods away from heaven, so the gods were now very unhappy, and they went to Brahma, Vishnu and Maheshvar and told them their unhappy story. When Brahma, Vishnu and Maheshvar heard what the demons had done to the gods, they became angry, so very angry, that from their anger a devi was born, her name was Durga.... leave the tea here, hope you put enough milk and sugar this time, I'm not used to putting anything in my mouth that tastes skimpy, you see." Shambhu looked at the maid servant from the corner of his eyes who was curiously staring at the unfinished idol as Shambhu threw those inflammable words at her. Then, as if something within her suddenly perked up and so she began to cackle like a hen at

Shambhu, "yes, your majesty, if you should find my tea so skimpy, why don't you go have your tea from a roadside hovel, or do you not have a paisa in your pocket to buy it? You belong there, anyway." Before he could open his mouth in retaliation, the maid servant left the site giggling and swaggering her hips, almost teasingly. Shambhu had not realized until then that he had just poked his finger in the hornet's nest, for she had decided to act like a scullion whenever they ran into each other for the remaining of his days there.

"Don't mind her, Shambhuda. Tell me, where did you read the story of Durga?" Dhruva tried to lighten the mood.

"Aaaa... I didn't read it anywhere... I would only if I knew how to... like you people do," said Shambhu slurping loudly into his cup of tea.

"Then how did you know the story?"

"Aaaa... my grandfather told me... believe it or not, my grandfather was a wonderful story teller."

"Well! where did he read all those stories? asked Arundhuti.

"Aaaa... when I don't know how to read and write, how do you think my grandfather would know?... He heard from his grandfather and his grandfather heard from his grandfather and so on and on."

"Then what happened to Durga?" asked Arundhuti.

"Aaaa... let see... then each god gave something to her, like... Shiva gave her a beautiful face; Vishnu gave her arms; Moon... a pair of breasts; Indra... abdomen; Varun... thighs; Brahma... legs; mother earth... buttocks; let's see, what did Agni give her... Agni gave her three eyes and Yama... yes! Yama gave her long black hair; Ocean gave her ornaments; now... what did the Sun give her... Oh! yes, the Sun gave her a golden complexion... then finally Durga came to the battlefield riding on a lion given by the Himalayas. She had ten arms for ten directions. The gods also gave her one weapon for each arm... they were sword, wheel, club, conch shell, three pronged spear, scepter, thunder, bell, bow and arrow." Shambhu had the list of Durga's weapons all by heart.

　　　　　　　　A WOUNDED TIGRESS

In the meanwhile, Devangshu Mitra came down to see how far Shambhu had progressed. He sat himself down in a lawn chair under a palm tree looking well rested after a siesta.

"So, how far have you come, Shambhu? I see you've already started working with clay, so, not much is left I suppose."

"Oh, no sir, I've quite a way to go, sir, after I coat it with one more layer of clay, I've to take my time and let it dry first. Then, the paint job will start, and then the draping and the hair do and the ornaments and so on."

"I see, so you do have quite a way to go." Then looking at Arundhuti and Dhruva, Devangshu Mitra asked, "are these children bothering you, Shambhu? Let me know if they are."

"Oh, no, no sir, they've been very good, sir." Shambhu was as humble as he could be.

"Grandpa, do you know the story of Durga?" asked Dhruva anxiously.

"I most certainly do," replied Devangshu Mitra.

"So does Shambhuda. Grandpa, do you know the story of the Raja of Rupnagar? and did you know that the mermaid on the sand dunes was really Durga?" said Arundhuti with great gusto and amazement.

"What story is that... hey...hey...hey?" Chuckled Devangshu Mitra, amused by Shambhu's fable.

"So, Shambhu, what have you been telling them?"

Shambhu looked embarrassed.

"It was during my grandfather's time, sir, but the part about the mermaid, sir, some say it's only a fable. I've never seen it myself so I really don't know, sir" Shambhu sounded almost apologetic for indulging in heresy.

"I see, so how far did you go with the story of Durga?" inquired Devangshu Mitra authoritatively.

"Sir, I just finished telling them how Durgama got her weapons for her ten arms from the gods. I think they would enjoy listening to the rest of the story from you, sir," suggested Shambhu.

"Alright," said Devangshu Mitra looking at Arundhuti.

"I'll do even better, I'll read from the book. But before I start, I want you to run along and tell the maid to bring me and shambhu some tea. There's no fun in telling a story or reading a book without a hot cup of tea, hey...hey...hey... what do you say Shambhu? You should know, you're an excellent story teller, I presume."

"You're right, sir." The potter most respectfully agreed with his client.

Looking at Dhruva, Devangshu Mitra made a gesture with his hand. "yes, you... I want you to go upstairs to my library and get the book that is bound in red with the name written in gold, it's at the very top shelf, but, I see you've grown quite tall, so, you should be able to reach it."

Shambhu was warily moving along inch by inch shaping and reshaping every single curve and contour of the idol.

"Face is very difficult to make and especially the eyes, most difficult of all," with a grave look in his eyes Shambhu reflected on the artistry of pottery, "it is in those eyes where I have to bring forth the expressions of kindness, gentleness, and at the same time power and fearlessness."

Devangshu Mitra nodded his head in agreement. Within moments, both the children were back — Dhruva with the book and Arundhuti with two cups of steaming hot tea.

"Now let see... where shall I start?" He was merely thinking aloud as he flipped through the pages of the book when the sculptor offered his suggestion.

"Sir, how about the Mahishasur vadh? I think the children will enjoy that, sir."

Devangshu Mitra sipped into his tea with great relish, "good suggestion, Shambhu," then cleared his voice and began.

"Durga rumbled with laughter. As she laughed louder and louder the earth vibrated, the mountains trembled, and the oceans tormented. Humbled by her overpowering disposition, the gods and the rishis began to extol her glory. The battleground echoed with animosity. Mahishasur, the king of the demons, with his battalion of armoured soldiers struck the Goddess. To Durga, the prowess of her rival was only infinitesimal and so she retaliated accordingly. With every breath she exhaled, an army of dauntless soldiers was born. To its contrast, the demons weakened as they lost their soldiers in thousands. Soon, Mahishasur found himself all alone in the battle- field, his spirits dampened by the loss of his army, and he followed a different course of action as his last resort. In the guise of a ferocious beast, he attempted to connive the Goddess and her army. But Durga was invincible. She beheaded Mahishasur and thus the battle between the gods and the demons ended."

While the grandfather read from the book, Dhruva saw glimpses of Durga in Arundhuti. Even earlier, as Shambhu was describing the subject of his craft, Dhruva found a semblance of some sort in his imagery of Arundhuti. In Dhruva's eye, she was much more than just a little girl named Rini. She was gradually emerging into a goddess, gifted with an intrinsic power and beauty that would hold Dhruva mesmerized for days to come.

Arundhuti was on the terrace right after her bath, hanging a load of washed clothes on the line, when Dhruva followed her from behind. The clear blue flawless sky without a flake of cloud, like a huge chunk of sapphire, hung over their head. Arundhuti looked up at the sky. The sun was up in its usual brilliance. Soft autumnal breeze blew across their faces. It was a day that was all around more than clement. Dhruva was looking for one such opportunity. So, he wasted no time at all in letting her know of his new born feelings towards her. Dhruva, bashful as he was, his face turned ruddy, as he opened his heart to her.

"I suppose, I am in love with you. It happened from the moment I set my eyes on you, Rini."

Arundhuti was at first taken aback and then overcome by a sense of embarrassment. How could he even think of it?

"You don't have to say anything, I know exactly what's on your mind." Dhruva tried to ease his way into her heart.

"How do you know what's on my mind?" asked Arundhuti, still embarrassed.

"You're probably thinking, how can this be? We are related!" said Dhruva in a matter-of-fact tone.

"But aren't we?" asked Arundhuti.

"Yes and no," replied Dhruva with a twinkle in his eyes, as if behind that twinkle lay a beautiful secret. Arundhuti wanted to pluck that secret from the twinkle in his eyes.

Dhruva was tall, unusually tall for his age and slender. His eyes were rather large that took prominence in his small, oval shaped face. He was probably in his late teens and had an exceptionally intelligent look about him. He was shy and yet bright, he spoke little but impressively that gave him an over all charming disposition. She did not know what to say and stood there feeling awkward.

"Looks like there's a secret to our relation." Said Arundhuti rather amusingly.

"Yes, and I want to share it with you and that's why I am here."

"R..i..n..i..." Just then Arundhuti heard her mother yelling at the top of her voice from downstairs, "R.i.n.i... how long does it take to hang those clothes... come right down this minute. I need you in the kitchen." Savitri sounded exasperated. Dhruva clinched his teeth impatiently.

"I have to go," said Arundhuti nervously.

"Can't you wait for just a moment? I need to tell you something, it's important for both of us," urged Dhruva.

"Not now... I've to go... please... we'll talk another time." She pleaded with him.

"Please, Arundhuti... I'll only take a minute... it's so hard to find you alone... I beg of you." If Dhruva would let go of her now, he would probably not get another chance to see her until the next day or the day after. With a house full of people, there were just too many intrusions and distractions. Earlier, when Dhruva tried to corner Arundhuti in the dark attic, or the day before on the terrace, or in the dark narrow alcove the other night under the staircase, or even in their backyard last week behind a pile of wood and charcoal stacked for the kitchen, they always got caught by somebody and this was something that could not wait. Dhruva could not afford to lose her this time.

"I'll come and see you at night." She had to rush.

"Where and when?" He wanted to scream but instead whispered in a clear sharp tone.

"Right here, after dinner," she whispered back to him.

The bitter sweet yearning that young lovers go through to meet secretly have always been the highlight of any romance and so were Arundhuti and Dhruva waiting impatiently for that moment. But, in the manwhile that evening they sat across from each other at the dinner table like two strangers. The dining table was rather large but not large enough to accommodate all of them at the same time. So they ate in groups. As many as ten could eat in each batch. They were among the first batch of children. Next would be all the male adults in the family, then followed the females. The servants ate last but not at the table. They crouched on a wooden plank on the kitchen floor and ate from large brass plates with a giant-like appetite. That day Arundhuti and Dhruva ate very little, especially Arundhuti. She could hardly put a morsel in her mouth and when she did, it would not go down her throat. Dhruva's presence had suddenly made her overly self-conscious. They never said a word to each other at the table and yet they both communicated perfectly well. At first they only looked stealthily at each other, away from everyone's attention. Then, slowly Dhruva made his first move. With a quick askance, he indicated her to the terrace. Arundhuti acknowledged the hidden indication in his askance with a flickering smile, which she had to quickly hide behind her tight lips, while the rest of the children, much younger than them and quite a bit rowdy, created a lot of commotion at the table. They yelled and argued with each other, spattered food and spilled water accidentally on each other's plates and all over the table, while the two adolescents behaved perfectly like two adults pre-occupied in their own secret world aloof from the rest.

Arundhuti could not sleep that night. Dhruva's soft voice kept ringing in her ears. It was not until she had known of his roman-tic feelings for her and learned about their inconsanguineous relationship, that she could suddenly care less for any sort of qualms that one might have about their feelings for each other. After all, he was a very charming young man, who adored her and at their age falling in love simply felt heavenly. But what about their parents and the grandparents and all the uncles and aunts and cousins. Even the servants would raise their brows if they ever had an inkling of what was going through Arundhuti's mind that night. Perhaps, their feelings were rather augmented by the taboo — the social contempt towards romantic indul-gences amongst youngsters and that too within the family — that could have provoked an all too incessantly a powerful long-ing for each other.

Durga Puja brought along with it a maddening revelry and now that it was over, a sort of uneasy calmness prevailed in Devangshu Mitra's residence at south Calcutta. Shambhu made the most enchanting idol of Durga in the neighborhood and Devangshu Mitra, unlike the Raja of Rupnagar, immersed the idol on the day of Dashera, so that Shambhu's fable of 'the mer-maid on the sand dunes' would not be repeated. Guests departed one after the other just like they had arrived. Devangshu Mitra finally breathed in relief. "Krishna, I'm so glad you could come and help me out. I don't know what I'd have done without you."
"Oh! no, you would have done just as well without me."
Unlike her usual self, Krishnamani chose to be rather modest with her brother, one man she revered more than anyone else, more so for his divine sense of intuition that held him in high esteem all her life. It was due to his divine intuition that he could

predict her early widowhood long before she was even married. Now, before leaving for Poona, she had one last request of her illustrious brother. She wanted him to predict Dhruva's future. Devangshu Mitra looked at his sister in despair, rather exhausted from carrying the burden of guilt mixed with a sense of helplessness all around. "Why do you want to know the future? Like a fair maiden, it's most charming when cloaked in mystery. Let's just leave her at that." His voice sounded like a whisper in a graveyard, and then with a heavy sigh the astrologer reclined into an austere silence. His words of stoicism alarmed his sister. His life long perusal and his ceaseless zeal for his vocation had gradually, for some unspoken reason, petered out. That day without further adieu, as Krishnamoni was never accustomed to, told Swarnalata to take good care of her husband and left with Dhruva for Poona. Devangshu Mitra sat still and looked on as he had nothing much to say to his sister or to anyone else for that matter. With the end of Durga puja, it was as though he had resigned from life, for he had just finished his last sacred duty as a mortal to appease the gods and the goddesses and now drawing closer to the twilight of his life, he looked at everyone, rather philosophically, as if they were each a moth that hovers around the flame of life until it drops over and burns itself to ashes, some only sooner than others. Steeped in a mood of philosophical melancholy, Devangshu Mitra seemed rather aching in solitude.

True to his namesake — Dhruva, the north star, that enjoyed the reputation of being perennial — Krishnmoni's son also took an oath of perennial love to Arundhuti before leaving for Poona. Thus, Durga Puja that year marked the beginning of a romantic chapter in their life. While they both finished high school and went to college, Dhruva in Bombay and Arundhuti in Calcutta, Dhruva, inclined towards literature signed up for English as his major and Arundhuti intrigued by the depth and the scope of ancient wisdom of India decided to study eastern philosophy in her honors course. Each living more than a thousand miles apart, it was their long and passionate letters which they wrote quite frequently that bridged the gulf and kept their love vigorously aflame. During the day they spent several hours writing letters while the nights went by dreaming of one another. In the beginning Arundhuti was more cautious and less bold, less direct than Dhruva in opening herself up to him, while Dhruva was right from the beginning straight forward and honest to an extent that seemed almost unworldly. Though, he was by no means indiscreet, yet, when it violated his sense of candor, he opted for the latter. Their letters carried their dreams and aspirations to and fro. Soon, their dreams, their love and their lives all entwined into a single thread of existence. Years rolled by in the meanwhile. Both of them got their Bachelor's degree and well into their final year of Master's program. Dhruva selected Shakespeare as his special paper.

Over the summer holidays that year, after the examination, Dhruva's English Professor, Dr. Pritish Sen decided to stage Shakespeare's latest and his finest philosophical allegory — Tempest. Dr. Sen, a fresh arrival from Oxford preferred Dhruva over a dozen other students who had auditioned for the role of Ferdinand. Shakespeare's Ferdinand was a rather brawny, lofty, precious child of nature that grew up in her lap, but Dr. Sen was willing to compromise, for he was quite taken with Dhruva's sonorous voice and told him that he had picked him over all the others for two reasons — the clarity in his speech and the modulation in his voice. Dhruva was quick to adapt the Elizabethan diction and that pleased Dr. Sen immensely. But his talent, though matchless, now posed a new problem. The question was who could he pick to play Prospero, the exiled Duke of Milan? Certainly Dhruva's overpowering talent as Ferdinand must not be allowed to jeopardize Prospero's role. After all, the author had mirrored himself in Prospero, so, one could not possibly do a greater disservice to Shakespeare than to play down that profound role. After a month-long gridlock brought on by a fruitless search for the perfect cast, Dr. Sen himself, perfectly at home with Shakespearean dictum, came up with the obvious choice. So, Dhruva was now playing against his own professor. That summer the university auditorium resounded with an astounding power of eloquence as pupils, parents and professors sat spellbound as the drama unfolded through Tempest. When Arundhuti learned of Dhruva's artistic endeavor, nothing arrested her attention more than the thought of that girl who might have won Dhruva'a heart on stage while playing Miranda. So she wrote:

My dear Ferdinand:
I am jealous of your Miranda, do write to me about her. I am dying to see her through your eyes..... etc. etc.

In reply Dhruva warily avoided mentioning a word about the 'Miranda' in the play and instead wrote to her:

My dear Miranda:
'O if a virgin, and your affection not gone forth, I'll make you the Queen of Naples'...etc.

Arundhuti in reply to her 'Ferdinand' playfully rebuked:

My dear Ferdinand:
I object to the first four words of your line — are you by any chance questioning my chastity? As to 'my affection' you must know that you are the only possessor of it and as for the last part of your line, I'll be quite content to be your queen, as I have no desire to rule Naples.

There again, in response to Arundhuti's letter Dhruva wrote:
My dear Miranda: 'The very instant that I saw you, did my heart fly to your service; there resides to make me slave to it; and for your sake am I this patient log-man.' Then, if you should ask me

as did Shakespeare's Miranda, 'Do you love me?' I'll reply as your Ferdinand, 'O heaven, O earth, bear witness to this sound,....... I, beyond all limit of what else i' th' world, do love, prize, honour you.'

Thus, all through that summer they continued playing Tempest through letters, until a tempestuous chain of events tore their lives apart. Lately Biplav had begun to sense something in Arundhuti's disposition that triggered his suspicion greatly. He had engaged more than one matchmaker to fetch him just the right proposal so that she would not have the heart to decline. Arundhuti, on the other hand, did not have the gall to confront her father directly for she knew only too well that, had she even dared to mention her true feelings for Dhruva, he would be among the least persuadable to such a proposition and that it would only end in a family debacle. It was a quandary in Arundhuti's life that stuck like a fish bone in her throat which she could for the life of her neither swallow nor remove.

So, Biplav decided to take things in his own hand and so on a warm July dusk without Devangshu Mitra's blessings and against Arundhuti's will, the Brahmin priest tied the nuptial knot between Arundhuti and Malay, the pharmacist boy picked by Biplav. Not too many guests attended the wedding for the same reason that carried a lot of weight and apprehension in their minds. Those that declined from attending the ceremony per-ceived this wedding as a recalcitrance between father and son. Caught in a precarious position, Arundhuti's love for Dhruva lay buried and matters of moral obligation took precedence. Fulfilling the roles of an ideal daughter and a loyal wife were the moral obligations that weighed heavily on Arundhuti's mind and was therefore compelled to avow to it. Malay was happy to have Arundhuti as his wife and regarded their marriage as a true bless-ing from heaven. Biplav was happy to prove to his 'incorrigible' father that unlike all his other siblings, he would not succumb to father's astrological hocus pocus. Arundhuti, in turn, took complacence from the fact that her father and her husband, both men in her life, had found their happiness through this marriage.

The newlyweds had been away to Darjeeling since past week. Malay only wished he could extend their stay for at least another week and enjoy the solitude and the grandeur of that neat little town tucked away in the north eastern corner of the country, cuddled in the lap of Himalayas. They had been rising in the wee hours of predawn every day to capture the much-talked-about sunrise of Kinchanjungha, and every day they have been returning to their hotel disappointed, as flakes of cloud came in their way forbidding that glorious sight. However, the newly weds cherished just being away from home and everyone else since it gave them the opportunity to know each other intimately. But the rush of professional duties brought on by the pressure of a new job urged Malay to return that day. The drive back home from Darjeeling via Siligudi to Calcutta exhausted them totally. They just could not wait to get home and go to bed.

But as the car turned to enter into their street, they noticed an ambulance parked right in front of their house and couple of police officers at the gate struggling to keep the crowd away as men, women and children choked the entire street. Neighbours were rubbernecking from terraces, verandas, balconies and windows, hawkers, passing by, stood still outside their gate and even the paanwalla from the next street closed his paan shop temporarily to steal a glimpse of the tragic incidence. Instantly, the thought of mother came into Malay's mind.
"Maybe something happened to ma." Malay wondered aloud, but it was not her.

It was practically from the street that they could hear a frantic voice wailing and cursing her new daughter-in-law. The moment Arundhuti heard her name being uttered with such contempt, she wondered as to how she could have caused such provocation to her mother-in-law. They have hardly known each other and for most of the time that she has been in this family as a daughter-in-law, she has been away with her husband. Frightened by the row all around, as she floundered up the staircase, headed for her room, she heard her mother-in-law again, "your majesty may go inside and see for yourself."

At first she only saw a couple of police officers inside their bedroom discussing in a low voice. She glanced over their shoulders, her palpitation heightened, a rush of cold sweat came over her, and her vision gradually blurred. She almost fainted when someone from the back held her and asked her to calm down. "Do you recognize the body?" She shuddered from the icy tone in his voice.

"Could be a case of suicide, but we don't know yet, maybe you can help us," the other police officer stated in a matter-of-fact tone without taking his eyes off the corpse.

"Oh, no!... no!!... no!!!... Dhruva! Dhruva!" screamed Arundhuti in a frenzy, "how could you?... how could you do this?"

At first Arundhuti's voice fluttered and then broke into a loud and helpless sob.

Malay stood there looking cadaverous, wondering if the sky had suddenly fallen on him or was he walking through a nightmare? Who's this man lying dead in their bed? How is he related to his wife? Why didn't she mention a word about him? The last few days have been so wonderful that he felt he certainly could not have asked for more from life. He had just begun to feel so close to her. Whenever he held her in his arms, he felt a sense of belonging, all her pains and pleasures, her hopes and fears, her past, present and future, everything, everything belonged to him. Yet, how could she have nurtured such a secret from him all this time that they were together? Even while she slept, he gazed at her and wished he could be a part of her dreams. But, now he wondered, if he knew her at all, or were these last few days with her only an illusion?

"I see a note... must be written by him," said one of the police officers and then looking at Malay's mother, "could you tell us how it all happened?" he asked as he pulled out a small note book and a pencil from his pocket.

"He asked me if he could see my daughter-in-law..."

Malay's mother, terribly shaken by the mishap, slowly mustered up her will, got her bearings and continued, "I asked him who he was... he said... he said... he was her cousin... so I let him in, you know...what else could I have done?... and told him that...that, they must be on their way home from Darjeeling... I handed him their wedding album to look at... then..." Malay's mother needed to take a deep breath. She had cried herself hoarse and looked terribly sapped. The officer tried to comfort her.

"You are doing just fine, madam, carry on, then...?" He tried to refresh her memory.

"Then... then... he started complaining of a headache... so I told him to rest and showed him to their bedroom... the only room that was empty since all the other rooms were occupied and then I sent the maid with a cup of tea... and then I heard a scream... so I ran into their room and saw him lying like that... just like that... with that empty green bottle right next to him." The police officers busily scribbled down every word as she struggled to give a complete scenario between her frequent bursts of sobbing and gasping. The police inspector managed to put the bits and pieces tidily together, then ordered a few snap shots of the carcass from various angles, of the immediate surroundings in the room, took a sample of the tea, fingerprints on the teacup, the note written by him and the empty green bottle that lay next to him. Thus, the investigation continued tediously with flurries of repetitious questions and answers that dragged every single member of the family into it including the servants and the neighbors. Dhruva's body lay there in their bed cold and stiff, his eyes fiercely open and enlarged, and stains of white liquid froth that had dribbled from the corner of his mouth. Everything around Arundhuti spun dizzily, something inside her stomach churned severely forcing upward a gush of vomit, and then everything around her suddenly turned black and mute. Arundhuti fainted.

My Dearest Rini:

By the time you will begin to read this letter, my life will have ended. I leave this world with a strange compound of feelings and emotions, but before I do so, I feel I should say a few words. They may not mean much to you, at least not anymore, since you will be spending the rest of your life in the arms of another man, perhaps quite happily, while I will be gone forever with these very thoughts in my heart. As I envision you in love with another man, I could not but seize that everlasting sleep for myself, that sweet and blissful sleep which alone can give me my peace of mind. I never could imagine that my Rini could ever belong to anyone else. Many times in the past when I would sit down to write to you, you would enter into my thoughts with a lovely smile on your face just like the full moon that slowly appears in the night sky shimmering with light. Today my moon is eclipsed and will remain so forever. As I write to you, I feel I had been stabbed in my sleep and then when I woke up I found myself fallen by the wayside of my life bleeding to death. Today, I am not about to question you as to how it all happened, why it happened or even if you could prevent it from happening. I assume, one does, only what one is capable of doing. If I had expected you to be otherwise, the fault lay in my perception of you and not in you. Nevertheless, my world without you feels like a dark abyss and my mind is immensely overshadowed by the fear of insanity. Therefore, I thought it best to end my life. But before my body is burnt to ashes, I want you to look at me for the last time, just so that you can at least see the pain in my eyes, if not feel it. The pain I will carry with me just to remain yours truly for ever and ever. But before I say goodbye to you, I would like to read to you one of my very favorite Shakespeare's sonnets:

'No longer mourn for me when I am dead
Than you shall hear the surly sullen bell
Give warning to the world that I am fled
From this vile world with vilest worms to dwell.
Nay, if you read this line, remember not
The hand that writ it; for I love you so,
That I in your sweet thoughts would be forgot
If thinking on me then should make you woe
O, if I say you look upon this verse
When I perhaps compounded am with clay,
Do not so much as my poor name rehearse,
But let your love even with my life decay;
Lest the wise world should look into your moan
And mock you with me after I am gone.'
Yours truly,
Dhruva

It was past midnight. Arundhuti must have read the letter for the
umpteenth time. She sat on the terrace all by herself staring pen-
sively at the empty space, dry eyed and sallow, after reading
Dhruva's letter one more time. She still had not recovered from
the consternation, and in lieu, intense pain, fury and guilt had
enervated her totally. She wished she could see him just once, so,
she could ask him, why in the world did he do this to himself and
to her... why?... why?... why couldn't he wait to hear her side of
the story? Arundhuti wanted to scream her heart out. It has been
over a month since Dhruva killed himself. After the postmortem,
the legal hassle finally died down, but, a cloud of vicious smoke
still lynching in the air throttled Arundhuti. The judgmental
society around her held her greatly responsible for it, and worst
of all, her own mother-in-law ostracized her, which had a debili-
tating effect on her husband. Within a week of that fateful day,
Arundhuti was left with no choice but to leave her husband for
good and since then she had been living with her parents in Lake
Road. The thought of Sita nestled on Arundhuti's mind. In the

Ramayana, when Ravana eloped with Sita and later Rama rescued her, the ignorant launderer accused Sita of sacrilege to which Rama acquiesced. He abandoned his virtuous wife for the sake of his subjects. Arundhuti wondered about such a world, the world around womanhood clothed in a charade of chastity. How could she ever gain empathy from such a world? What could she have done differently that would have alleviated her fate? Could she concede to her father about her love for Dhruva? That would only expedite her marriage. Could she elope with Dhruva? There too, he would hunt her down and get her married to the man of his choice or disown her for the rest of her life. So, what could she have really done? The more she mused about it, the less certain Arundhuti felt about her estranged husband and their future together. She was still a bride, but Dhruva's death, ironically enough, brought a sudden widowhood in Arundhuti's life. She seemed to have lost the taste for life. But, what would she do with herself? Where would she go? How would she survive? There must be a way out, somewhere in this world where she could be herself, just herself, and be able to breathe in the fresh air of life again.

Arundhuti had been revisiting old memories. Her father was always at an odd's end with his father, until the day she left her husband and came back home. Biplav had stopped talking to everyone completely since that day. He had virtually shut himself up against the rest of the world and went into a deep seclusion, a silent protest, perhaps, against everything he believed in including his own self! Nothing is more harsh and painful than to have fallen in your own esteem. That is how she remembered him, her last day at home. He had nothing further to say to her, when he finally learnt that she was on her way to Banaras to become what his father had long predicted.

Devangshu Mitra was in no better frame of mind either. She had found him rather weary from reading everyone's future. It was as if he alone could read from a cosmic page of an invisible book wherein was etched in bold print, the past, the present and the future of every living soul. And much of what he knew was too painful to share with anyone else. So, he kept it to himself until he could hold it no longer. He only wished he could change the destiny of all his loved ones — Biplav, Arundhuti, Dhruva, Krishnomoni — for he could see it approaching like a deluge, that would affect so many lives, but there was nothing he could do to prevent it, for he also knew that human destiny is far from a frivolous act of nature. She remembered him, always conforming to the enlightened wisdom of the ancient sages that vindicated the universal law of karma.

"Can you ever escape from bearing the fruit of your own past actions? No, certainly not, only you are responsible for all your actions," he would quietly nod his head, as though, he would soon lapse into a quiet contemplation, but he would once again continue, picking up the momentum in his voice, "so, my dear friend, the only way to redemption for all your past follies is through kind, just, noble and selfless deeds in your present life, the only way to redemption for your next life."

Devangshu Mitra must have uttered these very words a million times in his life to all those that came to him for astrological reading. Arundhuti recalled how everyone that listened to her grandfather and tried to grasp the meaning of karma would begin to take solace from their miseries for now they had no one else to blame but their own actions.

To this day, she remembered those words so distinctly, those words that came from deep within himself had touched her soul. She had felt a strange vibration within herself, a surge of faith renewed in her. It was the day before she left home for good, "go on, my child," he rumbled, "the path you are to follow will bring you infinite joy and bliss, go on and never look back, remember my words."

She had not looked back until this day. Arundhuti remembered Malay, his mother and so many others, all those whom she had left behind had been on her mind all day long. The voice of her mother-in-law echoed harshly. It was the night before she was driven away by her husband. Malay came home late that night. Since the mishap Malay had been looking for excuses to stay out after work and came home late every night. His immediate circumstances at home had virtually turned into macabre, and especially, with a shrew around for a mother, he just could not brave it any more. Unlike others, he did not hold his wife wholly responsible for whatever Dhruva did, but nonetheless, he was vexed that his family was wantonly dragged into the calamity.

Esoterically, of course, he could not stomach Dhruva's love for his wife. It seemed as though, through death, Dhruva had won his wife's heart eternally and therefore to the rest of the world the broken-hearted lover emerged chivalrous and that made Malay feel dastardly about himself. Overwhelmed by such personal humiliation and bedeviled by his mother, he cold heartedly turned away from her leaving her in utter misery.

"I am saying this not because he is my son," Malay heard his mother still bickering over the mishap when he came home that night, "but any other woman in your place would treat my son like a god, especially, for a woman like you with such a wonderful past, it's so wonderful that it shamed us all. We can't even show our face to the world now."

She dished her chiding with such sarcasm that it needled through anyone, no matter how thick skinned one was. Malay stood right there looking awkward and pitiful at first. He could not say a word to either of them. But his mother went on and on babbling repugnantly about how characterless her daughter-in-law was, and when that did not satisfy her, she started to gab offensively about her father and her grandfather and so on and so forth.

"Instead of sitting and mourning in my house, why don't you go to your father's house and weep over his shoulder for your late beloved and leave my son alone?" Malay could not take it any more. "That's enough, ma, can't you at least forgive her?" Incensed by her spite, he retorted.

"Don't ask me that question. See, if the rest of the world will forgive her. Don't forget, she has smeared our face with mud," the mother snapped.

"Why blame the rest of the world, when we ourselves don't have the generosity to forgive her. Besides, why even worry about the world, they don't feed us?" said Malay, provoked by his mother's insensitive words. Malay's mother had found her daughter-in-law a little too proud for someone who had a love life that had been divulged to the rest of the world.

"What is it with you? You seem to be oozing with love for your pious wife, what magic does she have, I'd like to know," the mother scoffed at her son for favoring his wife so openly and so shamelessly, "how could you even see her face after what she has put us through?"

"Ah! ma, don't you have anything better to talk about, it's been a week now, the neighbours can hear us, you know." Malay turned furious. He wanted to put a lid to this infamous ordeal once and for all.

"I'll say whatever I want to in my own house. How dare you raise your voice at me like that?" then turning to Arundhuti she rebuked, "you wicked woman! you are the root of all this, first you throw smut on us and then you turn my own son, my own flesh and blood against me, you'll not be spared. Just mark my word."

So saying, the mother burst into tears. Just then, in a maddening rage, Malay walked into Arundhuti's room, ordered her to pack her bag and baggage and leave until things cooled off completely. Falling at his feet, she begged him not to be so ruthless to her. But he stood unflinchingly to his decision. That day, for no fault of hers, Arundhuti felt like a convict pleading for mercy and it was denied.

The sun is about to set. Soon, the twilight as lovely as it is will look lovelier when a thin crescent of the moon will slowly emerge on the eastern horizon and adorn the autumnal sky. By midday the cremation was over and the burning pyre was slowly cooling off. Arundhuti comes back to Manikarnika's ghat. Ever since she saw Malay this morning, something stirred within her. Malay had left. Arundhuti felt a sense of void within herself for a few moments. But, why this sudden desire to turn around to look for something that she had consciously discarded — this material life — as a heap of rubbish. She had left home and come to Banaras to find peace and contentment, where she could also finish her doctorate in philosophy from the well reputed Banaras Hindu University. Or was she only trying to escape then, and now that she found out that Malay still wants her back, her mind once again swings like a pendulum.

From a distance the sweet chiming of the bell and the melodious chanting of the Sanskrit mantra from the temples resonated through the vast expanse of the sky above her head to the Ganga flowing below her feet. She recalled those words of wisdom from the Gita: 'Embodied beings, however, are bewildered because of the ignorance which covers their real knowledge. Therefore, the doubts which have arisen in your heart out of ignorance should be slashed by the weapon of knowledge...' As a student of philosophy, her scholastic approach towards the Book had enriched her perception of this material life all through her university days and during her stay in Banaras, but it was far from offering her the wisdom or the spiritual insight to see through the very fabric of this worldly life — a life caught in a web of maya, the divine illusion.

This brief, yet dramatic episode with Malay — his sudden reappearance at Manikarnika's ghat at daybreak and then again his disappearance by sundown, although, momentarily shook the ground on which she stood — yet, for the very first time it all revealed to her like a mirage. Arundhuti began to think of herself as kasturi mriga, the deer in the forest that wanders around madly seeking the source of the fragrance, not knowing that it is within its own body. After all these years, for the first time, she began to feel truly detached to the world outside. She realized that peace and contentment lay within and not elsewhere. Enlightened, at last, at the end of her odyssey, the sanyasini blissfully retreats to her ashram.

In the
Silence of
the Night

That night Janaki never closed her eyes. She lay there waiting for the town of Govindpur, that would slowly emerge, with the light of dawn, as a town forever unkind and now unforgiving to her as long as she would live. She lay there like a carcass, her eyes anchored in an empty gaze, her tear-stained face looked pallid, her mouth slightly open, as if a thought just embarked from her heart, perched on her lips, and then flew away into oblivion. Her thoughts seldom sought any expression, ever, and if at all they did, they were more unwelcome than otherwise. Janaki's parents made no bones about the fact that it was in their longing for a son, that she had arrived into this world. So, when her entry into this world, so ruefully disdained, how dare she assert it with self-expression! That there would be little tolerance to such audacity, if any, was not unknown to Janaki. Whenever Janaki screamed, or cried or laughed, or smiled, or even talked to someone, the world usually turned her a deaf ear, except one person and that was Sukumar Mahato, that harijan boy from the squalor.

"Janu, I hope you can forgive me, please, don't get me wrong, please, Janu, you know I could never wish you any harm, but I had no choice." Pleaded Sukumar as he leaned over her anxiously. That day as Janaki lay on the mud floor of Sukumar's one-room thatch- roofed hut in their slum, her tender lovely face seemed more dead than alive. Sukumar agonized over Janaki's misfortune, about everything that happened in Janaki's life since last night. Since the last three weeks actually, all of which precipitated last night's event. So Sukumar finally did what he had to do in order to save his Janu from the misfortune. But could he really save her and give her the security every girl dreams of, or did he simply pull her out of the jaws of a hungry tiger and then plunge her into the well? Such was the misfortune of being one of many daughters in a poor Brahmin family.

Enraged by social bias and depravation, Sukumar nervously scurried around bare footed, engaged in a lengthy monologue that gave the impression of an untamed beast that would not acquiesce even under the sharpest of lashings or the appearance of a babbling lunatic except that everything he said made a lot of sense. But there was no one to listen to except Janaki, and she had heard them before. Such provocations always left Sukumar in anarchy against the viciously domineering force of the society. His volatile and impetuous reactions always left him swimming against the strong current without any shore in sight. His drive for such 'radicalism', if you will, was as natural as any atomic reaction, or the annihilation between a particle and an antiparticle in a science laboratory. Sukumar was bound to scream louder, cry harder, and fight better for Janaki than anyone else could, for Sukumar himself was a victim just as vulnerable as her in a different form and with a different name.

From behind the cloth curtain, stained with turmeric and soiled heavily with soot and grease from the cooking, dividing their little room into two, emerged Sukumar's mother. She was carrying a glass of steaming hot beverage that she had carefully made for the Brahmin girl. "Come, my girl, get up and drink this. I make this my own hands. I know, what you thinking. I know you not suppose to eat or drink anything we make, untouchable, but you now under our care and we do all we can to make you comfort. It be a sin to let you starve when you under our roof. So, I bathe and change and did my puja before I go to the kitchen like you

Brahmins do. Come, drink it. You feel better." Sukumar's mother reminded Janaki of her own mother who once, not too long ago, nursed Janaki back to health when she was struck with typhoid, when the entire family almost gave up all hopes, except her mother. It was only her mother who listened to her own intuition and never stopped for a moment to think that her Janaki would not live. And Janaki did live, but only to see this day. Janaki thought to herself in despair, as she buried her face in the hollow of her palms and burst into an avalanche of tears.

"Now, don't cry like that, my girl, some things happen for better." Sukumar's mother tried to console Janaki.

"How can anything get better after this? I've let my parents down, my whole family, each and every one from my caste must be cursing me now." On retrospect, Janaki had a lot to regret. She was terribly saddened by the thought of its repercussion that her family would have to now endure.

"Oh! so, now you mean to tell me, you'd be better off by marrying that soovar?" retorted Sukumar angrily. "I just couldn't bear the thought of seeing you married to that dirty, old rich man. That man who's forty years older than you, god alone knows how many mistresses he keeps and how many bastards he has fathered, he has no business marrying you just because, just because he's a Brahmin, son of a zamindar and sitting on heaps and piles of money, black money, that is. I can't believe, just can't believe your family fell for that soovar, and you too!!"

But Janaki had another plan. "Oh, don't get me wrong," she said to Sukumar. "I'd never in my life marry him because I'd not stay alive to get married." In doing so, she could have at least saved herself from being branded as an outcast and Parvati, poor Parvati, no father will ever want his son to marry Parvati now. Tears trailed down her face at the thought of her young, innocent sister, and the price she would have to now pay for her own action.

Parvati, born with a complexion that glowed like liquid gold and of petite frame, with an oval-shaped face often compared with the shape of a betel leaf, dainty features made prominent by dark and dreamy eyes, fine rose pink lips and delicate chin. Endowed with such unsullied beauty, she drew the attention of many parents in search of a bride for their sons. Elders in the town found a somewhat divine quality in Parvati's looks. On the other hand, Janaki, brown as wild honey, moderately tall, with a stunning figure, long luscious hair and large black eyes, somewhat earthy, had something very seductive about her. While all the young men in Govindpur gawked at Janaki, the elders in the town saw an image of a goddess in Parvati.

"Believe it or not, that was my biggest fear," snapped Sukumar, "The moment I heard about your marriage to that soovar, I remembered those two sisters from the Bada Bangla." Sukumar was referring to the two sisters in their neighborhood who recently hung themselves to death because their father could not afford dowry for their marriage. They knew, they would be tortured and then burnt alive once they arrived at their in-laws, so they had decided to quietly take their own lives. "I know you only too well to let you go through it, at least, not as long as I'm alive," said Sukumar. "Ram Ram, how you think like that, my girl? This life god gave and you destroy it like that?" said Sukumar's mother whose voice was so full of love and kindness. "What's left to be destroyed, when my fate has destroyed it all?" Janaki once again broke into a bitter sob.

"Don't blame your fate, it's really the fear in you that destroys you." Sukumar was angry, very angry with everyone including Janaki, whom he loved so dearly. "Fate is only an excuse we use to hide our fears, our inhibitions and our own inabilities." Sukumar spoke with conviction while his mother lovingly cajoled Janaki to take the drink. "Come, come, now drink this while it still warm. It give you some strength, you need it."

A draught of cold January wind blew in from under the door. The bottom of the door was eaten up by the rotting from heavy monsoon flood. Sukumar's mother wrapped the shawl around herself neatly as she felt a chill in the air inside their little hut. A shaft of morning sunlight pried through the cracks of her tiny grilled kitchen window throwing a few sparkles on her brass pots and pans neatly shelved against the wall. Sukumar's mother was up well before dawn preparing this special drink for Janaki. She took a pot of water and added a few chunks of sugar candy, then stepped out of her kitchen to pluck some fresh green leaves of tulsi that she once planted just outside her hut, threw it into the pot along with some freshly ground ginger-root, some black pepper and then went out and borrowed some cloves from her neighbor, added that and boiled the pot for an hour or so until the ingredients became almost indistinguishable. A warm glass of boiled milk instead would have sufficed but Sukumar was in no mood to run any errand that morning — to the milkman's hut was out of the question altogether. "It give you strength, go on, drink it; you turned blue with cold and fear; I bring you another quilt." Then, she looked at her son and said, "now leave the poor girl alone till she find some peace in herself first. She be alright, I know."

Janaki lay there reminiscing. It was just yesterday and yet it all seemed so far removed from her life today, as if she woke up to another aeon. For a Brahmin girl to take refuge in the house of a shudra, share their food and spend a night under their roof was as unholy and scandalous an affair, the little town of Govindpur could ever take it, though, as modern as it claimed to be. According to the rigid Brahminic scruples, Janaki was polluted beyond purgery. Until yesterday she was a daughter of a Brahmin, today an outcast. Her notoriety would now make the infamous sisters from the Bada Bangla look like suttee. Elders of Govindpur would cast her away from their thoughts and memories indignantly. Young women in company would quietly whisper under their breath about the Brahmin girl that disappeared on her nuptial evening to lose her virginity before her marriage, and that too, to a shudra!! Of course, the world would never know the truth, for it would remain buried in the silence of the night. The truth, borne out of a respect for human dignity, the lack of which in their world created a common bond between them since their childhood.

Born in a caste that was perennially cursed by the rest of humanity in that part of the world, Sukumar Mahato was like the primrose on a dunghill. He had the instincts of a warrior who believed in fighting against all odds for equality. The anathema of being born as a Shudra turned into a catalyst in Sukumar since his early childhood. Because of his often too-radical characteristics, his mother, a poor illiterate widow herself, lived in constant fear of losing him in the hands of those slumlords, 'gundas' as they were called in common parlance. In a communal riot, not too long ago, Sukumar, the Mahato boy, as he was fondly called by his people, escaped by the skin of his teeth. But to Janaki, Sukumar was her savior today. It was Sukumar alone in whom she could confide and seek advice.

In the backwater of the fast approaching urban tides, in the gender-biased, caste-ridden little town of Govindpur, a girl who went beyond the eighth standard, if anything, was deemed as overly qualified and therefore 'harmful' to the society. Given the opportunity, she would grow up to form her own ideas and opinions even on matters that were always governed by men. That itself could pose a threat to the predominantly male society. So, like all her other sisters, Janaki too, was told to stay home and help her mother and her little sister Parvati with their household chores, until she could be married off to a suitable boy picked by her parents.

Janaki and Sukumar knew each other from the time they went to Govindpur Primary School and became friends ever since. Despite their social disparity, they both quietly reveled a sense of attraction for each other, though, they were too shy to openly admit it to one another. Sukumar was one of the brightest pupils in school. Once, when he was in the eighth standard, he won a prize for scoring the highest marks in mathematics.

The prize was a biography of the mathematics genius Srinivasa Ramanujan, the poor, lonesome and peerless Brahmin from the South who grew up along the bank of river Cauvery in a small town called Kumbakonam. Often described as the world's most creative mathematician of the century and compared with none other than Euler and Jacobi, Ramanujan was the first Indian ever to attain the Fellowship of the Royal Society (FRS). It was not until G.H. Hardy, from Trinity, Cambridge, mesmerized by his genius, invited him to come to England, and E. H. Neville, Hardy's colleague, having met Ramanujan at Madras and looked at his notebook persuaded him to take the ship to England. Sukumar also learned from that book that Ramanujan's note-books, riddled with mathematical equations, have left scholars around the world intrigued by its brilliance even decades after he died prematurely. Infected with tuberculosis from England, while at Cambridge, Ramanujan came home severely ill in 1917 and died on April 26, 1920. He lived to be only thirty-two.

That book became such a revelation to the young mind of a school boy, that ever since then, Sukumar decided to devote himself to mathematics, so that some day he too could explore into the world of Ramanujan's genius. Later, as he was one day lamenting over the brevity of Ramanujan's life, he quietly expressed his fondest wish to Janaki, "you know, Janu, I only wish Ramanujan had lived to be as old as Bertrand Russell or Isac Newton or Albert Einstein, then, maybe, just maybe, he would have lived to prove the famous 'Riemann's hypothesis'."

"Maybe he left it for you," said Janaki half teasingly, and then broke into a peal of laughter.

"Then, come to think of it," continued Sukumar with the same melancholy in his voice without minding her insensitivity to the matter, "a mathematician, though, not necessarily, is at his best when he's young. Look at Galois, he died at twenty one, Abel at twenty seven, Ramanujan at thirty two, Blaise Pascal was already a well known mathematician at fourteen and died at thirty nine. Bernhard Riemann died at forty. O! and how could I forget our very own? The earliest extant book on Algebra was by a twenty three year old, Aryabhatta — the fifth century mathematician and astronomer. But, if you look around, you find poets and philosophers rather start to blossom after thirty or maybe forty, with a few exceptions like Shelly who died at thirty and Christopher Marlowe at twenty nine." Janaki quietly wondered, how does he know so much; when does he have the time to read all that. Janaki could not think of anyone in Govindpur quite like him. This harijan boy from the squalor was more learned than most Brahmins she knew in the town.

While Sukumar was still breezing through mathematics, scoring the highest marks all through high school and college, a great social leader of the time drew his attention. Soon, Sukumar began to follow his footprints. It was Dr. Ambedkar, the man who rose from the same social mire as himself to become a pioneer of the Indian Constitution. Dr. Ambedkar, a graduate from Columbia University in New York, dreamed of saving his people from the oppression of untouchability. In 1946, Ambedkar authored the Indian Constitution, and in 1947, Babasaheb, as he was commonly known, was appointed as the Law Minister of the Indian Government, outlawing the discrimination of untouchability. For someone born at the bottom of the social pit, it was a great height to attain and of course, at much greater cost. So deep rooted was the caste system in the Indian soil that to escape from its heinous practice, on October 14, 1956, on the day of Dassera, Dr. Ambedkar renounced Hinduism and became a Buddhist. That day Sukumar's faith in his idol shattered forever. Still, the harijan boy remained unfettered to the cause. Just seven weeks later, his fallen hero succumbed to death.

In Govindpur, a little town near Patna, the state capital of Bihar, was a town so small that it would take one by surprise, if it could be spotted on the map. In the early fifties, it started gaining prestige among neighboring towns and villages with the emergence of its own high school — a red brick L shaped two storied building with a long impressive corridor — a historical landmark for a town on its way to progress.

A medical clinic, staffed by a couple of doctors and a nurse who commuted from Patna everyday, was the next thing to happen in the way of modernization. Till then the homespun and ancient Ayurvedic treatment made from various herbs and roots prevailed widely. Once, when Parvati sprained her foot from a fall off a mango tree, the treatment was available right in their kitchen. Their grandmother cooked up a steaming hot paste of powdered limestone and dried roots of turmeric, applied a thick coating of it on the sprain, and that was all there was to it. For cuts, bruises and insect bites, juice extracted from ground leaves of marigold served as an elixir. During an epidemic of small pox, the treatment did not start with the patient alone, but with the entire household disciplining their diet to a stringent form of vegetarianism, for those that were not vegetarians otherwise. Once, as a child, when Sukumar suffered from smallpox, he practically survived on neem leaves, for he was fed, bathed and even fanned with neem leaves. Camphor purified drinking water. Also aloe juice; fresh garlic; and one's own urine were some of the excellent potions of great medicinal value that prevailed not just in Govindpur but in the bucolic life of India. The midwife, a rural proxy to an obstetrician, delivered babies at home. In keeping with the ancient eastern philosophy that says, 'diet cures more than the doctor,' food — coarse, unadulterated and fresh from the farm — played an all important role.

As daily commuting, via Siwan by bus between Patna and Govindpur, became more and more a way of life, the emergence of a railway station in the town became imminent. An unpretentiously small brick structure with red tiles for a roof, sitting at the center of an equally small cemented platform, was all that was needed for the steam locomotive to swoosh away busily through the heart of Govindpur carrying passengers to and fro every day.

Then, there arose a need for a post office, a sort of makeshift cubicle of a structure with a corrugated tin shade at the top. Inside the cubicle sat the postmaster. Earlier, a postman with a knapsack on his back running through the town like a marathon runner in the Olympics, humming away folklore to the rhythm of his pace was a familiar sight. Now he was a modern man provided with modern transportation, a brand new bicycle.

Next, an equally unimpressive looking police station took over the rural system of justice. Almost overnight, they were replaced by a hierarchy of police officers. These new institutions proved to be quite functional as each one of them served a purpose, though at a slow, restful pace like a painting that fitted well within the background of the slowly emerging town of Govindpur.

And now a movie theater! Its recent advent brought new excitement to the life of Govindpur. Indian movies, as always frilled with songs and dances, had the magic of creating a world of fantasy to the minds of both young and the young at heart. Until then it used to be the village barber with his inexhaustible well of gossips, who provided their main source of entertainment, and once in a while during the long drawn summer evenings, even the gram panchayat provided quite an entertainment. Of course, all said and done, it was Ramlila that topped the list of entertainments, their most eagerly awaited annual event in town.

Janaki lay there thinking of that day, a few weeks ago, the day

Prakash Thakore called on her family. It was for the first time she saw the man of whom she had lately heard so much, especially from Sukumar. Thakore's sudden visit that afternoon took Janaki's father Vishnupriya Pathak quite by surprise. At first he did not know what to make of it. In his white crumpled dhoti and his sacred thread hanging from his shoulder diagonally across his bare chest, the father trotted about in the presence of this all-important visitor for awhile, like a jolly little puppy that was being unleashed by its master. At first, Janaki saw the two men exchanging words in a low voice that spelled nothing short of confidential. Then, she watched her father, a little hesitant, humming and hawing to her mother while the stranger patiently waited behind the curtain of their scantily, yet neatly kept outer room. Mother's ruddy face leaning over a flaming hearth as she stirred a boiling pot of lentil soup, suddenly turned pale and remorse. At first she drew a blank and then her eyes slowly glistened with tears. As Janaki gleaned, her eyes like a pair of ping pong ball shuttled back and forth between her parents. Their low whisper from across the room came floating in an inaudible blur as the warm stuffy air in their dim, tiny, windowless kitchen stenched with conspiracy that was being broiled by her parents. Father seemed a little preoccupied and a great deal perturbed, actually. Of course, at first Janaki mistook the stranger for a moneylender. He must be demanding mother's last pair of gold bangles or the fine gold chain she wore around her neck ever since Janaki remembered as a little girl.

"Is that man in the other room from the pawnshop, mother? Is he here to strip you of your last bit of gold from your body?" Janaki asked her mother in dismay. To be jeweled in plush gold was the traditional image of a Hindu woman that best described her wealth and her fine status. It was not until she lost that status to either widowhood or to a state of impecuniosity that her image condescended to a new dimension. Janaki grew up watching her mother drudge through hardships day after day with utmost devotion, the kind of tenacity and resilience one would find in a beast of burden. Often, a sense of empathy and adulation for her mother would strike a gentle chord in her inner self. From early on in her life, as she painfully recalled bearing the brunt of poverty and humiliation, she found this all-too-familiar road to struggle never ending but only getting steeper.

"No, my child, it's not for my gold that he is here. He is asking for a lot more," the mother replied vigilantly.

"You stay out of it and speak only when you are spoken to," scolded the father without looking at Janaki directly, "and next time try to show some respect when you talk to your elders."

The father, as always irritable and exacting reverence that he failed to earn, yet, never refrained from demanding it.

"What else is left of us that we can give away?" asked Janaki without paying much heed to her father.

"He wants to marry you." The mother struggled to hold back her tears.

"And let me tell you something," added the father excitedly, "he is so rich that he can probably weigh you in gold and then give it away in charity without giving it another thought. He was just telling me how he would treat you like a queen. What more can a poor Brahmin poojari like me ask for?"

The father looked pitiful. It was as if he was asking for his daughter's mercy. Janaki saw in his father's eyes a culprit that begged her not to judge him so harshly.

"If he is such a wonderful match for your daughter, then why do you look so distressed and why is mother in tears?" Janaki defied her father like never before, as if she was possessed by a spirit of a dauntless soul. Father wasn't like this before. Janaki recalled her father as a morally scrupulous, orthodox Brahmin, especially, when it came to selecting a husband for his older daughters, Durga, Uma and Shivani. He always looked for their ideals before picking them as his son-in-law. He never cowered down like this. Never before had she seen so despicable a sycophant in her father.

Despite his modest means, Vishnupriya Pathak always took a great deal of pride as a Brahmin. Yes, he was a poor Brahmin maybe, but a full-blooded Brahmin no doubt, whose only duty on earth was to uphold the righteousness and integrity of his religion. Whatever happened to all that? Poverty certainly had its satanic power that could suck the virtue out of the very best, and sometimes even the idealists and the moralists have failed to escape from its grip.

"What's the matter with you? I've never heard you talk like this before?" Janaki's audacity had shocked him.

"It's because you never tried to sell your daughters before. That man looks as old as you are. Have you no shame? How can you do this to me?" Janaki exploded in rage.

The father slapped the daughter across her face and rushed towards the outer room leaving both mother and daughter in tears.

The stranger had quietly left, leaving behind a jewelry box that contained a gold necklace studded with diamonds and pearls and a little handwritten note saying, 'I am leaving behind something very small for your beautiful daughter. If she can ever accept me for whatever I am worth, I will wait for an answer. Prakash Thakore.'

"Oh! What a nice man, How very kind of him, I wonder if God will ever forgive me," Janaki's father wailed in humiliation. "Only if you foolish women could see, here was Prakash Thakore, son of a zamindar, an epitome of Lakshmi at my door step asking for my daughter's hand! And what does my family do? Chase him away like a street dog! Oh! How much I must have sinned in my past life to be cursed with such a foolish daughter."

"Prakash Thakore! that traitor! that imposter!" Janaki could not believe her father could give in to such desperation. How low can one stoop to get his daughter married? What if I decide not to get married at all? Why is this marriage to that imposter so very important that father is even willing to look the other way? There's not a soul in Govindpur who doesn't wince at the mention of this infamous man? Why? Janaki could not understand the rationale behind this that could be so very compelling to her father. So ludicrously lopsided are some of the values of the Brahmins! And more so than anything else, it was their vaunt and inflated sense of moral superiority that she found intolerable.

"Why don't you go and fall at his feet. He's probably waiting to forgive you, anyway. Don't forget to return the jewelry. He might need it for his next catch — another poor Brahmin's daughter like me," said Janaki in contempt.

Deep down, she was more angry at herself than anyone else. She blamed herself for being born in such poverty. She blamed herself for being their daughter. Why couldn't I be their son instead? The son they always wanted to have. How different my life would have been then.

"Don't talk to your father like that," uttered her mother in her husband's defense, "can't you see your father and I are helpless? If we want to live in a society with respect, we have to do certain things even if it hurts us a little. I don't believe it's a sin to get our daughter married to a rich man, as long as he treats her well. He seems like a nice man to me."

The mother attempted to make some sense, though her attempt only gave away a lurking suspicion hidden behind those words 'as long as he treats her well'. Her belief, if at all, was shaky. They were bound to come out that way for she never really believed in a rich man, even now as she spoke to her daughter, she hid behind those words. The rich would sometimes trust the poor, but the poor never trusted the rich and certainly Janaki and her parents were no exception to that, and yet, today, she was willing to make a sacrificial goat of her daughter! Janaki was appalled.

"Nice man! You call him a nice man? Isn't he the same man who set fire to the harijan slums, the one next to the movie theater, so he could build a restaurant right there?" Janaki fumed in rage as she continued, "and then, afraid of getting caught, he bribed them all from the SP to the constable. What's so respectable about him?"

"Go on, ridicule me as much as you want. A poor man deserves no respect, not even from his own child." Griped Vishnupriya.

It was not a plea from a father to his child alone, but a much larger plea to the world outside. Deep down the father lamented not for what he was about to do to his daughter, but for what has been done to him. He was sinned and not the sinner.

The grinding stone of poverty crushed his pride and left him a broken man, so now he was ready to take up on this offer — a crutch to move on and perhaps up in life.

"But I'll tie you down with a rope if I have to and get you married to him." Retorted the father in a rage.

"Why don't you tie a rope around my neck and hang me instead and you can do the same for Parvati too." Janaki was furious that day.

"Don't talk like that, like those two girls from Bada Bangla, everybody is talking about them. They brought nothing but sorrow and humiliation to their poor parents. Is that what parents deserve, tell me?" Janaki's father screamed at her.

"Did they have any choice? Tell me. They would have been burnt alive anyway, at least, this way they died peacefully. Besides, what have I done that I should deserve this?" She screamed back at him, "why didn't you let me finish school? I could have tutored some children and brought home some money. I could be as worthy as any boy."

Or why couldn't I be like cousin Smita? She thought to herself. Janaki had heard from Smita that girls from big cities enjoyed a lot of freedom. Their parents allowed them to go to college, find jobs and bring home money like men do? Why couldn't she be born in a modern family like Smita's? Janaki had never been to a big city, but once when Smita visited her over the summer holidays, she had heard all about city life. City girls were even allowed to wear bras and talk to boys. That day Janaki listened with awe. Smita also told her that people from small towns have small minds. Janaki's feelings were hurt. She thought Smita was being a snob. But that was a long time ago when Janaki was a little girl herself. "Whatever gave you the idea that you could be as worthy as a boy? Besides, it's not like he's asking you to be his mistress. He wants to marry you and what can be more honorable than that?"

It was as if Janaki's father saw no wrong in that man. After all, how could he? By the time he had his third daughter, Shivani married, he was dragged to near destitution. Had it not been for Prakash Thakore, he would not have had a roof over his head today. Of course, at the time, Vishnupriya Pathak was not in the least aware that he would have to someday pay for it so dearly.

The family priesthood, like most ancestral estate, followed its family lineage and also that of its client's. Thus Janaki's father and his forefathers had been the family priest in zamindar Thakore's household for several generations. Priesthood, viewed as next to godliness, survived and thrived at the altar of the client's benevolence. Today, the same being severed, the priest's daughter spewed with sacrilege.

"To be buried alive." The daughter looked her father straight in the eye. "You know very well what he did last year during the riot, how his own men raped the sisters and daughters of those harijans that refused to take part in the riot, we all know who set fire to the harijan slums, his dirty pact with those dangerous slumlords, you know very well how corrupt he is and you still think I deserve this?"

"What men do outside their home is not your lookout," snarled Pathak, "your duty as his wife is simply to take care of him and his family and that's all. Women have no business interfering in the men's world. Haven't you learnt anything from your mother?"

Janaki was left with her only weapon that day, her tongue.

"Yes, I've learnt not to be like her and I mean it."

There, she spat it out in absolute distraught.

The father and daughter saw the world through very dissimilar eyes. The father, imbued with age-old beliefs and burdened with poverty weighing heavily on his back, as he groped through the jungle of servitude, this sudden prospect of a wealthy and influential son-in-law loomed before him like a divine aura. While the daughter influenced by young Sukumar's idealism that virtually opened her third eye, the eye of wisdom, so to speak, had brought to light the bigotry and the chauvinism that was intrinsic in her society. After that, a conflict between father and daughter was only imminent.

"What!! What did you just say?" screamed Janaki's father, as if he was just electrocuted. Janaki's mother stood there timidly, as timidly as the dark shadow behind her husband.

Janaki could not stand it any longer. She rushed into their little puja room next to the kitchen, slammed the door behind her and knelt down on the floor with tears melting down her fiery eyes. She wept before the icons of their family deities, asking for their blessings, to guide her through the right path and not let her astray and to give her all the strength to withstand this ordeal and not give in. It was then that she saw Sukumar's face appear and reappear before her. With her eyes closed steadfastly, the blurred vision took a distinct form. It was as if he was right there to rescue her. But could that be possible? If she ever went to him, could she ever return to her family? Wouldn't her father abandon her for good? The warm air in the little room suffocated her, those narrow walls fiercely caving in on her. Next thing she knew, she was stealthily stepping out of her house without anybody seeing her and running breathlessly towards the harijan slums.

It was sundown. Janaki sneaked through the dark, narrow lanes across the town, and as she headed towards the maze field at the outskirts, she fell flat on her face on a wild shrub that grew by the wayside and often went unnoticed until one tripped over it. Just then an idle call of a panduk came floating with the river breeze... koook... koook... koook... through a throttling grove of tall, slender stalks of sugarcane standing erect and way above her head much like the bamboo grove. The call of that dirty brown unimpressive looking bird always reminded Janaki of the squeaking noise of the grinding stone in a flour mill that went koook... koook... koook. At the brink of the maze field lay a pond that almost choked with an abundance of overgrown water hyacinth. Every now and then a gorgeous blue, beautiful kingfisher, the master diver and fish hunter, dived into the pond and spooned out a small fish in its long stout bill. Halfway around the pond, the thatched roofs of the harijan slum began to emerge in the horizon.

Janaki's eyes squinted and her brows furrowed as she tried to see Sukumar from a distance squatting down in an upright position, cross-legged on his mud floor with a hurricane lamp hanging over his head from the low thatched roof, throwing a giant shadow behind him, giving its owner the appearance of someone as if in meditation. He's probably working on his thesis or correcting papers, she thought. Sukumar was working on his Ph.D. in mathematics while he held an assistantship at Patna Science College. He lived with his mother in one of those desolate slums, a part of which was recently burnt down by Thakore's men.

"Janu! what's wrong? You look so frightened." Sukumar was bewildered to find Janaki at his doorstep at this hour. Especially since the riot, none other than the harijans, the denizens of the slums, ventured here at this hour, and certainly not a Brahmin girl should ever trod this path. What could she be doing here?

"Is anybody chasing you? Has anyone seen you coming here? Come, speak up. Are you alright?"

Janaki was gasping for breath and feeling slightly out of sort.

"I didn't want to be seen by anyone, so I ran. I was also afraid, I might miss you. You have to do something for me and soon."

"What's wrong? Tell me. I'll do everything I can to help you. You know I will."

"My father wants me to marry that zamindar's son, Prakash Thakore."

"That criminal!!" blasted Sukumar like a dynamite. "How can your father do this to you? Doesn't he know how many innocent lives he has ruined and gotten away with it... that soovar has a daughter older than you. Has your father gone mad? Have you talked to him?" Sukumar felt like shaking an answer out of Janaki as she stood there dumbfounded and trembling nervously.

"Yes, I have, but...but he says, he'll... he'll tie me with a rope if he has to," Janaki stammered.

"I'll do whatever it takes to stop the marriage. Just leave it up to me. Now, let me walk you home before they start missing you. Plus, the evening show is about to break and people will pour out of the cinema hall like ants. I don't want you to get caught in that crowd."

For rest of the way Sukumar wore a grave expression on his face. He was deep in thought. Wonder what's on his mind? Is it about me? Janaki only wished he would share it with her. Deep within herself she craved for his favor. The longer she spent with him, the more she wanted to be with him. She wanted to belong in his thoughts, in all his private and precious moments from where everybody else would be barred. He seemed so much older to her, especially now, when he walked beside her quietly and solemnly with his hands firmly clasped behind him. Just the way they walked together, his sheer presence next to her vibrated a sense of protection and well being, who alone, she felt, could give her the sanctuary she was seeking. All his students from the college, not much younger than him, also felt the same way about Sukumar.

What was it about him, that made her feel so secured, even while walking beside him? Once, Janaki, enthralled by his act of courage and single mindedness during a communal riot that devastated many innocent lives in the Harijan slums, wrote him a letter with great fervour and adoration..

'My dearest Sukumar:' she hurriedly scribbled under a dim street light that found its way through her window after everyone had gone to bed, 'You always seem older than your age, wiser than a sage, I wonder what it is in you that makes a true man of you and the rest of them all look like eunuchs! Is it your faith in you, your compassion for the underdogs, your ideologies that give a true meaning to the term 'man' as it did for Ram in Ramayana and Arjun in Mahabharat? I just want you to know that in life's journey, if we ever go apart, never mind the earthly distance, I will always worship you no matter where you are. Your Janu.'

Next morning before the day broke, on her way to the milkman, Janaki took a detour, a longer route than the usual with the letter hidden underneath her blouse. Rather than taking the shortcut through the mustard field, wading across a sea of tiny yellow flowers glinting in the sunlight as they sway with the breeze, Janaki made her way through the maze field, the road she usually takes to visit Sukumar. A sweet sickening stench exuded from the liquid waste material that flowed into the open field outside the sugar mill, fermented under the tropical sun. The milkman's hut stood right behind the sugar mill and the harijan slum only a few yards away. She stopped abruptly for a split second in front of Sukumar's hut, looked around stealthily to make sure no eyes were on her, and then quickly slipped the letter under the door and left. That morning as the letter spread a sunny smile over his gentle face, he murmured to himself: only if she knew how much I care for her.

"So, you're sure, you can stop this marriage?" Deep down, Janaki knew she could trust him. Yet, she feared, what if he failed? Many great men failed in their lives. Failures did not make them any less of a man. It only made the feat greater. This was no small matter for Janaki, nor was it for Sukumar. Perhaps, Janaki would never know how great a feat it was for him, thought Sukumar to himself, and how sweet its reward would be. In the meanwhile, anxiety was riding high on her mind.

"Yes, I'm sure," replied Sukumar, "I don't know what I'll do, but I'll do whatever it takes to stop the marriage. Believe me. Now, don't you mention this to anyone, not even to Parvati." He cautioned her sternly.

"Mention what?" she asked innocently.

"That you talked to me; not a soul should know about it," he repeated.

And not a soul knew about it, but, only for a day. The word, from one mouth to another, whirred around like a cyclone, started by a slumlord who saw the two together as Sukumar walked her home that evening. The word, as feared, poured fuel to the fire that was already ablaze in Janaki's life. Since then, Janaki's parents kept a hawk-eye on her and 'clipped her wings off' as the father, vexed with her undue indulgence, metaphorically referred to her freedom. She was to remain that way until the marriage vow would sanctimoniously deliver her in the hands of her husband, the savior of every Indian girl.

It was only yesterday, at the wake of dawn, with the loud and lilting music on Shehnai, marking the august occasion, all the women in the bride's family gathered around Janaki, smearing her with turmeric paste before she took her bath. In his desire to oblige the bride's family, Prakash Thakore, the youngest son of the late zamindar Priyanath Thakore, refused to take any dowry from the bride's father, and in lieu, took fancy to a conspicuous consumption that threw the bride's family in a daze. He sent for

A WOUNDED TIGRESS

the young bride a whole new wardrobe, an endless repertoire of gorgeous silk saris woven in various parts of India and named after them, for instance, the pure silks from Kanchipuram, Mysore, Tanjore, Banaras, Kashmir, Garwal, Patan, Murshidabad, Cuttack, not to mention the Tanchoi silks, the Gajji silks and the gold brocades or the kinkhabs of Surat, each distinct with its special texture and blend of colors, some of them painstakingly embroidered with gold threads and others meticulously handpainted. With exotic jewelry of gold and platinum and pearls imported from Japan and rubies from Burma to match with the saris and lots of other accessories, with baskets and bouquets of fresh flowers, Persian attar and Bengali sweets, it was in all a lavish display of Prakash Thakore's enormous wealth and generosity, an object of envy to the bride's other relatives and friends and a matter of great pride and vanity to her immediate family. The aura and the spectacle of it all swooned young Janaki.

To the clever Thakore — that he was — it was merely a trade off, one which he considered as more than fare, for he was getting in exchange a young beautiful virgin, younger than his own daughter and what could be more appetizing, more stimulating to the sexual fantasies of a middle-aged widower than a tender virgin for a wife. For a while, Janaki would have probably mustered all her will to preempt all his actions and would have soon come close to dominating his entire life, enslaving him with her youth and lust until she attained motherhood, her prized position in society. After that Janaki's reign over him would begin to decline and our Prakash Thakore would have once again wandered off in search of new pastures. When the mighty gods like Indra, Vishnu and Shiva have fallen prey to the aphrodisiac power of the apsaras, what power would our Thakore have against the frailties of humanity?

Janaki was dressed in bridal attire of scarlet Banarasi silk, gleaming with gold jewelry and floral ornaments, her face veiled under a ruby red chiffon. She sat there frightened, terribly frightened, like a little bird chased by its predator before it learnt to fly. She knew she had no recourse; no doors would open to her that she could escape through, except one, that one inevitable and final exit open to all daughters driven by sheer atrocities. Though the day that Janaki's parents talked to her about the marriage, she ran for Sukumar's help, yet, later on, she began to have second thoughts. She begged him to forget that she had ever asked his help. In fear of losing him to those gundas, she urged him to stay out of it. She knew that Thakore's men would not be so kind as to spare him his life if they sniffed even faintly of his involvement in the matter. With each passing day, Janaki's mounting fear grew larger. She had to pull Sukumar out of it, or else he would be compelled to pay for it some day and very dearly. After all, once the elders made up their minds, there was no turning around. She had agonized over Sukumar's fate in the hands of those gundas and the state of his poor old mother who depended upon him. How could she show her face to his mother? What would she tell her if anything ever happened to Sukumar?

The auspicious moment crept slyly like a deluge that was about to devastate Janaki's life for good. It would wash away all her dreams, the very foundation of her faith and hope in humanity would come tumbling down. Sukumar and Janaki spent many hours in the past debating over the flagrant dichotomy of their society. Sukumar had pointed out to Janaki the many paradoxes that lay beneath the garb of puritanical ideologies in their society. While Sukumar had been her mentor, she had been his inspiration. After that last communal riot, they had taken a promise together to never give in to any kind of social bias and boycott all its advocates.

Janaki could hear the shrill music of the bugle piping over a distance and growing louder and shriller by the minute, as the band in its stately attire smartly strode through the main streets of Govindpur leading the bridal procession amidst a pageantry.

Fireworks crashed into midair, splashing the night sky with luminous colors. Young women from the groom's family adorned in shimmering silk and sparkling jewels, with fresh flowers on their head adding glamour to their delicate features, sang joyous wedding songs, while young men danced madly on the streets. Curious villagers from far away walked for miles to gain a glimpse of the princely groom. Dressed in beige tasar kurta and churidar, with a garland of red roses around his neck, his face veiled behind strands of marigold, a part of nuptial headdress, the middle aged and flamboyant figure of the groom on horseback cut quite an elusive profile to the eyes of the villagers.

"Is he not the one whose wife died that day?" whispered the farmer's wife to her husband.

"I suppose so," responded the husband nonchalantly.

"How long a man mourn? After all, he need to go on with life you know," replied a village cobbler overhearing their conversation in the crowd.

"Yeah! is only us, our life end after our husband die," argued the loquacious young milkwoman.

"Watch your tongue, woman," cried another farmer, "don't like our women talking like city folks."

"Yeah! We know that, truth bites, isn't it?" she rebuked in a loud hoarse and then spat out a blob of chewed paan from her mouth right next to his feet.

"If you man enough then tell your woman to hold her tongue," yelled the farmer to the milkman. The colour of his face turned bloody, yet, he would not stop, "you feel sorry for womenfolk, go give speech at panchayat and you need crowd? I let lose my cattle," he cackled.

"What you say?" snapped the husband whose masculinity was questioned, the biggest insult any man could ever swallow, so raising his voice to prove his masculinity, "hey, what you mean by man enough? What are you? huh! Thakore's chamcha?" Then with an ugly, obscene gesture of his hand pointing to the groom on horseback, he scoffed, "is yours also itching like his to get on top of a virgin, huh?" having now put him in his place he chuckled, as the crowd around them broke into a loud, boisterous guffaw. Thus, the villagers kept poking fun at each other until it got out of hand and was not fun any more. Despite the clamour and the commotion on the side, the main procession moved on with a lot more dignity than the crowd of vilalge rabbles could offer.

As the groom pompously arrived at the bride's house, everyone from the bride's family rushed frantically to catch a glimpse of the grandeur that the illustrious groom had to offer, leaving Janaki all to herself to fight against her destiny. But before Janaki could make her move as she had planned, Sukumar sneaked through a narrow dingy opening of their neighbor's compound, slouched through a red brick broken wall that looked more like the half-opened mouth of a dead animal with its teeth broken unevenly, snaked his way up the staircase to the terrace, hopped into the adjacent terrace which was Janaki's, climbed down a few flights of dark staircases, and hid in an alcove behind a pillar before he spotted Janaki in their outer room. Then, with no questions asked, Sukumar briskly picked her up into his arms, turned around, followed the same route backwards and then through the narrow scruffy lanes of Govindpur, they crisscrossed their way to the outskirts of the town while Janaki with her eyes closed and her arms locked around his shoulder, she clung tightly to Sukumar.

As the jackals looked up to the night sky and howled in melancholy, an owl atop a branch of a nearby neem tree hooted ghoulishly and the crickets chirped incessantly, Janaki shuddered in cold fear as they groped their way through a vast stretch of maze field until darkness swallowed them whole. Sukumar had, after all, answered to Janaki's inner voice for there was not an iota of doubt in his mind that Janaki would have otherwise paid with her life to flee from this marriage.

The thought of Parvati nagged Janaki. In the last couple of years, matchmakers bringing in new proposals for Parvati had almost become a weekly ritual in the Pathak household. This was long before Prakash Thakore came into the scene. But it was not until Mihir's father, a Brahmin pundit with a social standing approached Pathak for his youngest daughter, did Pathak actually consent to the betrothal of Parvati and Mihir, a bright young professor at Patna Science College. Both fathers agreed on one condition, that the marriage would have to wait until Pathak found a suitable boy for his older daughter, Janaki.

One afternoon, Parvati curiously stole a glimpse of Mihir from behind the curtain of their outer room, when Mihir was visiting the family. Ever since then, she had been secretly and most fervidly nurturing a budding love come to a tender bloom. In many a frivolous moment, Janaki felt it in Parvati's eyes. As far as the young professor goes, he had an eye on Parvati long before she knew of him, right from the time he first saw her years ago at Govindpur's Durga Puja festival. After what Janaki did last night, would the father, being an orthodox Brahmin himself, allow his son to marry her sister, or would she have to bear its brunt for the rest of her life? Janaki grieved at the thought of Parvati's ill fate that awaited her.

Pathak girls were gifted with good looks, so finding a suitable boy for them was never a problem. The problem was purely monetary. Along came Prakash Thakore's proposal for Janaki. In Pathak's eye, he was godsend, for Prakash Thakore had now worn the garb of a philanthropist and that dazzled the Brahmin poojari. He had convinced Pathak that to him money was no object.

"Poojariji," said Prakash Thakore ostentatiously, flapping a fat bundle of hundred rupee notes before him, "this money that you see is only the dirt off my palm. Sometimes, I wonder, what is it like to be poor, but that can be a problem too, you see."

"You! you have a problem!! What can it be, if I may ask?"

"I have no one to share my wealth, that's my problem. As you know, I only have one daughter and she's the wealthiest woman in town. She's also married to a zamindar, as you know. You see, ever since I lost my wife, I promised to sacrifice my life in the humble service of the poor and the needy and that's my only reason for asking your daughter's hand, if I may. Now, it's up to you."

As Pathak listened to him with mixed emotions, half in disbelief, half in adoration, he wondered, if there could be such a philanthropist living in a selfish world as theirs and particularly in Govindpur. He felt ashamed, remembering the times when people of Govindpur misjudged him and how he himself had been unfair to him by listening to those that bad-mouthed him. Prakash Thakore not only offered to pay all expenses for his own marriage, but also assured Pathak that he should from now on consider him as his son, the son that he never had, and that he would be only too happy to take care of Parvati's marriage expenses as well. Prakash Thakore was only reaching out to a drowning man. How could the poojari turn his face away from such noble a gesture.

Suddenly, a boisterous commotion outside Sukumar's hut jolted Janaki out of her reminiscence. Sukumar's mother, like a scalded dog that fears cold water, tried to guard her son from any violent upheaval that might be brewing outside. Of course, Sukumar, without any such apprehension stepped out of his hut to see what the row was all about. It was a zesty little boy in the Harijan slum who was yelling himself hoarse — fresh news of the day! hot news of the day! Copies of a local Hindi news bulletin were selling like hotcakes in the slum and everywhere else in the town. Those that did not buy, looked over his shoulder to catch a glimpse of the glaring banner headline that gripped the imagination of the pedestrians. He quickly bought a copy of the bulletin and began to read it aloud to his mother and Janaki. Thus ran the story:

CROCODILE STEALS THE BRIDE WHILE GROOM CONSOLES THE FAMILY

A poor Brahmin poojari and his family mourn the death of his nineteen year old daughter, Janaki, devoured by a man eater crocodile while bathing in the river hours before her wedding. The Brahmin girl, recently engaged to a widower, Prakash Thakore, the youngest son of the late zamindar Priyanath Thakore, disappeared only hours before the marriage could take place. Later, a relentless search along the bank of the river ended as one of the family members found a remnant of the sari and a few broken bits of glass bangles worn by the bride. The bride's family, plunged into shock and grief, found solace in a turn of event, when the groom offered to marry Parvati, the youngest sister of the deceased, who is now seventeen. Shraadh for the peace of the departed soul will be observed on the full moon.

The brilliantly fabricated story that killed two birds with one stone threw Sukumar at his wit's end.

"This is how Thakore plays his game!" his voice raised to a feverish pitch, looking at Janaki. "He couldn't come up with anything better, so he cooked up this crocodile of a story!! and your family fell for it!! I guess, he pretty much convinced your father that he could save his face by this crocodile story in exchange for your sister. That soovar, that ruthless bastard must be very happy today. He must think he played his game fair and square. That soovar should be put to stake and burnt alive." Sukumar, nodding his head and pacing back and forth, gnarled in rage.

"As they say," murmured Sukumar's mother beneath a heavy sigh, "Prakash Thakore killed the snake and not break the stick." Having had a daughter that eloped with a shudra, at least, the story however bizarre it may sound, it swept the facts under the rug for awhile if not forever, which saved the father from humiliation in exchange for his youngest daughter.

"So he thinks," spurned Sukumar, "I'll break his stick if I have to, but I'll not put up with this sham, this shady game of his."

"Now, don't forget my boy, you only a small fry. Besides, a leopard never change its spots, you know," cautioned the mother of Thakore's cunning.

Janaki grabbed the bulletin from Sukumar's hand, hastily ran her eyes through the bold headline and onto the raucous story, which she read over and over again. Seeing is believing; yet, she could not quite believe what she saw. Disillusioned by the cunning and knavery, she fell on the ground and in a loud uncontrollable spurt, cried out helplessly, "How can it be? How can my father do this to me? And my mother! My poor mother! They'll do my shraadh when I'm still alive! And Parvati! Oh! poor Parvati, please, forgive me, Parvati, I didn't mean to hurt you at all, believe me." Reading her own obituary in the bulletin and learning about Parvati's marriage with Thakore, simply tore Janaki apart.

Sukumar's mother gently held her in her arms. "Calm down my girl, calm down. We here for you. Think me your mother. Everything be alright." Sukumar's mother continued, "don't worry, my girl, parents hold no grudge against own flesh and blood. They come looking for you soon. Like fire in a haystack, give it time and things soon cool off." Those soothing words embalmed Janaki's fresh wound at the time.

"Ma, stop dreaming, the world is not as beautiful as we want it to be." Sukumar knew that his mother was being only too naive. "Don't listen him, my girl, I know what I say."

Then, changing the subject quite abruptly, she added, "we not be in this wretched place too long, you know. Just you wait till my Suku find his first job, and then we move to a strong brick house. Won't we Suku? At least, we be able to sleep in dry warm bed, the damp cold nights killed Suku's father, you know, he died consumptive fever. If he live today, he love you like his own daughter. He's godlike, no bad habits, never beat me in life, not even once, like other men do to wives." The mother drawled in sweet reminiscence.

Sukumar threw a quick smile at Janaki.

"Don't let ma scare you with all her talk. To her all men are bad except babuji. By the way... I'm not one of them."

Janaki could not help smiling for she never had any doubt about it. Her face still smeared with tears, the sudden spread of a smile did wonders to her looks.

"You ever be a bad husband, I take it as insult to my womb. You better remember, my son," the mother scolded affectionately and then continued, "we treated lowly in this world but in god's eye we just as good as any good Brahmin... Suku's father one of them."

Her eyes slowly moistened with tears.

"Ma misses babuji a lot," Sukumar could not bear to see his mother in tears, so he interrupted, "she likes to talk about him, especially to someone that she likes."

Janaki was touched by their warmth. Sukumar then looked her in the eye and reached out for her hands, "Janu," he said, "I'll do anything to make you happy, believe me, Janu, I will."

GRANDPA'S LEGACIES

Against the backdrop of the eastern horizon, as the rising sun darts out gleaming through the July sky, Kaveri strolls along the bank of river Sonali. Especially, in the early hours of a misty morning when the grass is still moist with raindrops from last night, she loves to crush the mass of pearls under her bare feet. She finds it cool and refreshing for both her mind and body. Every now and then she stoops to pick up a handful of tiny pebbles from the wayside and then unmindfully throws them into the water one-by- one. Kaveri is dressed in white cotton sari. She will never again dress in fine silk or wear any jewelry or make-up that will enhance her youth and beauty. Quite haplessly, she has entered into a dreary catacomb of life, where even an occasional indulgence to any sort of worldly pleasure would be scathingly denounced. From now on, the rest of her life, marked by austerity, leaves her listless. In her thirty years, already exhausted of all the springs and the summers of her life, she now stands at the threshold of only autumn and winter, with one departing and the other approaching, her heart impinged with a sense of emptiness. She drops those pebbles one-by- one and then stops to watch the multiple ripples forming a sort of rhythm in the water. Perhaps they remind her of the ones that are hidden underneath her placid exterior. Ever since Kaveri lost her husband six months ago, a somber mood looms over her mind. From a distance one could easily mistake her for a sanyasini in absolute beatitude.

If widowhood to a Hindu woman is looked upon as ungodly, Kaveri's marriage which was conventionally, and much to her reluctance arranged by her parents, was not of any innocuous nature either. Her parents, enamored by Priyankar's affluence and social stature, lapsed into an awe as they watched the real hero behind the silver screen, their hero — handsome, enigmatic and ingenious. Kaveri's parents had dropped in at Priyankar's studio to see him in action and they certainly liked what they saw in him.

Of course, he was also twice her age. But that was not of any real concern to Kaveri's parents. After all, no match is perfect. At the age of thirty-six, Priyankar had reached the pinnacle of his film career. He had been immensely prolific in the last few years, directed quite a few films in quick succession, but it was not until his most recent and much acclaimed 'Thunderous Moon' a masterpiece production, by his own admission, that earned him not only a nationwide recognition and prestige in film making but won many accolades in the international film festivals as well. Priyankar's mother, Mrs. Pratima Roy, a widow herself, basked in the glory of her son's recent fame, but not without poignancy.

Like any other mother, Mrs. Pratima Roy, wanted her son to settle down happily and raise a family. Happily — only from her own standpoint — of course. But Priyankar kept refusing to get married, until one day she threatened him with an ultimatum. Mrs. Pratima Roy had waited long enough for his consent. Now she was only waiting for an opportunity. So, finally one Sunday when Priyankar was spending an evening with his mother over tea, an evening of leisure that was much sought after between his busy schedules, Mrs. Roy dropped the bomb right then.
"From now on," said Pratima Roy sternly, "I have decided to consider myself a childless widow. So, now my only wish is to leave for Banaras and spend the rest of my life there. By the way," added Mrs. Roy, her gaze fixed far away where the twilight

sky kissed the Arabian Sea, "I'd like to leave before the next full moon." That did it. The son almost choked over his hot cup of tea. Though, Priyankar, with his brilliant career and gifted with a demeanor that could charm anyone beyond belief, yet, deep down had a soft corner for his mother that virtually made him into a stuffed doll in the hands of a little girl.

The father, a lawyer by profession, had a great talent as a stage artist. Acting was his hobby and was superb at it. While on stage, he mastered the role of Lord Krishna, known for his devotion to his consort, Radha; paradoxically enough, when at home with his wife, the great actor assumed a diabolical character. As a young boy, Priyankar, helplessly watched his father torture his mother day in and day out. The painful memories of childhood forever haunted Priyankar, so, to undo the wrong that was done to his mother early on, Priyankar took it upon himself to see her happy at all times and at any cost.

But Mrs. Roy, well aware of her son's soft spot, used it to manipulate him whenever she needed to and it worked every time. From then on there was not a moment to waste, for she already had a girl in mind. So she seized the propitious moment to approach her childhood friend Srilekha for her daughter's hand. Coveted by the glamour of his wealth and success, the parents of the bride-to-be considered this offer a miracle.

"It's our daughter's fate, I suppose. She's born to live like a queen," the father vaunted. "Now, can you imagine a goldsmith for our son-in-law? As a Brahmin, I'd have lost my prestige in the town. I must thank my stars for saving me from such humiliation." "Yes, by the grace of Ganesha, we couldn't have asked for a better match. One could only dream of such a son-in-law like Priyankar. After all, she's the granddaughter of a zamindar. We can't marry her off to any hoodlum." Srilekha gloated.

Kaveri eavesdropped while her parents prattled over tea in their veranda about this princely character, Priyankar. That is how she came to know of him. Not that they wouldn't have mentioned it to her, but they would have waited for the opportune moment to put it to her which they did. It left Kaveri emotionally lacerated. That day, she pleaded with her parents untiringly, but all she got from them was an icy cold stare which only implied, how would you know what it takes to find a match as prestigious as this, so why don't you just stay out of it, while we fulfill our moral obligation. And then they openly shunned her for being a feckless adolescent infatuated by a village rabble. Since then Kaveri spent her days and nights in forlorn while her parents went about busily preparing for the wedding with all sorts of conspicuous consumption. In keeping with their social status, both families tried to outdo one another which only turned the ceremony into an inexhaustive play of vanity. The wedding ceremony lasted for five whole days.

On their first night, Kaveri, like a wounded captive, sat in their nuptial bed, dazed by a plethora of feelings. Despite apprehension and deep remorse for having to immolate the love of her life, she waited for her husband to join her in their bridal suite. But, quite unfortunately, the nuptial bed, canopied with a decor of rajani gandha, lay cold and empty. Little did she know, that having fulfilled his mother's wish by bringing her a daughter-in-law, the bridegroom chose to be someplace else, rather absorbed in his make-believe world. So, Kaveri sat there lackadaisically, with tears raining down her eyes. She pondered over her fate. While the village boy — yes, that's what Kaveri's mother disparagingly called Sidhartha — had stolen her heart, ever since she was a little girl, here she was waiting to receive the man and hoping to seek his love, the man who had not yet set his eyes on her, nor held her in his arms. It was a long and a lonely night that marked the beginning of a lonesome journey in Kaveri's life.

Kaveri and Sidhartha had fallen in love fairly early in their life.

Sidhartha's family, goldsmith by caste and occupation belonged to Anantapur. Ever since Kaveri was a little girl, she spent her summer holidays with her grandparents in Anantapur, one of the several villages her grandfather came into possession after he married Mohini grandma. Actually, what later became the Choudhury estate was originally one of Ananta Choudhury's wedding gifts from his father-in-law. In due course, Ananta Choudhury acquired the stature of zamindar along which came enormous property and prestige. Kaveri's mother, Srilekha, the only daughter of Choudhury was married in her late teens to a well renowned architect and owner of a consulting firm in Bombay. Kaveri, though born and raised in Bombay, always nurtured a special affinity for Anantapur. Every year as the schools closed for the summer holidays, Kaveri and her mother looked forward to their journey across the country from the cosmopolitan city of Bombay to Anantapur, a village on the east coast. For little Kaveri, visiting Anantapur was like entering into the pages of a fairy tale, and grandpa's Indrapuri seemed like an enchanting castle to her — there was something magical about that mansion.

Indrapuri, impressive with its granite exterior of gray, an array of tall pillars at the front entrance that stood like sentries on guard, and long corridors of white marble skirting all around it. A three-storied structure divided into four quarters, one in each direction and named after it. Each quarter consisted of several suites; for instance, the suites in the north and the south quarters were occupied by zamindar's eight sons and their families. The east quarter, exclusively designed as the main residence of the zamindar, had a special suite right next to his built for Srilekha and her family. All the suites in the west quarter were meant for overnight guests. At various festive occasions around the year, Choudhury entertained friends and family from out-of-town and they were always welcome to stay overnight and sometimes for weeks together. An assembly hall at the center of the mansion with a high, dome-shaped and intricately carved ceiling, added a special characteristic to it. In the heyday of zamindari, it used to be the center where Choudhury would meet with all his subjects once a month not only to collect revenues for the government, but also to listen to their woes, settle their disputes, sanction financial and other special grants, and encourage them in their academic and cultural upliftment through many philanthropic gestures.

Indrapuri was a large household. Each quarter had two kitchens, one for the non-vegetarians and the other for all the widows who were restricted to one simple, wholesome, vegetarian meal a day. Curiously enough, only widows (not the widowers) were subjected to a rigid code of social ethics referenced in Manu's Dharma shastra formulated in 500-600 AD. Such norms, though, have gone through quite an evolution since the beginning, yet, to this day they are still quite prominent and vindicative of the puritanical attitude towards women. Adjacent to the widows' kitchen were built a granary, husk pedal shades, and two store-rooms, one containing stone grinders to grind all sorts of grains and the other filled with yearly stock of tons of grains, dried beans and pulses in big brown sacks; glass jars filled with a variety of spices, sweet and sour pickles, dry fruits, almonds, cashew nuts, nutmeg and saffron; tin canisters filled with ghee; and round, wicker baskets piled with seasonal fruits like mangoes, jackfruits, jamuns and watermelons. There were times when Kaveri and Sidhartha filched into that dark room for a handful of dried cashews or raisins, jamuns or mangoes which were stocked under strict supervision by Kali charan, an old, faithful servant. Once inside the room, their eyes burned and the tip of their nose tingled from the heavily pungent odour, a blend of all the dried spices and pickles that were neatly shelved high up against the storage walls.

As the Choudhury family grew in size, the mansion needed annexation. Indrapuri, built several generations ago, both architecturally and also otherwise as the nucleus of now Choudhury Estate, stood majestically at the summit of a hill, with its landscape all around rolling down to a gentle slope. Thus, from its terrace one could feast his eyes to a panoramic view of Anantapur and the surrounding villages. Now flanked on either sides by north and south cottage, the newly designed architecture gave the grand mansion an appearance of a bird in flight from a great distance. The designer was none other than zamindar's only son-in-law, Kaveri's father. The north and the south cottage accommodated both near and distant relatives of Choudhury. They were the ones who were not very well off and could never afford a home of their own. At the back of the mansion stood a cluster of servants' quarters where all of Choudhury's personal attendants including butlers, chefs, gardeners, coachmen, oarsmen, a host of club-men and gatekeepers lived with their families. Just as a drop of honey attracts a swarm of bees, so did Choudhury, a slew of sycophants and carpet knights shamelessly lived off his benevolence all their lives.

Twice a day, once at daybreak and again at sundown, everyone in the Choudhury family bathed in the ponds, built within the estate. Men and women bathed in separate ponds. Children were allowed in either one and so they swam for hours together. Widows, who were supposed to bathe thrice a day, took a quick dip once at midday before lunch. The women's pond, fenced with young plants of papaya, guava and lime along the wharf, served somewhat of a privacy to the bathers. Black marble wharves around the pond rendered a perfect venue for all the young adults and the children of the joint family who gathered around for recreation on moonlit nights especially during the warm season. Those were the times when the women sang songs, recited poetry, ate kulfi and made merry while their children played hide and seek or staged their own little plays.

In the winter times, the zamindar invited local drama units and paid them handsomely to perform Ramlila, the all-time favorite of the rustics, that depicted scenes from one of the two greatest

Hindu epic plays — Ramayana, one of the two most popular themes ever to evoke a plethora of human emotions and the highest ethos of Hindu culture and the other, Mahabharata — the Odyssey and the Iliad of India, if not in any semblance of contents, at least, in their scope and magnitude. During the nights of Ramlila the entire household of Indrapuri, including the servants, hummed with joy and excitement.

To pamper his whims, Ananta Choudhury had built himself a spacious cottage nestled in the woods at the outskirts of his farm, a vast stretch of thousands of acres of farm where herds of cattle grazed about lazily all day long. On special occasions, the zamindar entertained himself at the cottage, usually called as baagaan baaree, to a night of musical extravaganza. Renowned classical maestros like Bijli Bai with her professional ensemble traveled all the way from Calcutta to his baagaan baaree in Anantapur to grace the occasion. After a few sips of imported wine from a silver glass, zamindar Choudhury's eyes would begin to twinkle with a special fondness for his Raat ki Raani — a name he had affectionately given to Bijli Bai. A lightning of a smile flashed through Bijli Bai's face as his eyes met hers. With her voice and her eyes, both sensuous and seductive enough to pierce through the hearts of her male audience, 'Raat ki Raani' reigned all night long through the early hours of the morning. She had such absolute power over her voice and her eyes that she could use them at will if and when she chose to. During the early hours of the evening, she flirted with her audience, that is, if she fancied a lighter mood; and if not, she mesmerized them into an aura of romance. But then as the evening matured into a deep and somber night, with the zamindar all by himself in the audience and enslaved by her charm, the notoriously capricious Bijli Bai would begin to communicate with him at a much higher level, almost spiritual in its intensity, and all this through the lovely music in her voice. One of her many favorite Urdu ghazals that inevitably elated the spirits of choudhury was:

Yeh dil koi shisheki jaam tho nahi
    ki jab chaahay laga lee labsay
  Aur jab chaahay reza reza kar dee zaminpay
(This heart is not a wine goblet made of glass, that you can raise
it to your lips as you wish, and shatter it into pieces on the
ground whenever you feel like it). Enraptured by the passion
evoked in the ghazal, the zamindar would close his eyes in contemplation, until she would very seductively go over the same
line repeatedly, the line he adored most: reza reza kar dee zaminpay (shatter it into pieces on the ground), with a delicate varia-
tion or a slight nuance in the tune every time, at which point he
would raise his right hand in a gesture of applause: "wahh!
wahh!! wahh!!! wahh!!!!" Hypnotized by her music, he would
remove the diamond ring from his finger and gently throw it at
her feet as a token of appreciation from the grand aristocrat. Bijli
Bai would then craftily imprint his heart with her precious 'Raat
ki Raani-glance', pick up the piece of jewel from the ground and
while still holding it in the cup of her palm, she would daintily
bow down and do adaab.

None from the family of the grand aristocrat was ever allowed to
the interior of the baagaan baaree, of course, with the exception
of his cortege. Kaveri recalled that night watching with awe, that
gorgeous woman from out of town singing to her grandpa, as
she and Sidhartha sneaked into the wooded backyard of the baagaan baaree and quietly peeked in from outside the window.
That night little Kaveri standing on tiptoes and stretching out
her neck like a duck as her little heart roused with curiosity to no
end. "What was so great about her music that Grandpa seemed
so immersed in?" Kaveri remained puzzled. Instead, what really
caught her fancy was the way she dressed and behaved and ogled
at grandpa, so differently than her grandma, or for that matter,
any woman she ever knew. She just did not know what to think
of her — that gorgeous woman from out of town that kept her
grandpa mesmerized. Kaveri knew that all female members from

the Choudhury family were supposed to stay away from the baa-gaan baaree, so she was careful not to breathe a word about it to anyone, not even to her cousins, a deadly secret that only the two of them shared.

The women of Indrapuri usually stayed aloof from men during the day and remained occupied in their household chores. During the afternoon the elders recited from Ramayana and Mahabharata, while the younger women poured over renowned biographies and novels written by classical or contemporary authors. Some engaged in needlework and others leisured over a game of chess or cards. Women of the Choudhury family were cultured and considered quite sophisticated, for there were learned resident tutors appointed by the zamindar himself to instruct them regularly on various subjects including classical and modern literature, ancient history, philosophy and astrono-my. Some of them who were artistically inclined wrote songs, poems, and short stories; some painted portraits and landscapes; and others learnt music.

Often, in the lingering glow of a tranquil summer evening, to please his own fancy, the zamindar would leisurely sail along the bank of Sonali in his luxurious houseboat, immersed in the plea-sure of reading Tagore, Ghalib and Kalidasa. Needless to say, Choudhury himself was a man of great learning and culture. As a son of a learned Brahmin, Ananta Choudhury had acquired knowledgE in various fields such as ancient history, astronomy, mathematics and classical literature.

Unlike the popular notion about zamindars, Choudhury was not just a creature of comfort. He was not only highly adored by his people, but almost placed in a pedestal for his wisdom, his lion-heartedness, and his patrician like characteristics. He was often compared to Bhishma for his nobility. Anantapur was one of the largest villages around with its own high school, a college, a medical clinic, and a library all built under the patronage of Ananta Choudhury. In two remarkable instances in particular, his power and influence were well put to the test. Once, when he approached the Central Government of India to have a railway station built at the outskirts of Anantapur to facilitate not only his own subjects but also others that lived far and apart from his domain. At another instance, he filed a petition to prohibit hunting of wild games in the forests in and around his territory. Unlike other aristocrats, Choudhury was a pacifist. He saw hunting of wild games as too primitive and predatory by nature to be considered pleasurable.

Yes, that was when it all started. At the approach of summer the day Kaveri would arrive at Anantapur, without wasting a moment, she and her cousins would take off with Sidhartha for a swim, while chasing ducklings and plucking lotuses that grew abundantly in the ponds. Kaveri was quite a tomboy. With the village boy as her mentor, she quickly learned to climb those tall coconut and betel nut trees. Sometimes they sat on the wharf underneath a papaya plant and threw stones at the tadpoles or tried their skills at frog-leap throw in the water. Or they played hide and seek in the quiet afternoon when the rest of the village slept through the scorching heat. Grandpa's stable used to be Kaveri's favorite hideaway. She would clumsily make her way through the ankle deep swamp and filth that stenched from the concoction of clay, urine, dung, half-eaten grass and fodder, all turned soggy and fermented by the tropical heat, and nettled by the mosquitoes and gnats that droned around her. Though she grew up in a big city, it didn't take her long to learn the traits of rural frolics. In the heat of a summer afternoon, like a pair of squirrels, the two youngsters climbed up a jamun tree that stood at the brink of the pond, plucked those ripe jamuns bursting with juice to quench their thirst until their mouth turned deep purple and then briskly dived from a branch hanging low into the cool water below. They laughed and they giggled as they mimicked each other with their purple lips and purple tongues. At the end of a summer storm, the children rushed to the mango grove behind the baagaan baaree and rompously picked up mangoes from under the trees. There never was a dull moment in their lives. On a pitch dark moonless night, the two ghoulishly groped through the woods in search of glowworms. Those were their days of childhood romance amidst an exuberance of rustic innocence and pure joy.

But as Kaveri approached her adolescence, her disposition towards Sidhartha changed noticeably. By now Sidhartha had lost a play mate, but little did he realize that he had quietly won her heart. Kaveri was no longer interested in climbing trees or diving into the pond or sliding down the haystack with Sidhartha like they used to. The naughty little girl was slowly growing up into a dainty and bashful young lady. Curiously enough, in his presence, Kaveri became ostensibly quiet and shy. At times, they hardly ever spoke, but just the smile on her lips or the look in her eyes told the tale on her.

"Kaveri, did you know there's a carnival in Sonapur at the other end of your grandpa's farm. Come, let's go there this evening?" Sidhartha was gasping for breath as he had to run a long way to find her. She was by the village well, under a tamarind tree, plucking sweet and sour tamarind for pickles.
"I would, if you weren't so busy with all those silly sports of yours." Kaveri laid her rules down with a firm voice.
"What's the matter with you? Ever since you came back this summer, you have been acting strange. If you don't like me any more, just tell me so and I'll be off." Sidhartha could not take it anymore. Her strange attitude was beginning to get on his nerves. Kaveri tried to calm him down. "You don't understand, I'm not a little girl anymore, you know."
"So! does that mean we aren't friends anymore?" Seemed like he was questioning her allegiance to their friendship.

"Don't be silly. Sure, I'd like to be with you. I just don't like to monkey around anymore. In fact, you don't even know how much I care for you. You've been on my mind ever since I left Anantapur last summer. But, what's it to you; you don't even care."

The village boy felt a slight tremor in her voice. Her face had suddenly turned florid, and she could feel the warmth of her blood gushing down her veins especially around the neck and behind her ears. Kaveri had just poured out the deepest secret of her heart. It made her all the more bashful, for she was so shamelessly blatant about it too, but how else could she have done it? She had to get the message across while she had this one chance, away from her cousins, or else Sidhartha would have never known how much she loved him, though, she wished there was a better way to do it.

"Really! do you really mean that?" Sidhartha looked her in the eye, and his eyes sparkled like a pair of jewels as if he had just discovered the greatest wonder of the world. He never knew until that very moment that falling in love could be so very fascinating. "Do you know something? I missed you too! Kaveri, I wish you would never ever leave Anantapur."

Kaveri had never felt such tenderness in his voice before. Now that she knew that Sidhartha does care for her, Kaveri's heart raced at an astronomical pace and then god knows from where a sudden sense of awkwardness overcast all her thoughts. It was a similar feeling she once experienced, when one day one of her male cousins with whom she was very close, accidentally opened the door of her dressing room when she was changing. That day she swore she would not show her face to him ever again as long as she lived. Kaveri could not rest her eyes on Sidhartha, for strangely enough, she felt as if they were both standing naked and that too in broad daylight. She wished she could vanish into thin air. Without lifting her eyes, she murmured, "I have to go," and then with a swift twirl she left the scene running towards

Indrapuri as fast as her feet could carry her. As she ran, she felt a sudden spasm in her stomach, a sort of discomfort she felt every month before menstruating. Amused by her shyness and thrilled with excitement, Sidhartha yelled after her, "don't forget the carnival, I'll be waiting for you." Kaveri's heart pounded like the feet of a racing horse. The mansion which stood within her sight seemed so far away that day. Kaveri wanted to get there as fast as she could and share her excitement with her cousins and Lali, one of their servants' daughter who would be the only ones to understand how she felt about Sidhartha.

Why did he have to yell like that? Couldn't he be a little discreet about it? It embarrassed Kaveri to no end. She covered her ears by pressing her palms against them, as she sneaked through one of the side gates trying to avoid the attention of the old gate-keeper at the main entrance of the mansion. The village women by the well, where they usually gathered for their midday chat, stopped prattling and gawked with their mouth half-open and then burst into silly giggles. She was afraid of that. Kaveri knew that those women by the well would now churn it into another slander. Just as she feared, no sooner had she disappeared behind the iron gate of Indrapuri, the women started chattering like sparrows.

"That lad is in for big trouble!" one of them exclaimed.

"Isn't he our goldsmith's son?" inquired another.

"That lad needs to be told off, you know... it's not wise for a midget to reach for the moon," the third added.

"If the zamindar ever found out, I wonder what would be the fate of that poor lad. For all I can think of, Choudhuryji might order his club-men to throw him out of the village and along with him, the goldsmith and his wife too. Did you see how quickly she has grown?" the fourth joined.

"How can you not see with those heavy breasts of hers tossing about, while she runs around like a horse." They all broke into a loud guffaw.

"Those shameless city girls just can't keep their eyes off boys," she continued peevishly. "If Munna's father ever finds our daughter running around like her with a boy, he will simply bury her alive." Thus, they went on and on with their scatological remarks.

But Kaveri also knew that gossip of this type, though momentarily, can and does spread like fire in a haystack. Yet, eventually they all die down with the most inconsequential end. Especially, since she knew her grandparents, who could be very unorthodox when it came to certain matters. After all, grandpa himself, as impoverished as he was in his youth, defied the prowess of the zamindar of Sonapur and married his only child Mohini. Mohini grandma, a learned woman and a highly spirited anarchist during British Raj, daughter of a Kshatriya, pledged to marry none other than Ananta Choudhury. Until her last, Mohini grandma would always take pride in grandpa and her eyes would begin to sparkle as she would relate to the brilliance of his mind that held her stupefied when she first met him. She knew right then that if she were to ever marry, it would have to be him. In those days, that was considered highly unconventional, but then again those were the days that saw the advent of Hindu reformation culture. Mohini Grandma would reminisce, "it was your grandpa's knowledge of ancient history and literature, his command over Sanskrit, Latin and Persian, that drew me like a moth around a glow of light." So, how could they, of all people on earth, ever object to their love.

That afternoon Kaveri had worn sari for the first time. A turquoise blue of fine organdy with a matching blouse trimmed with fine lace around the neck and the puffed sleeves. She had her black wavy hair down to her waist. As the evening breeze played with her soft, silky hair, Sidhartha sat beside her in one of her grandpa's carriages in absolute awe. He had never sat in a horse carriage so spacious and so richly ornate with velvet cushions, silk curtains and Persian rugs. As the pair of white Arabian horses galloped through the rugged country road along the bank of Sonali, Sidhartha felt like a prince in armor with his beloved princess next to him.

They were on their way to the carnival. Never before did he realize how very attractive she was. When did she grow up to become so ravishing? What have I done to deserve her love? Am I dreaming or is it real?

"Dreaming of what?" Kaveri looked at him before Sidhartha realized that his thoughts had already formed into words and quietly escaped his lips.

"Never mind, I was just thinking aloud." Sidhartha tried to brush aside her question. He didn't quite know how to respond to her. Suddenly, he found himself clumsy with words. He had been pondering ever since she made that sweet confession to him earlier that day. But Kaveri was persistent. "You have to tell me about your dream. Or is there something you don't want me to know? Please, tell me, or else I'll never speak to you."

Sidhartha flustered. "Don't be silly". He grabbed both her hands and squeezed them gently in his grip. "Don't you threaten me like that. There's nothing that I'd like to hide from you. Believe me. You are my sweet dream, my only dream." Kaveri sat there like a china doll. She had never felt more alive, her blood gushing down her veins, his gentle squeeze and his low, husky voice had done something magical to every nerve and sinew in her body.

They were at the carnival taking a ride in a giant wheel that spun like a top, and the dizziness continued for a while even after the wheel stopped. But it was still nothing compared to how she had felt after Sidhartha had uttered those fateful words to her. Sidhartha wanted to buy her something at the carnival, anything that would please her, but how could he possibly afford anything that would please her fancy. After all, she was the granddaughter of an aristocrat. Kaveri, warm and sensitive, knew not to be demanding. So, she discouraged him from buying her anything.

Instead, they ate Kulfi and watched a puppet show at the carnival. The puppet show was from Kalidas's Shakuntala, who lived with her father, a sage named Kanna in a hermitage ensconced in the forest. Once, as she was lost in thoughts of her beloved King Dushmant, a sage named Durbasha called on them. Beautiful Shakuntala was so engrossed in her sweet reverie, that she became unmindful of his presence. The savant took it amiss and thought she had deliberately ignored him. He felt humiliated and enraged. Durbasha was notoriously known to have had a bad temper. So he cursed her, that, whosoever had stolen her heart away would forget her from that instant onward. So powerful were the minds of the rishis, that before the words could escape his lips, King Dushmant became totally oblivious of his Shakuntala. Until years later, through a chain of events that turned fate in favor of the lovelorn couple, did the king finally remember Shakuntala, and their plight ended in a happy reunion.

"Oh! poor Shakuntala! No girl deserves to go through that," said Kaveri at the end of the puppet show. But Sidhartha looked at it a little differently.

"It also tells me how much they loved each other," said Sidhartha, "or else they wouldn't have been together again."

That evening, as the two of them sat on the wharf, next to the guava plant, under an open sky, Kaveri looked up to the heavens and said dreamily, "if everyone of us were blessed with one magic spell in our life, can you imagine the happiness we could find in this world? Don't you think so, Sidhartha?" The puppet show had stolen Kaveri's heart. Sidhartha sat there poised as the evening drifted away. "I've already found my magic spell, haven't you?" He looked at her. Kaveri looked at him and wondered, what if she woke up one morning and realized that it was all a dream, or could it be possible that Sidhartha too, just like King Dushmanta, would forget his Kaveri.

That was their last summer together. At the end of the holidays, after Kaveri came back to Bombay, they received a telegram from Anantapur. It was brief yet shocking: 'Zamindar Choudhury expired.' The family rushed back to the village to pay their last homage to the grand old aristocrat. Kaveri missed her grandpa a lot for she was the apple of his eye. Also, there was someone else she terribly missed in the village. Sidhartha had already left for his college in Calcutta. About a couple of months later there was a letter from Calcutta. It was for Kaveri. Sidhartha had written:

My lovely Kaveri:
The day you left, everything in the village suddenly seemed so listless. Even the ducks and the lotuses, the palm trees and the mango groves, the summer breeze and those flickering glow worms in the twilight, they all seemed to have lost their splendor. It was as if they were all saying something to me. As I was wandering along, it felt as if our beautiful village of Anantapur was struck by a sense of melancholy. Needless to say, I miss you, Kaveri. I want you to come back soon. Another summer is much too far. I want you back sooner, much sooner. Write to me, please. I will meet you at Anantapur. I will be counting every moment until I hear from you. Till then with love from your one and only.
Sidhartha

Sidhartha never heard from her. The letter accidentally fell in the wrong hands. One afternoon as Kaveri came home from college her mother held the letter right in front of her, infuriated, "What is going on? How can he dare do such a thing to our daughter? Sure! You are a great catch for him; after all you are the granddaughter of a zamindar, but what about our prestige in the society? To have a goldsmith for a son-in-law would be so much beneath our dignity, do you at all realize that? Or don't you even care about us anymore?"

At that point, Kaveri's father came from behind like a ghost and intervened, his voice rumbling like a thunder. He straightaway got to the point, "I want you to listen very carefully as I speak. Your mother and I, for your own good (with emphasis on those last four words) have decided to get you married within a year. Since our family is presently bereaved by your grandfather's death, I decided to wait until spring or else we would have had the marriage earlier. We have met the young man and are very impressed with him and his family. He is both very successful in his career and genteel in manners, unlike some plebeian (the last few words pricked her like a thorn). He has a charming personality. His mother is a childhood friend of your mother, so we know the family pretty well. Now, if you wish to meet him sometime, we will make the arrangement. Other than that, we have nothing to say to you." Having said that, he marched off from the scene like a generalissimo, leaving behind the lovelorn adolescent frozen to the bone with fear and shock. That day the eighteen year old girl had felt tremendously intimidated by their threat. With that threat came the end of a romantic chapter in Kaveri's life. The heavy hand of parental discipline wantonly crushed the budding love that had all the potential of emerging into a beautiful relationship in Kaveri's life.

Now married, Kaveri arrived in her husband's new bungalow, built on the beach, with an ocean view front and a terrace garden of luscious tropical plants. The large iron gate to his bungalow looked ostentatious, its arch entwined with a beautiful vine of bougainvillea. To countervail for what he could not offer to her, he showered her with all the comfort that money could buy. Prior to Kaveri's arrival in their new Bungalow, Priyankar had already employed a host of servants along with a chef, a gardener, and a chauffeur who would be at her beck and call. Later, Priyankar made the effort to apologize to his bride for staying away on their first night. It was not until a week later, that Priyankar could actually bring himself to face up to her. Painfully curt, as he was to her, he made it amply clear that he was a prisoner of his own past and that she should not try to approach him ever. If he could, perhaps, some day free himself from his own emotional bondage, he would come to her, if not, she was free to choose her own life. Being trapped in an unhappy marriage, what else is left of an Indian woman, that she could pursue on her own and if there were such women out there who could, she certainly was not one of them, thought Kaveri to herself.

In her flamboyantly furnished boudoir, there was a large glass picture window, which quickly became her closest companion. Every day, she sat next to it and quietly watched the evening sun dip into the Arabian Sea. Then, in the placid aura of twilight, she gazed at those bohemian sea gulls hovering over those tiny fishing boats along the shore, or with their wings spanned across, roaming the sky in a lordly fashion. Sometimes, in the dead of night, she lay in her bed all by herself and awake listening to the roaring of the tumultuous waves in the sea. Thus, through that window, she had silently built up quite a relationship with the world outside. The sea had plenty to offer her, and Kaveri, in return, offered long and lonesome gaze. Its sun drenched bed of sand glittered like gold particles in the noon. Waves laced with pearly white froth heaved like women's breasts. The color of the sky went through a delightful metamorphosis according to the time of the day, and the sea frequently borrowed its color from the sky. From dawn until dusk, all those fascinating sights and sounds of all the activities along the shore on the other side of her window became an integral part of her lonesome life. Like a lagoon, Kaveri's life was perennially cut off from the mainstream of ever flowing life, with its own little ripples caused only by the sights and the sounds along the shore. While the highly talented benedict kept himself preoccupied behind the camera — his only passion in life.

Priyankar devoted all his precious moments to his craft. Only a

genius like him could portray sometimes so vividly and sometimes so very intricately those various and often highly complex
facets of human life through the eye of a camera. His camera
never blinked, even when it was a matter of focusing on the most
subtle nuances of human sentiments and emotions. But strangely
enough, he turned blind when it came to his wife. He was not
quite insensitive, but, certainly lacked the emotion one would
expect of a husband. As though, she was an absolute miscast in
his life. Despite his counseling on their first week, Kaveri sometimes of her own volition went out of her way to please her husband. But Priyankar found her much too common to excite his
intellect or evoke any passion in him. It was as if she was not
meant to be there. It did not take her long to realize that she was
there only to fulfill his mother's demand of a daughter-in-law.

There were times, in an act of self-pity, Kaveri would call into
memory all her cousins from Indrapuri, that she knew were now
happily married and had children of their own. She recalled
Rupa, who was married to a physicist and lived in New Dehli.
She was the oldest among all the cousins and was married in her
teens. Unlike most of her other cousins, Rupa never even got to
meet the man she was to marry. All she saw of him before their
marriage was a black and white photograph taken during his
graduation. Today, they have a son who is now on his way to
become a physicist like his father. After Kaveri's marriage, Rupa
wrote several letters, inviting the newlyweds to visit them in
New Delhi. In return, Kaveri thanked her for the invitation but
could never bring herself to invite them back. Neela, married to
a college professor, now mother of two daughters, settled in
Calcutta. A couple of years after their marriage, Neela and her
husband made a trip to Bombay to visit both Kaveri and their
other cousin Kajol. Neela had tears in her eyes when she saw
how lonesome Kaveri was. Kajol just became a mother of twins
after eight years of their marriage. They lived in Bombay and
not too far from where Kaveri lived. Kajol's husband, an airline

pilot, was often away from home, but when they were together, there was so much love between them. She had told Kaveri that they had fallen in love on their very first night. Kajol kept in touch with Mukta and Panna who settled in Anantapur, and always talked about them to Kaveri.

It just seemed as if everyone around Kaveri were infinitely happy and content in their marriage, though none of them knew their husbands before their marriage. She even thought of her own parents with envy, whom she always thought as one of the happiest couples she had ever known. There were times when she would feel like a wounded tigress struggling to tear away from the vicious trap of destiny. Not that the thought of Sidhartha never crossed her mind, but she would never do anything that would make a cuckold of her husband. Often, her heart writhed in pain thinking of Sidhartha, but over the years she had learnt to tuck that wound in the deepest crevasse of her life and just live on. It must be, she thought to herself, one of destiny's cruel designs that placed her as a proxy in Priyankar's life. It was this stoicism that kept her going and served as her only potion to an unhealing bruise. While Priyankar lived the life of a debonair, Kaveri, on the contrary, quietly lived right beside him as his consort, yet, a stranger to one another.

About six months ago, just last winter, with the sudden and premature death of her husband, Kaveri is left to bear the brunt of widowhood without ever knowing the joy and the excitement in a marriage. It was not until very recently, that Priyankar had finally begun to confide in her the most intimate part of his life, when she had least expected. Whether Priyankar acted on the dictates of his conscience or his intuition or if it was something that was preordained or simply a matter of coincidence, she will never know, but in any event his rapport with his wife during the last days of his life saw a remarkable change. The metamorphosis he went through in his final days could not have been a cry in the wilderness, for it gave him an enormous sense of peace and left him with a sense of catharsis before he breathed his last.

Finally, after more than a decade, Priyankar, one day of his own volition led his wife through his desolate past. He told her that in his early youth, he had met an exceptionally talented young artist and fell in love with her. They shared all their hopes and fears, their disappointments and their dreams together. As a budding film director then, he felt great affinity towards her. Theirs was a union of art and intellect, a veritable bond of two souls. They could not live without seeing each other even for a day.

Soon, his mother came to know about it, and so one day she called her son aside and told him that she would even go this far as to disown him if he ever considered marrying her, for two reasons, firstly, she was a film actress, in her opinion, an absolute riffraff who could not be brought into an aristocratic family as theirs and secondly she was not a Hindu.

"But, mother, she wants to give up acting once she's married and what difference does it make if she's not a Hindu? Do you know, we come from the same Aryan descent? History has recorded our past." "Now, why would I need to take history lessons to find you a wife? Don't I have enough common sense to know that a girl from Zoroastrian faith who grew up worshipping the Ahura Mazda would not mix well in a Hindu culture? She would look very odd among us, trust me," was Mrs. Roy's response as she walked out the door.

But, more importantly, what Priyankar did not know was the fact that Shirin was carrying his child until it was too late. She did not have the gall to mention it to anyone, not even to Priyankar. For an Indian girl, nothing can be more disgraceful than being an unwed mother, it is the ultimate sin a maiden can bring upon herself, so, as naive as she was, she quietly guarded her darkest secret in fear of losing him. Until one night, Priyankar received a devastating phone call that broke him completely. He had just come home after seeing her. They had a very emotional discussion that evening. Knowing how much he meant to her, he did not have the heart to tell her how his mother felt about their relationship until that evening. Priyankar had mustered up his will to finally let her know that they had no future together. At that point, though Shirin struggled to bring it to her lips what she had suppressed in her breast all that time, she just could not for the love of him. Instead, all she did was to beg him to leave her alone. So, after Priyankar left her house, she wrote him a letter, then doused herself with kerosene and set on fire.

After he had unfolded his gruesome past to his wife, he begged her forgiveness for not being able to give her the love and affection she deserved. He told her that his greatest irony in life was the fact that his mother whom he would put before everything else in this world was the one who inadvertently hurt him the most. He told her that ever since that day he has not been able to forgive himself for dragging Shireen to her death, but he also hoped that maybe one day he would be able to turn to her for love. That day never dawned. After that, it was only a matter of months when one night in his sleep Priyankar died of a massive heart attack.

Another summer has dawned in the quiet village of Anantapur. Not much has changed, except the tamarind tree by the village well and the guava, papaya, and the lemon tree along the wharf. They have thrived so well, that they instantly reminded the young widow of the girl in her adolescence, when youth had just made its sweet debut. It rained all night and continued through the wee hours of the morning. The coastal plain of the Bay of Bengal is just as pluvious as the shore along the Arabian Sea. Raindrops dripped from tips of morungas that hung like green sticks from the branches. A mourning dove on the morunga tree, that usually filled the air with its dirge, sat quietly, pitifully drenched from the shower. The sky looked washed out of its color. Kaveri felt a chill in the air that stenched heavily from the swamp mixed with a sweet scent of neem and hijal flowers strewn all over under the trees. As a little girl, Kaveri had learned from Sidhartha how to extract blobs of glue by scraping the bark of hijal tree. The ferryboat just arrived with such a clamour bringing in commuters to the village from the town across river Sonali. From the heavy downpour all through the night one could see how Sonali had swollen like an expectant mother.

As he stepped down into the slush from the ferryboat, carrying a briefcase in his right hand and a black umbrella under his left arm, Sidhartha's eyes suddenly fell on the dark silhouette of a young woman at a distance. Sidhartha had grown beard and his complexion darkened from the sun and toil. His eyes reflected a sense of profound serenity and his quiet composure gave him the appearance of a poet/philosopher rather than a physician. Sidhartha is the only surgeon around who has sacrificed an urban living, his only mission being to be of service to the villagers amongst whom he grew up. He makes house calls, commuting from one village to the next on ferry. He was coming home after treating a patient in a town across the river. He felt a little exhausted as he was up all night.

Sidhartha had never expected to see Kaveri again, who was once the girl of his dream, much less in a widow's attire. She was long gone from his life, or was she really? Although, many years had come and gone between them, one glimpse of her made all that time seem just like yesterday. Sidhartha could hardly believe his eyes. What should I say to her! Would she remember me? How should I address her? After all, she was married to a famous film director. What if she doesn't want to talk to me? As he wrestled with this sudden gale of thoughts, her eyes momentarily met his. She was at the prime of life, yet, wearing a facade of age and serenity.

"Kaveri! is that you?" Sidhartha exclaimed. "I am so sorry to see you in this... state," he warily dropped the word 'widow'. What's the matter with her! Doesn't she remember me? How could she ever become so cold to me? He began to despair. But he needed to talk to her. "What brings you here after all these years? Of course, I'll understand if you don't wish to speak to me. After all, you come from the world of glamour and riches, and I'm only a village doctor." The words seemed to fling out of his mouth like a handful of sharp-edged stones. He really did not intend to be sarcastic to her, but then again there was so much pain he had suppressed for so long now, that, seeing her, it finally found its way out.

"I am here to visit. Since grandpa died, never came back to Anantapur again. It's been ages since I saw my uncles and aunts and cousins." She paused for a moment and then continued, "it's been a long time for us too... thought you'd have forgotten me by now." She was prudent. Sidhartha sensed a biting chill in her voice, as if his Kaveri was long dead and it was only an echo of her voice he heard. With the life long gone, the echo still lurked in an abyss. "I wish I could have forgotten," Sidhartha replied, "it would have saved me of, Oh! I don't know... I don't know... how many days and nights of pain and agony. What happened to you? I was waiting to hear from you. You never came back to Anantapur since that summer." Sidhartha wanted to bring his Kaveri back to life. He could have gone on and on, if it wasn't for the storm that was fast approaching from across the river. Sonali looked livid, as if in rage. The tiny ferryboats rocked like cradles as the waves bellowed in the river. They could see the strong gale sweeping and swaying through the paddy field far away. The birds flew in disarray. There was a dreadful commotion in nature. But Kaveri looked as calm and composed as ever.

"Let's look for some shelter first, or else this storm will swallow us alive." Sidhartha floundered as he guarded her against the strong gusts of wind that blew in every direction and led her towards the ruins of an old Shiva temple next to a banyan tree. A broken roof that hung between the massive pillars on the temple portico was all they could seek as far as a little shade was concerned.

"I don't want to be seen like this by anybody." Kaveri stealthily looked around with the corner of her eyes, a little perturbed.

"You know how the village folks are, they'll start fabricating stories the minute they see us together," she said.

"Never mind the village folks, don't you have anything more to say to me after all these years? I want to know what happened. Why did you suddenly disappear from my life?" Sidhartha interrogated.

"What's the point in opening up an old wound?" Kaveri chose to remain cryptic about her feelings. She did not want to raise her emotions to the surface and certainly not before him. They are better off buried where they are, deep within herself. It was bad enough that she ran into him like this. It would be very unbecoming of her as a widow to cry on his shoulder today after all these years. After all, he has his own life... maybe also a ... beautiful wife... and...children...a happy family, which she never had. Like a vulture, the thoughts ripped her heart apart. She was on the verge of tears.

"Please, let me go, and don't ever try to see me anymore." Struggling to keep herself in check, her voice trembled.

"You must be out of your mind. I can't let you go like this. I want to know what happened between us, where did I fail?" Sidhartha was persistent.

"You did not fail — not, at least, in my mind. Believe me, it was my parents. When they found out about us, they quickly arranged for my marriage. They wouldn't even listen to me."

"Did you try to escape from them?" Sidhartha interrupted.

"I thought about it a lot, but I didn't have the courage. Where would I go, to whom, tell me? I was so frightened. I just couldn't. Believe me, Sidhartha, I wouldn't lie to you."

Sidhartha had no reason to disbelieve her.

The storm had just settled. Kaveri could see from a distance one of the servants from Indrapuri walking towards them. She had been out long — long enough to be missed by the family. The old aunt ordered one of her servants to look for her.

"I have to go." Kaveri hurriedly wiped off her bleary eyes with the back of her palm and was just about to leave when Sidhartha held her hand and requested her to see him that evening in the mango grove behind her grandpa's baagaan baaree.

"Do you realize what you're doing? I'm a widow, for god's sake. I couldn't be seeing you. Let me go, please." Kaveri begged as she tried to shake her hand off his grip, "besides, don't you have a wife at home, waiting for you this very moment as we speak?" She needed to remind him of his sense of fidelity which seemed terribly lacking.

"Well, that's an issue I'm glad you brought up. We'll deal with it when I see you this evening at the mango grove."

By then the servant had walked much closer to them. Kaveri waved at him, as she yelled, "run along, I'll be home shortly, oh! Keshav, please do me a favor?" She lowered her voice vigilantly, "don't mention this to anyone. You know what I mean?" Indicating Sidhartha with an askance.

"Oh! don't worry, mem sahib, I won't mention this to anyone." The old servant nodded his head with a smirk on his face as he trudged along towards the mansion. Kaveri then turned around, looked Sidhartha in the eye and gave him a piece of her mind, as she tried to fight back her tears at the same time, "look, we have no right to ruin another life, and let me tell you something else, if we start seeing each other, a day will come when we both will regret and never be able to forgive ourselves for that."

"Stop, stop right there." Sidhartha felt like he needed to interrupt to amend the situation before it got out of hand, "wait a minute, whose life are we about to ruin?"

"Your wife's of course." She retorted, "who else?"

"I have no wife. I never married." As Sidhartha carefully spelled out every single word, she stood there gazing at him, her hands still clasped together tightly in his grip. Soon, her rage melted like dew drops that melt at the first touch of a warm sunshine.

Ever since Priyankar died, Kaveri had coerced herself into a life of continence and complacency. But just this morning after having met Sidhartha by chance, and having learned that he had never married, Kaveri's prism of life picked up a splash of fresh colours. Today, after so many years, Sidhartha had ignited a blazing fire in her. She was never driven by such a furious yearning ever. Even as a newlywed, she had never encountered for a moment, such overwhelming emotions.

"Sidhartha, what have you done to me? I always took life as it came, and never knew what it is to defy. But, today for the first time, I feel so differently! Tell me, where will it lead us to?" Sidhartha could feel the agony in Kaveri's voice.

They were nestled in the mango grove. She was sitting on the grass leaning against a mango tree. He was lying on his back, with his head on her lap. Sidhartha looked so content today. The grove echoed with the relentless call of the lonely cuckoo just like in the past. In the warmth of a summer day, even the shy and the secretive blackbird sounded impatient for love.

"Kaveri, can you think of anything that is sweeter than love?" Sidhartha put the question to her as he played with her hair.

"What kind of a question is that, how can anything be sweeter than love?" She wondered aloud.

"To find one's lost love, ah! the joy of it, I know now."

For a fleeting moment Kaveri's attention escaped to a different time and space where the thought of Priyankar lurked in her heart.

She wondered, if Priyankar too might have found his lost love, if not in this world, perhaps, on a higher plane, where the spirits dwell. Kaveri looked so pristine that evening as the setting sun pierced through a rush of leaves in the grove and warmly kissed her eyes. Sidhartha could not help laying his eyes on her as he quietly wondered: How can I let her waste away her life? Just like the shefali in autumn that blossoms in the woods and withers away quietly, unseen, unadored forever.

"The longer I see you today, the more I feel that this was the moment I have been waiting for," said Sidhartha, "this moment makes everything else worthwhile, our parting and the pining, the agony of not knowing how I'd continue with my life without you, the sleepless nights I spent just thinking of you, and everything else that I have endured... everything."

"Sidhartha, you should have been a poet." Remarked Kaveri.

Then, overcome by passion, he lay her down on the ground, leaned over and said, "of course, I am a poet, and don't you know, you are my poetry?" While the young widow lay there, her heart throbbing like a boiling cauldron of passion, he murmured again, "this reminds me of a poem I had written about us after I found out that you were married."

"Oh! please, tell me, I want to listen." Kaveri impatiently waited, while Sidhartha tried to collect his thoughts together.

"Let me see if I can remember all of it, alright, here's how it goes. I've named it:

At the Dawn of Love

In a quiet moment of reflection
beneath a soft, twilight sky,
as I was writing your name
in the sand, time and again,
a warm drop of rain fell on my lips
that quietly stirred me from deep within.

A warm drop of rain on my lips
brought back a flood of memories
from the days of our sweet innocence
while we were still young at the art of love.

How we tremoured like an autumnal leaf!

while our hearts throbbed, stormed by passion,
and then calmed as love melted into
our first gentle kiss like a drop of dew."

"Oh! Sidhartha, how lovely, how very lovely!" Kaveri was ecstatic. "Do you remember that afternoon? It was our last summer together," he asked.

"Oh! How could I forget, we were on our way to the carnival at Sonapur, it was as if we had just discovered something magical," she fondly reminisced, "we were, like you said, in our days of sweet innocence and young at the art of love. How well you have treasured those memories! Sidhartha, you make me feel so special. Tell me, do you still have that sonorous voice? Remember, those beautiful songs you'd sing to me? Whenever I felt lonesome, I'd think of you and hum those tunes for hours together... remember those Rabindra sangeet you'd sing to me...

The shadow of my beloved floats in the sky,
along with the rain drenched breath of remorse.
and then another...
You have given away rainy day's first blossom of kadam,
I have come to offer you my songs of monsoon."

"After all these years, how can there be a song left in me? In fact, soon after I found out that you were married, I gave up singing and that's when I first started writing poetry, I must have written hundreds of those. I just couldn't bear the thought of you with another man."

Kaveri felt a sudden gloom in his voice. She would do anything to take his pain away, so, she started talking about her marriage, which she otherwise seldom did. Having since found out about Priyankar's ominous love life which had caused him irrevocable damage to his emotions, she had learned to take a kinder view of him, but until then her married life remained a trying one.

"If you can believe, Priyankar and I lived our lives together but never really belonged to each other. For some reason which I might tell you another time, we always remained strangers to one another. Believe me, Sidhartha, my marriage was the greatest irony of my life," she tried to ease his pain, "anyway, tell me there's a song left in you, somewhere, for me, please?"

"I'll try if you promise me something," Sidhartha briskly got up and sat upright, still holding Kaveri in his arms.

"Promise me you'll never leave me again, no matter, what? Do you remember the puppet show we saw that afternoon?"

Kaveri had to interrupt, "but, don't forget, Shakuntala didn't get married to another man and become a widow, while she was separated from king Dushmant." Kaveri's voice riddled with despair, "how can we ever have a future together? Tell me, who'll approve of our marriage? I'm so torn between the two, today, I just don't know what's right or wrong any more. A part of me wants to be yours forever, and then there's a part of me that tells me it's not right... it's not fair to you."

"Then, what is fair? That we both should be lonesome, miserable and yearning for each other for the rest of our lives, when you know there's no one else in my life." Sidhartha sounded so grave as if he was giving a sermon, "you must break open that shell and come out of it, Kaveri. Listen to me, together we must set a precedent in our village. I know, we have come a long way since the days of suttee, but don't you see we have a long way ahead of us? We have to walk that road and I want you right beside me, all along. Kaveri, please, I want you as my wife and mother of my children." Sidhartha's voice resonated with faith, hope and passion. His power and strength of character so closely resembled that of her grandpa's, the man she revered all her life. As if, unbeknownst to her, grandpa had left behind in Sidhartha his very own legacy in Anantapur.

The next day, as the two of them were taking a grand tour of the baagaan baaree, Kaveri fondly remembered her grandpa. Only if he was alive today. If he had not died that summer, Kaveri's life would have taken a different course altogether. In her childhood days grandpa's baagaan baaree was one of the greatest taboos of all time. In Kaveri's mind it was always an abode of undying curiosity coupled with her wildest imaginations. Today, as she wanders around glancing through every nook and corner of the place that was once shrouded with mystery, she finds it all so incredulous. Grandpa had left behind one more legacy that truly depicted his proud demeanor.

As Kaveri entered into the main parlor, which once used to be the banquet hall of the grand aristocrat, embellished with crystal chandeliers, velvet curtains and Persian rugs, bronze decanters and tall, brass, finely engraved vases, the air thick with rose attar and lilting with Bijli Bai's gifted voice, her eyes fell on an ivory figurine displayed on the mantlepiece. It was of Gandhi — who fought for the abolishment of untouchable in the nineteen thirties — eating from the plate of a Shudra. There were sculptures of great martyrs, the warrior queen of Jhansi carved in onyx and robust statues of Tippu Sultan and Sirajudulla, all those who fought for freedom and gave their lives during British Raj.

The walls of the cottage exhibited impressive portraits carved in bronze and copper plates — portraits of such pioneers as Raja Ram Mohon Roy, and Vidya Saagar, the two men who had championed the cause of suttee abolishment and widow remarriage in the eighteen hundreds. As a student of Indian History, she had studied all about the abolishment of suttee and the pioneers of widow remarriage, but at the time they seemed so intangible in the pages of her textbooks. Today was a day of grand revelation for Kaveri which she wanted to share with the rest of Anantapur. She wanted the people of Anantapur and all the others to know that her grandpa's baagaan baaree, unlike many others, was not after all a haven for all the clandestine affairs of a grand aristocrat. Why was it then such a taboo? Could it be because of the age-old tradition of protecting women against blasphemy — a reflection from the Moghul period of their puritanical attitude towards women? Today, she was driven by the fervor of a historian to convert her grandpa's baagaan baaree into a museum which could restore the wealth of bygone days. One of its kind on the entire east coast, that would proudly display the culturally enriched legacy of a zamindar.

Kaveri was awake all night. She was contemplating all that Sidhartha had said to her in the grove. Had it not been for Sidhartha, a man liberated enough to believe in women's cause, it would remain a cause unchallenged in Anantapur for generations to come. It would not have been easy for Kaveri, all by herself, to walk away from all her doubts and fears, from those dark and sham taboos that had always intimidated her in the past. Despite her modern upbringing, the thought of a remarriage, until yesterday, seemed rather sinistrous. But, today she could envision the beginning of a new day and age dawning in Anantapur.

THE
PHILOSOPHER AND
THE PHILANDERER

A bullock cart went jingling and jolting, its wheels squeaking as it rolled lazily along the muddy road. A dark silhouette of a young village woman, with a slim contour, curved delicately along the breast line slowly diminished into the yonder. A herd of cattle raised a cloud of dust, drawing a veil of obscurity for a while. On their way home, the doves formed a perfect crescent in the twilight sky. I am reminiscing along the country road.

Monsoon is usually severe along the coast of the Arabian Sea. A torrential downpour of heavy rain all through the night quenched a thirsty earth and made it cooler than usual. Suddenly, I hear leaves rustle and then out of the exuberance of greenery, there appears before me a pair of innocent eyes of a fawn, like a divine intervention to my train of thoughts. As if terrified by my encroachment upon its domain, the lonely denizen sprang to its feet with a tremor and within a flash of a lightning leaped away into the hazy distance. The wet earth and the fresh greenery together exude an aroma that waft the air all around me. With each deep breath I must have drunk a goblet full of the forest fragrance and felt it gushing down through my blood stream. I am home at last.

It has been a decade since I left home. I have barely recovered from the jet lag. My mind is still unwinding itself from another age, time, culture and people. The slow, calm and open Indian country road dazed me. As I walk down the country road, far away from the big city, I see bees and butterflies dipping themselves into the bosom of bakul and champa for a sip of the nectar. Oh! What flirtation goes on in the wilderness! I remember once Mohan saying, "would you believe, Nandini, that more romance goes on in the naked wilderness than one can ever imagine?"

In this rugged country road I see robust men carrying fresh produce of the village farm to the nearest market place in preparation for the next day. Tall slender village women, carrying hay stacks on their heads, parade in a queue. Their weather-beaten complexion has a shade of bronze, their sharp and sturdy features remind me of those Egyptian statues I had seen at some of the international museums. A villager passing by, with a pair of baskets hanging from his muscular shoulders, left a trail of sweet aroma behind him. Might there be freshly plucked jasmines in those baskets?

Oh! How sweet can nature be! The sight, the smell and the sound of it all bring such nostalgia that all my senses are begging to belong to her today. I have never felt like this in a long time. Not since that late summer afternoon when Mohan had held me in his arms for the first time, sitting by the bank of river Shivangini and later on, as we walked through this very road in the rain with his arms around me. We were taking a stroll down the country road after a movie. It was one of Mohan's weekly assignments for his paper to review all the current English movies in town.

That was a long time ago. He was trying to talk me into not leaving him like this. He said my absence would make his life void and meaningless. That he would not be able to endure it. "Please don't destroy me like this, Nandini!" he begged. Why did he have to wait all these years to say this to me? I thought to myself. What took him so long? While I spent sleepless nights longing to be caressed and loved by him, he walked beside me like a stranger. He never said a word about how he felt for me, nor did he ever care to find out my feelings for him. All he talked about was my writing. That I should give more insight, more depth to my writings. Why, why now? "It's too late now, Mohan." I wanted him to stop cajoling me. It was ripping my will apart.

Yet, I knew I had to go. My passport was ready. It was now only a matter of days. Many parents in educated middle class families, cherish the dream of sending their sons abroad for higher studies. Since I did not have a brother, we were only two, me and my baby sister who is much younger than me; so my parents brought me up like their son. I dreamt the dreams of my parents. After all, I am their firstborn. How could I disappoint them? I would never be able to forgive myself if I did. My father's voice echoed, "Nandini, let me tell you something, life is full of temptations, but don't let those ever lead you astray, that's what I call strength of character." Besides Mohan had always taken me for granted. He never thought that I could leave him for something like this. "How can your father let you do this?" he paused to take a moment's breath, "when he should be seriously looking for a husband for you?" I had never seen him so perturbed before. The news of my going abroad really took him by surprise.

"I never knew that you wanted me as your wife." Besides, my father thinks that in the long run a good education comes more handy to a woman than a husband."

"Handy! huh!" chuckled Mohan, "an interesting choice of words! Well, anyway, haven't you had enough education already? And now that you know, I care for you and I want you as my wife, shouldn't your father, Mr. Liberal, reconsider this decision of yours?"

"Call him names if you wish, but you have to admit that there aren't too many Indian men of his generation who would want their daughters to go abroad for higher studies."

"Humm! That makes me wonder. Is he a feminist by any chance?"

"Well, I don't know that he is or he isn't. But I can certainly say this, with millions of male chauvinists like you, this world can use a few good feminists like my father, that is, if you think he is one."

"I find you very cute when your face turns red and puffy over those all-important-global issues." I sensed a pinch of sarcasm in those last few words.

"You never take me seriously, do you?" I accused him.

"Sure, I do. Why do you think I am begging you to change your mind. Nandini, I need you as my wife. Please, don't do this to me. If you want, I'll be more than willing to talk to your father."

"I only wish you took this stand much earlier. Besides, what about my journalism?"

"Well, you can be both. My wife and a journalist."

"You must be joking! Once I become your wife, I'll be compelled to abandon that idea for good."

"Why do you think so?"

"Don't you see? I'll be like a creeper, leaning on you. You're so lofty in the profession, like an old banyan tree, standing tall and indestructible. Here I am, a budding journalist, just starting to get my byline."

"You make me feel so special. But I suppose, I'm still not good enough to be your husband. I've not met a girl as ambitious as you are. By the way, that interview of yours with that beauty queen... Miss India... what's her name?... Sangeeta... Sangeeta Chandani was pretty good. Shows lot of promise."

Much to my relief, our conversation gradually seemed to take a detour. "You really think so! I thought you would never mention it." Mohan seldom paid any compliments to my writing.

"I had a pretty good lead, of course. We both went to the same school and college, you know. By the way, I've quite a few assignments lined up for this week. Oh! Mohan, I have to tell you this." Like a little girl in a candy shop, I bounced with excitement.

"My editor wants me to do a story on Dr. Ranna, you know, the psychologist from V. S. Hospital, who's currently involved in some extensive research on hypnosis and is invited to attend the hypnosis and psychosomatic conference in Germany next month. I must say, it's very intriguing. He called me last night. He wants me to visit his clinic and observe some very unconventional cases before I start writing about him. So I went this morning. There were two cases that fascinated me most. One of them was a woman in her early stage of pregnancy," I paused to catch my breath, "though, it wasn't a case of psychosomatic, Dr. Ranna was pretty confident that with his hypnotic method he could definitely help her labor painlessly. So, I watched him suggest repeatedly to the expectant mother, that child birth was not only painless but that it was also pleasurable. A whole new dimension to childbirth! Can you believe it? An absolutely painless, natural childbirth! He's simply incredible, don't you think so, Mohan?" I could not say enough about Dr. Ranna's revolutionary step towards painless childbirth that day.

"Yes, I think so," said Mohan seriously and then after a moment's pause he continued, "my last childbirth was simply awful and yet it was better than the previous one. Oh! where was your Dr. Ranna then?"

"See, that's what I mean. You never take me seriously," I fretted.

"Well, how much more seriously can I take you? I am listening to you, am I not? Anyway, don't let him get too revolutionary with his ideas now. Who knows! he might even succeed in getting men pregnant with his hypnotic messages like: abraca dabraca diddle doo, let there be a child in you, and then the expectant father might suddenly wake up and say, "damn it! I didn't even get to take my pants off! It's not fair." "There should be a limit to your vulgarity, Mohan." Though he irked me for ridiculing Dr. Ranna, I could not help smiling at the hilarious picture I had already drawn in my mind.

"Well, my vulgarity is at least making you smile. What other incredible things did your Dr. Ranna do? Tell me, I'm all ears."

"There was another patient, a newly married young man who thinks he's impotent." I said, bursting with impatience.

"Now, wait a minute, did you say he's married?" Mohan interrupted.

"Yes, that's right," and I continued, 'now, this definitely is a case of psychosomatic, to be more precise, a case of psychosexual disorder,' Dr. Ranna told me before he called the patient in and sounded absolutely certain that he would be able to cure him."

"Did you meet his wife?" Mohan interrupted again.

"As a matter of fact I did. Anyway, as I was saying, Dr. Ranna made this young patient lie down and then..."

"If you will be so kind enough as to spare me the details about the poor impotent and tell me about his wife."

"Oh! no, he's not poor at all." I jumped all over him, "Do you know that his father is the owner of a..."

"Well! I don't care even if his father owns every bit of land from the peak of the Himalayas to the tip of Cape Comorin. To me a man who can't have the pleasures of life is a poor man, anyway, now tell me about his wife."

Mohan delighted in vexing me. "What about his wife?" The interruptions began to get on my nerves.

"Now, you are really embarrassing me!" Baffled by his strange comment, I asked.

"Embarrassing you! how?"

"Well, there's a newly married young woman who is in need of help and here I am wasting my time talking to you."

"Were you listening to me? It is the man who needs help." I was quite exasperated by then.

"My dear Nandini, do I have to spell out everything I say? Can't you see? A healthy young bachelor like me..." With both his hands pressed against his chest, his head held high, like a grand old mythological character on stage, he went on... "Oh! how my heart aches for his wife who's destined to spend all those loveless nights."

With those words and a touch of pathos tingling in his voice, Mohan teased me to no end. Quite an improviser he is! I thought to myself and then gave him a mouthful. "Well, if she is destined to have loveless nights, so will it be, even with you beside her. What gives you the power to change her destiny, may I know? Besides, how dare you say that! What about me?" I clinched my teeth in anger.

"What about you? You are leaving me for a career that you can very well pursue in our own country."

"You will wait for me until I come back, won't you?"

"I don't believe in waiting. Either now or never. You know what they say, out of sight is out of mind. Besides, who on earth gave you the idea that a degree from abroad will make you a better journalist?"

"It's not just the question of a degree. It'll also broaden my horizon, you know. Anyone with a penchant for writing needs a wide variety of exposure, which even all the libraries in the world can't give you. You need to travel, see places, meet people, learn their ways, speak their tongue. In other words, you have not yet begun to live your life until you have left your cozy little nest, and I don't intend to make a speech, but that's the truth."

"But you are making a speech. Anyway, you have my permission, so, go on." Mohan tried not to chuckle. I continued without minding him.

"As a writer, unless you've walked that huddled road, everything you write will be distastefully skeletal, superficial, unrealistic and may even be unromantic. A reader needs to feel the heartbeat of the characters portrayed in one's writing".

"And who may I ask gave you this piece of valuable admonishment, because surely it doesn't sound like you at all ?"

"Kamalda". I made no bones about it.

"Who is Kamalda? I see, that philanderer." Mohan pierced me

with a look of suspicion.

"He's not a philanderer. It's that Mrs. Chatterjee, the Colonel's wife at the base. Kamalda calls her his Diotima. You've heard of Diotima, haven't you?" I asked, "the woman who taught Socrates all about love and beauty and wisdom." A spontaneous ripple of a smile escaped my lips.

"Oh! for heaven's sake! Was he trying to impress you again?" Mohan had this 'don't give me that nonsense' look written all over his face, "his Diotima!" he mumbled, "she's nothing but a... well, I better not say it out loud."

"Well, maybe, so was Diotima herself. How do we know who she was in real life? We always have a tendency to idolize or at least romanticize the lives of those that have lived before us in the distant past, although, I don't know why we do it."

"It's my understanding, that within every one of us in this world there's an ultimate desire to become immortal, to leave behind something that will never die in us, that perhaps could be the reason? who knows what it is? but you are right, anyway, what else does your Kamalda say?" Mohan looked at me.

"Or, one better still, if not Diotima, she could be that Kamala in Hermann Hesse's novel Siddhartha. You've read that book, haven't you?" I looked at Mohan and found him amazed, perhaps, at my analogy?

"You probably didn't expect this from me, did you?" I asked.

"Yes, Kamala, how very appropriate! and you're right, I didn't expect this from you. I suppose, wonders never cease!" Remarked Mohan as he kept nodding his head trying to picture the seductive Kamala.

"Wonders never cease!" I repeated after him mockingly. "Well, you didn't have to be that blatantly candid, you know, just because I asked." And then continued without making a big deal of it,

"Kamalda says, a little flirtation now and then is good for the intellect. That's his way of pulling out some vital material for his writing. While flirting, quite often they also bare their soul to him, you know. It seems, it's an old technique women use to arouse men's sympathy. Obviously, that gives him the vantage point to peek into their bosom."

"A peek into their bosom!" Mohan's eyes danced impishly, as he played with those words over and over again. It annoyed me.

"Don't be so vulgar, Mohan." I said.

"You keep calling me vulgar, but let me tell you, I can't be more vulgar than your Kamalda even if I want to. You know nothing of what we know about him. All you know is that he speaks fluently in ten or twelve languages and writes fairly well, though highly controversial; and that he's a voluminous reader, your favorite one. But, if you truly care to know the real man underneath, you should listen to our editorial staff and they'll tell you what a sadist he is."

"If Kamalda is a sadist, then you people from the press are not exactly saints either. This is so typical of you journalists. All you care is to go through people's dirty laundry." I was furious.

"You mean dirty linen?" Mohan tried to correct me.

"What's the difference, they're both dirty. Besides, you shouldn't be talking about him like this. If only you knew how highly he speaks of you. The other day at the Rotary Club as we were having our lunch after the press conference, he said, 'tell me, Nandini, when is your Mohan going to become the editor-in-chief?' He thinks, you are one of the finest journalists in the entire west coast."

"You may thank him on my behalf," said Mohan rather mockingly, "for all the exaltation he showered upon my name, but that's not to say, that, it will ever change my opinion about him. Anyway, you were saying something about peeking into their bosom...?"

Quite zestfully, I picked up the fragment of our conversation once again, "Kamalda thinks those so called happily-married housewives are not really all that happy. For whatever reasons, they have a lot of pent-up frustrations in them, and despite all that they still have to act happy at all times, and oh! did you also know that quite often it's the frustration that leads them to an extra-marital relationship?"

My eyes must have given away to a great big wonderment because at that point Mohan enacted a vigorous look of astonishment.

"No, I didn't," he answered, and seemed like he just fell from the sky or something like that, only to ridicule my wonderment. Anyway, then he said, "but thanks for sharing that with me. These days your Kamalda has been giving you some in-depth lessons on married life. Does your father know about it? Isn't it a little too premature for you to be worrying about?"

"Not really. Better early than too late as they say."

"That too is said by your Kamalda, I gather." Mohan seemed to be gradually losing his composure. "Do you know what that man is turning you into?...a parrot... yes, that's right. Have you ever wondered, what magic he might have up his sleeves that he can manage to be so desirable to all these unhappy women?"

"I don't know, and to that extent I really don't care. He was just telling me the other day, every time the Colonel is away from home she likes to entertain him to high tea".

"High tea! haa... haa... haa...!" Mohan laughed fiendishly, "and what else do they have for entertainment, while the cat... I mean, the colonel is away?"

I chuckled as I caught him almost off guard and enquired if that was a Freudian slip.

"Yes, you may call it so, but, you make me laugh, Nandini, you're so naive. That's what I like about you. There are two things that drive me crazy about you. Your naivete and your figure. Did anybody ever tell you how well shaped you are. Well, on second thought, they better not set their evil eyes on my Nandini. How about your Kamalda? Didn't he ever...?"

"Don't talk rubbish." Mohan's attitude towards the man I revere so much annoyed me terribly. "He is my father's friend. We all adore him in our family. My father often refers to him as the philanthropist and the philosopher."

"I wonder, how on earth an impoverished rather impecunious that he is could ever become a philanthropist, and speaking of philosopher, your father could be referring to the Epicurean philosophy maybe, and you know how that goes." Snapped Mohan.

Brushing aside his comment, I added, "I remember Kamalda telling me once that he finds his idol in Russell, Bertrand Russell."

"That explains it," Mohan's eyes flashed like a torch in the dark, "Russell, if I recall, was a distinguished seventh wrangler from Cambridge, but he was also a world-class lady-killer, if I may add. Anyway, why don't you write a short story about those two and call it Lady Chatterjee's Lover and I assure you, it'll be published. With your niche for characterization, if you can place them both (I mean your Kamalda and Lady Chatterjee) in the context they are best suited for, I am sure you'll be able to make your readers listen to their hearts, not just beating but pounding." Mohan then burst out into a loud, uncontrollable laughter and choking as he tried to stop it. While still laughing and choking and with tears welling up in his eyes, he staggered out words in bits and pieces as if they could not wait,

"I can't wait to tell our editorial staff about this married women's frustration business. Oh! what a laugh they'll get out of it".

I fretted and fumed helplessly as he ridiculed my idol.

"Promise me you won't do any such thing, Mohan, I'll never forgive you if you do that to Kamalda." I was on the verge of tears.

"Tell me this," by now Mohan had pretty much brought himself together. Clearing his voice, as he pulled out a neatly folded white handkerchief from his pocket, which instantly filled the air with a sweet aroma that almost made me dizzy, he looked me straight in the eye and asked me, "Tell me Nandini, has he cast a spell on you or something? I am beginning to envy him. I wish you would feel the same way about me for a change, Nandini".

That very moment, quite impetuously of course, I felt like snatching that handkerchief from his hand and holding it close to my face and then maybe just once, if I could, I would have liked to throw my arms around him and bury my face over his chest and take in deep breaths of that aroma that surrounded him, even if it made me dizzy. By now, I was much too familiar with that scent. I must have smelled it a million times. Whenever he leaned over my shoulder to edit one of my writings, I would stealthily and fervently take in deep breaths and fill my breast with his sweet aroma. Only if he knew how much I yearned for him. But then, I also knew how to hide my feelings and desires like any other Indian unmarried woman.

I suppose I loved him a lot, but yet not enough to turn around and give up this once-in-a-life-time opportunity. As my father always said, "Nandini, mark my words, an opportunity like this comes knocking at your door only once. If you're wise enough to avail it, you are sure to make a go of it; if not you are lost in the crowd and then you are there only to rot amidst mediocrity for the rest of your life." Whenever the question of going abroad came up, he would stop me from whatever I would be doing at the time, look me straight in the eye as if trying to locate my mind, and then slowly but firmly imprint it with his grand oracle. To me it was like the voice that uttered the Ten Commandments to Moses on top of Mt. Sinai or the admonishment of Lord Krishna to his favorite disciple, Arjuna, at the battle of Kurukshetra, illustrated in the Gita.

"Its too late now, Mohan," I said.
"Too late! How easy it is for you to say. I never expected you to be that cold, Nandini".
"Cold!" I could not help raising my voice at this point, "God alone knows how much I wanted you to see the woman in me. The more I found you unapproachable, the more I was drawn towards you, while you were too preoccupied playing your part."
"And what part is that, may I know?" Mohan inadvertently opened a floodgate.

"I'll tell you, your part. You're always either criticizing my style of writing or...or...calling me long distance from wherever you are just to make sure that I cover this or that press conference." Then mimicking his voice: "Nandini, make sure you investigate thoroughly before you turn in your story at the desk," or "Nandini, do you think you can meet the 3 a.m. deadline?' That's all you cared about me as far as I am concerned. Did you ever stop to think that besides all those stale news items of yours, those cold headlines and stiff deadlines, there's a young woman in me who wants to be a part of you, and not your stupid, dull newspaper?" There, I said it all, unabashed, much to my own astonishment. Everything I ever wanted him to know. Didn't take me long to pour my heart out to him, did it?

Mohan was awestruck. "Nandini, I'm sorry you feel that way about me and my paper, but we are a part of one another, you see; I just can't help being that way."

Bewildered by this new and strange revelation, I raised that illustrious question to him, "so, who are you really?"

"Humm... now, that's quite a fundamental question. For that matter who are we all, really? Rishi, munis of bygone days have meditated for hundreds of years in search of an answer to this eternal question, but, I can simply tell you this," Mohan fixed his gaze at me with his index finger like a pointer pointing at me, "who are we?"

Little knowing that those three words would invoke a response so voluminous in both depth and scope, I waited for an answer.

"To put it in a strictly social sense," Mohan continued, "we are nothing but a gamut of roles that we play simultaneously, perhaps some well and some not so well, which again is subject to how one perceives a certain role, which further adds to the complexities of the many paradoxes in our human character." He spoke like a grand orator, adding more enigma to his speech in the process of unraveling it, as I listened to him, "now, if I may quickly point out to you one of the paradoxes in humanity that intrigues me most is that, on the one hand, we humans are gifted with such stupendous intellect that almost raises us to the stature of invincibility, like the mighty gods, whereas, on the other hand, we are just as fragile and vulnerable as an ant or an earthworm that can be crushed to dust in no time. Now, doesn't that fascinate you? But, to answer your question, philosophically that is, we are each a great piece of a grand infinite puzzle that this universe is." Mohan paused.

"Yes, as I perceive this very moment, you certainly and most faithfully do contribute to that puzzle," I said.

"And so do you, mademoiselle, you can be so naive at times and yet so witty other times. You puzzle me, infinitely." Taking a great deal of delight from the thought that he had finally put me in my place, Mohan burst out laughing and then quite abruptly held back his laugh, looked me in the eye and continued, "but at this point in time, I'm only interested in playing the role of your suitor and pledge nothing less than to do absolute justice to it, besides," Mohan's voice changed dramatically, "why do you think I keep telling you not to socialize with those male reporters?"

"Oh! Now you tell me why! All this time you told me," I responded mimicking his voice once again, 'watch out for those rascals, Nandini, or else they'll sneak up on you and steal your lead'."

"Yes, that too, besides, why do you think I always wanted you to join me at those international film festivals, those art exhibitions?"

"Because you wanted me to learn how to be a good critique."

"Don't you get it, that was my way of asking you out. How else do you think I could have you at those social galas?"

"Some strange way of saying things. Only if you had said these words a few months ago; why, even a few weeks ago before my passport was ready."

"Passport! Is that all you care ? Is it really all that important to you, tell me Nandini?"

"No, it's the commitment. I am committed to my family. I am committed to myself. You waited a little too long, Mohan".

"Yes, I see that, and I guess you are bent on making me pay for it for the rest of my life, aren't you?"

"I don't know what to say, Mohan. I just don't know. But I know you'll wait for me, won't you?"

"I've already told you about my feelings on that."

"Well! you'll at least write to me, won't you? I'll wait for the postman every day."

"Oh, how very romantic!" Mohan was always quick to spot the humour in any given situation. To him nothing was serious enough that he could not have a laugh over it, so he carried on, "I wish I could be that postman. I could at least see you every day," and on he went with his silliness, "see, what you have done to me! Now, you make me envy the postman!" But, I suppose there are times after all when one could only laugh so much. I noticed Mohan, suddenly turning his face away from me and then looking up at the sky with a heavy sigh, as if caught in one of those rare struggles between love and his wounded pride. If I recall, that was the only time I ever felt a true sense of solemnity in his company.

The rain clouds, like a herd of fleecy lamb, were slowly gathering in the horizon. Whips of lightning slashed across the sky. Soon, we knew the gentle quiet evening would be torn asunder by a storm. If we did not hurry home, we knew we would be drenched by a heavy downpour of the monsoon, but we could not care less. I felt rain drops on my warm neck, and then I saw a drop or two on Mohan's cheeks, and then another one on my lip, but it did not matter to us any more. Nothing could steal the crescendo of our passion now. Mohan had held me so tightly in his arms that it almost took my breath away. I must have been trembling like the frightened little fawn I just saw a while ago.

"Are you afraid of me?" Mohan whispered into my ears.

"No." I lied.

"Then, why are you shaking like a scared little bunny? You know I won't do anything that will bring shame upon you. I just want

A WOUNDED TIGRESS

to keep loving you. Won't you let me, please?" His steaming breath all over me, around my neck, behind my ears, on my forehead and everywhere as he kissed me all over, I felt I was burning up with fever. I could not keep my eyes open for my head was spinning like a top. Even in my wildest imagination, I could not think that there could be such a tender, passionate lover in Mohan. I wanted him to keep loving me forever and ever. I had my face buried over his chest. Every atom of me was begging to be a part of him. It felt like a brief but a powerful dream that left its lasting impression long after one is awake. That afternoon was the most spellbinding moment of our lives together. Neither of us wanted to part. "Nandini, I only wish I could hold this moment in my palm and never let it go, so I wouldn't lose you," he whispered again. I wanted to really ask him what kept him from loving me all this time. What magic does he have that drives me so wildly in love with him. Instead, I simply said, "it must be our fate that is drawing us apart, Mohan."

Yes, it must be some invisible power that dictates our course of action in our life or else why was there a part of me so dazzled by the glamour of a foreign degree. Like myriads of other ordinary Indian girls, I could have compromised too. Quite typically, I could have sought my future in my marriage. In lieu of that, I left behind someone who could have been the father of my children and flew across the Atlantic, to the Dawson of my dream, for a career that had meant so much to me at the time. While I was away from home, I must have revisited in my reverie that one stormy, rainy afternoon with Mohan beside me by the bank of Shivangini a million times over. How could I ever dispel him from my thoughts, though at times I could not help remembering him with poignancy. He was the love of my life that I had quietly treasured in my heart all through my young adulthood.

Then, of course, there was Kamalda, my idol forever. The two intellectual stalwarts had entered into my life at an age when one is highly impressionable and then their quiet exit left a void in me forever. I cannot fault them today, for leaving me with such a brief encounter, for they have left me with tender, sweet, ever-lasting memories. Kamalda was the one who got me into journalism. I remember one afternoon he came over to our house for tea and asked me if I had written anything lately. I was a little hesitant at first. The last thing I would ever want anyone to do is to ridicule my writing, especially a man of his stature. My father took one look at me and said, "don't you worry, Nandini, Kamal won't make fun of your writing. Instead, he might be able to help you improve. What do you say, Kamal? You won't laugh at my daughter's writing, will you?"

"Laugh!" he exclaimed, "to the contrary I might learn something." I knew he was being too modest, yet, his approach was so genuinely inviting that it suddenly sparked all my enthusiasm for his scrutiny. He quickly glanced through the pages and looked me straight in the eye and asked, "you have not seen twenty summers yet, how do you know what it is like to be old?"

"It's only as good as my imagination, I suppose, sir." I stammered.

"I suppose so", he nodded and posed another question, "tell me, have you read Plato's Republic?"

"No", I said.

"Strange as it may seem," Kamalda continued, "your whole idea of the poem, YOUTH IN MEMOIR closely resembles the essence of Sophocles's reply to the question in Plato's Republic: 'how does love suit with age?' Do you know what the aged poet answered?" Kamalda looked at me. Being embarrassed at my own ignorance, I could scarcely nod my head, when Kamalda, much to my relief decided to answer his own question.

"The aged poet answered: 'I feel as if I had escaped from a mad and furious master.' Having said that, he let out a deep puff from his pipe and then as if thinking aloud he looked at my father and mumbled, "must be purely coincidental".

Then, he asked me if he could take the poem with him. I was a little nervous at first. I didn't know what to say. So I told him that that was my only copy. Before he left our house that evening he assured me that I would get my copy back. A week later a peon arrived at our door and handed me a copy of the English Daily with a little handwritten note saying: 'Congratulation! Nandini, you are now a published writer. The editor would like to see you sometime. Try and make an appointment with him as soon as you can. Don't miss this golden opportunity. Kamalda.'

From that moment on, my life whirled with creativity and romance. I had just stepped into a new era, fraught with an insatiable appetite for the finer things in life. As a young reporter my heart steamed with aspiration. It was also quite invigorating to make new acquaintances and to have the opportunity of meeting some of the highly acclaimed virtuosos and maestros of the nation. That was when I first met Mohan. We were both attending a press conference. The host from the Ministry of Information and Broadcasting tried to make an impression on the press by flaunting their mission and their marvellous accomplishment of uplifting the bucolic mass and the evils of illiteracy in the villages across the country through the advent of television, while Mohan was bent on the arduous task of making an impression on me. Much later, once on our way to an art exhibition, I took the liberty of asking him why he was so keen on getting my attention that day.

"What day?" Mohan looked at me with a pretentious blank on his face.

"The day we first met at that press conference." And then I gave him one of those 'don't pretend' looks.

"Oh, that day!" He paused and then his face lit up in a moment, "I suppose, it's because I didn't have any choice that day. You were the only one in sari, the rest were all in pants."

I could see a naughty smile lurking behind that wit. Those days journalism was very much male dominant, even in big cities, like the one where I grew up. It did not take me long to find out why

I was so attracted to Mohan. Besides being tall, fair and charming, he was also extremely witty and well read.

Kamalda, short, dark, gaunt, his hair unkempt and shabbily attired was just as witty as Mohan. Of course, Kamalda's wit was quite often at his own expense. His ability to laugh at himself always landed him above reproach and won him great admiration. I must admit it had its own appeal altogether. He was outlandishly unpretentious, which much too often raised many eyebrows. As a true man of letter, he was also notoriously nonconformist. One autumn afternoon Kamalda asked me to accompany him to a funeral. According to Hindu tradition, a woman is seldom expected at a funeral ground. I asked him, "are you sure you want me there?"

"Yes, why not?" he said, as he plunged into a soliloquy, "it humbles your soul. For a while it also elevates your mind to a higher plateau from where everything beneath seems disgustingly petty and sham. Our life suddenly appears hollow and evanescent like a bubble. It opens your eyes to that what is inevitable, the grand finale of life. That one experience that you do not live through which makes it so unique. I think everybody should have that transcendental experience once in a while."

It was Kamalda who accompanied me to an evening of masterpiece theater — Macbeth. Another time he invited me to Sophocles's King Oedipus, and then on our way back lectured on Sigmund Freud and Oedipus complex. He was devastated when he found out that I had not read Freud, Darwin's Theory of Evolution, Marx's Das Kapital, Plato's Republic, or Aristotle's The Politics.

"But I have read some others like Chaucer, Milton, Shaw, Ibsen, Shakespeare, Tagore and also Pushkin, Dostoyevsky, Chekhov, Gorky, Tolstoy."

Thus, I hastily ran a list of authors I had read until I was almost out of breath. It hurt me to see him disappointed in me.

"Go on," he said, "why did you stop?"

Then having glanced at the empty look on my face, he continued, "but you have not read Freud, Darwin, Marx, Plato or Aristotle!" His brows furrowed, "how could you be so oblivious to these great avant garde and yet consider yourself a writer? You have not done your homework yet, my girl." At that point I felt a dire need to defend myself, so I said, "but what if I have the zeal and the originality as a writer, do I still need to steal their intellect to fill my pages?"

"It's like this, my dear girl," Kamalda began, "take for instance a human child with all its potential, who's brought up in the jungle. It'll be grossly incapacitated to speak our language, or behave like a human for that matter. Similarly, as a writer you need to first grow up in the right environs and have all the exposures you can get, even with all your originality and zeal."

Since then I have read them all and many times over. Of course, after having gone through all of the ones from his list of 'must read' books, I could not wait to report to him, so I could alter his opinion of me. Now that I had already taken the first few steps of a child, that once dared to march into the world of literates before learning to crawl, I could now face up to him without feeling small. It is ingrained in us from our early childhood and especially so among the educated middle class that academic excellence and accomplishments is the single most desirable quality one should strive for during their formative years, and those that fall behind in that race are looked down upon with pity. For that matter Kamalda was just as guilty as my father, Mohan and myself included in our prejudice against mediocrity. Both father and Kamalda have always been exceptionally pedantic and thought highly of any one who put discipline above all else in their lives. Father would go so far as to claim that even a genius may live disastrously if he lived without any sense of discipline. From early on, father took great care in instilling certain habits in me. He had schooled me to always read about the author before reading their works and having done that, he

could never emphasize enough how good of an idea it is to collect all our thoughts together and pen them down after reading
each book. To never put down the newspaper until I had read
the editorial, and to always rise before the sun for those are the
most vital hours when one can contemplate in peace and quiet as
our brain is most receptive then. "Gaining knowledge is more
like meditating," a phrase, father hammered down on me so frequently that it got to a point when I could almost see it coming
long before he actually vocalized it. Sometimes, he would go on
to say, "the human mind is never vacant. Now, if you can picture
a railway platform in a big city, our mind is even busier than the
busiest railway platform you can imagine, where passenger
thoughts keep rushing in and out, but, instead, our mind should
be like the engine driver whose only goal is to engine that vehicle
to its destination." But that was not the end of it, having said
that, he would now move on to the next step, "now, once you are
able to focus on something, then," clearing his voice father
would now come up with yet another analogy, "like a honeybee
you must learn to draw out the crux of the matter. As you know,
the word 'education' is derived from the Latin word 'educere'
which means to draw out, so, as I was saying, when you have
your heart set on something, whether it is reading, writing or say
for example, if you were to work on some mathematical formula
that will give us the exact age of our universe or its rate of expan-
sion, or composing a piece of music or painting, however great
or puny your task is, always consider meditating on it, and mark
my word you will accomplish." At the time, I was convinced that
it was one of his obsessions to ground me through his ancient
method of disciplining the mind through meditation to attain
higher and finer objectives in life, but, on hind sight, I can see
how invaluable a lesson it was.

I was one of Kamalda's chosen few who had access to his personal library. Quite often, when he would be lost in his own world,
much like my father, working on some research for his writing, I

would be stealthily browsing through his books stacked up close-ly rather crowdedly on the shelves.

"What are you looking for?" Kamalda asked me as he took a sip off his coffee and then let out a puff from his pipe.

"Homer's biography", I replied.

"I don't believe there's one". Kamalda seemed totally unaffected by its absence or the vacuum created thereby to the world of the intellects. But I was devastated.

"What? One of the greatest authors of all time and there isn't a single biography of him!" I exclaimed.

"That's right. Haven't you heard of the 'Homeric Question'? There's very little we know about Homer. All we know is that he was a trained bard and that he became blind in his later life. At least that's what I know, but then again what do I know, I could be wrong."

"No, you can never be wrong," I murmured to myself.

That afternoon Kamalda was engrossed in translating Tagore's Bengali poem 'Aamee' meaning 'I'. The poem, based on the dogma of 'Advaita' philosophy — the philosophy of 'cosmic monism' which immensely pleased Tagore's intellectual/philo-sophical palate. As Kamalda recited aloud the poetry, the air in the room began to echo impressively, and then he suddenly paused.

"Why did you stop?" The sudden break from the poetic spell caused me to pull from my train of thoughts.

"You recite Tagore's poems much better than any of us in town." Replied Kamalda, adding, "I couldn't help overhearing those boys... that evening after your recitation."

"What boys?" Ravaged with curiosity, I looked at Kamalda.

"Those boys at the club who were showering you with compli-ments at Tagore's birth anniversary function."

Compliments did not embarrass me anymore like it used to at the beginning. "Thank you," I said, "and could you please read the translation now?" I could not leave until he read the translation to me. Kamalda cast his eyes on his unfinished translation while I waited for him to read.

Aamee (I)
The colour of my inner consciousness
> manifested the green in jade,
> > the red in ruby.
> > I looked up to the sky —
> and it lit up
> > the east and the west.
> I looked at a rose and said, 'beautiful' —
> and so did beauty manifest.

> You might say these are divine theories,
> > not the words of a poet.
> > I will say it is the truth
> > and therefore it is poetry.

Kamalda paused for a moment, threw a long, lost gaze at the space, far beyond our immediate surroundings, and then as if merely thinking aloud, he posed a question, "doesn't this remind you of Descartes' famous phrase? — 'I think, therefore I am'." Then, as if, waking up from a reverie, he continued, "anyway, this is only the beginning, it gets very intriguing when it delves much deeper into the cosmic monism and the incorporeal and the amorphous aspect of the Brahma of the Vedanta Philosophy." Kamalda continued, "the poet visions our moon as an aged one with a cruel and cunning smile, as a messenger of death creeping towards the very rib of our earth until one day with its fatal attraction, the oceans and the mountains will rupture, all ending in a vast void with the entire human history blotted by the ink of an infintie night." Kamalda's face suddenly radiated with a blissful smile as if he was reminded of something more beautiful, "interestingly enough, if you notice, there's another dimension to this poem," he said, "which is based purely on the science of cosmology." After a quick pause Kamalda resumes his analysis, "through out the latter half of the poem, the poet describes a scenario based on the cosmological speculation of 'The Big Crunch'. Here, the poet envisions a gravitational imbalance which will eventually turn this orderly Universe into a chaotic one. He foresees it with a clearly scientific vision of the Universe, at the very collapse of time and space, when it is left to vibrate with an astronomical energy in its nucleus. But, from an anthropomorphic stand point, the poet imagines the Creator of the Universe — Brahma, sitting at the centre of it, at first bemoaning the loss of music, poetry, humanity, beauty and love; until he gets to the very last stanza of the poem, where he imagines Brahma at the wake of The Big Crunch meditating for eons together, so that once again through Maya the Universe may evolve manifesting love and beauty." Much like my father, Kamalda always fascinated me with his critical appreciation of Tagore. Had it not been for all the philosophical discourses on eastern philosophy father and I used to engage in, to which mother and my sister always listened with great intent, I would not have been able to appreciate Kamalda's translation and much less Tagore.

When I left my homeland in pursuit of a career in journalism, I had not the iota of a notion, what awaited me in that great land of 'milk and honey' so to speak. I had plunged into the unknown with a hundred dollars in my purse and a will of iron in my heart. Soon, I realized, the aspiring journalist in me was losing heart and fading away from my life. The question of survival took precedence and everything else seemed like an undue indulgence or a whim I could least afford. I ended up slogging in an assembly line in a factory called Mohawk Spring Company in the suburb of Chicago. The supervisor of the department, a middle-aged, bald headed, potbellied, beer guzzler would always instruct me in broken English, leaving me to wonder as to why he could not speak his own tongue correctly. Until later, much to my own amusement, I discovered that he had presumed I would not follow anything beyond 'hello'; 'good morning'; 'sorry'; 'thank you' and 'please' in English like the rest of my colleagues. At the time, the major portion of every factory in Skokie, a suburb of Chicago, where I worked, was peopled by a huge influx from the third world. A few weeks later, when he found out from one of my colleagues that I happen to be a university student, he courteously invited me to his cabin one morning, and as he handed me my last pay check, he pointed at my fingers and said that they were too feeble for the assembly line. I should look for a job at the university campus.

Weeks later, here I am working for a halfway house on North Winthrop Avenue in Chicago. A seven-storied brick building, a home away from home for the mentally ill. As the lady supervisor hopped from one floor to the next in an old rackety elevator, showing me around, introducing me to the various inmates, and familiarizing me with their idiosyncrasies to say the least, my mind kept fleeting back to
Dr. Ranna, the psychologist, whom I had interviewed before leaving the country. I was appointed as their social companion and helped them take their meals and medication, and the rest of the time simply keep them company. They were a bunch of harmless, affectionate and interesting people. Interesting, of course, from my point of view. I soon found out how extraordinarily intelligent some of them were. A few of them very well-read and one of them amazed me to no end when I realized how well-versed she was in Hindu philosophy and religion. Her name was Ms. Roberta Bogan. Roberta would always initiate a discourse on the subject of Hindu philosophy whenever we ran into each other and strangely enough, interrupt our conversation now and again to remind me that her husband, bent on killing her, shadowed her constantly. As I got to know her, I began to see Roberta's brain as a great storage of information that intermittently swayed like a see-saw between reality and fantasy. Dr. Ranna would probably call her schizophrenic with her enigmatic

scrambling of thoughts and garbled language. But she definitely reminded me of one of Shakespeare's lines which goes something like — 'Poets, lovers and lunatics are of imagination all compact'. Fleetwood as it was called could be the haven for any ambitious psychologist and very definitely the dream laboratory for Dr. Ranna.

My chapter on Fleetwood would remain incomplete without the mention of my hilarious discovery of a new alphabet in the English dictionary. One afternoon as I was busily taking the roll call of the inmates, (a part of my daily chore) I stumbled over a certain name and so I asked one of them to spell it for me since I could not decipher the hand written word. One of them volunteered to do so, but no sooner had she uttered the first letter of the name, I discarded it right away, assuming it to be the babbling of an insane who got her alphabets mixed up. But as she became more and more emphatic about the existence of such an alphabet, quite embarrassingly, I began to wonder as to how could I have lived to be this old without knowing all the alphabets in the English language. More so, since I have used the language so frequently and quite unpremeditatively as my only tool of expression. I asked her to write it in bold letter and no sooner had she done that, I burst out, "oh! you mean zed".

"Well, we call it zee," she said.

Oh! what a relief it was to find out that we were both quarreling over the same alphabet that the Americans called it Zee and the English Zed.

Now, as my days in the university drew to an end, my first instinct was to teach English literature. One afternoon, as I was being interviewed for a teaching position in the Washington metropolitan area, Mr. Richard Peterson, the principal, asked me a question which ever since has remained unforgettable in my mind. It was a question which was not in the least out of context, to the contrary, quite legitimate. Yet, it befuddled me to no end that day. Very blatantly the principal had put it to me, "tell me, coming from a non English speaking country, how do you feel so confident teaching English to the children of an English speaking country?"

I must have looked flabbergasted for a moment. Then suddenly something became quite transparent to me.

"Strange, you should ask me that, sir." I blurted out spontaneously, "quite pertinently, of course, you have questioned my ability from a perspective I was totally oblivious to. Somehow, I have never considered myself an alien to the English language. Perhaps, it was my upbringing." Then, on a lighter mood, I added, "if dreams could be dreamt in a language of our choice, I would probably choose English for most of them".

The Principal chuckled merrily and then he added as he nodded his head, "must be one of the legacies of the British Raj."

After that it was only a matter of minutes in which he quickly scanned through my credentials, and then with a gentle smile and a firm handshake, the principle requested me to focus on the writing skills of the students.

This is one skill where you come across pupils who either love it or hate it; in either case they do it with passion. There is no room for indifference. As luck would have it, all my students belonged to the latter category except one, who from the very beginning always seemed highly keen to master the art. That pleased me immensely. I started taking great pain in teaching him the basics of the skill and found a lot of delight in his zeal until a few months later, when I discovered that his interest lay more in me than my subject. I would be lying if I say I was utterly dismayed. In all truth and candor, I felt quite flattered though I knew such feelings in a youth are like vernal showers, sweet and brief. Not too long ago, I had the taste of one such sweet fantasy myself. In graduate program, when we were studying Shakespeare's tragedies, oh! how I yearned to be his Desdemona, when young and charming Dr. Munshi, our English professor improvised Othello in the class room. Sweet were those reveries that carried my heart away and placed it elsewhere, where it pined to dwell, though it was all for a moment. Anyway, it was an arduous task I took upon myself to convince David that he should pay no heed to such distraction and get on with his studies more seriously. Instead, he paid no heed to my admonishment and continued to enjoy his new found role of a cupid in the class-room which was of course short-lived.

One morning, the principal briskly walked into my classroom and requested me to see him in his office instantly. "It's about David" he murmured as he offered me a seat across from his desk. With one quick glance at his grim visage, I thought I knew what it was all about. As I staggered to offer him an explanation, I noticed at first he looked a little puzzled and then quite abruptly he put it to me, "I don't know what you are about to explain but I am sorry to say, David died in an automobile accident on his way home last night". A couple of hours later I found myself lying down on a bed, a nurse leaning over me, her eyes twinkling with a smile. "How do you feel now?" she asked. "Why, what happened to me?" I asked her back. "You had fainted. The shock was too great for you, I suppose. David was a sweet kid. We all loved him." The nurse continued with her kind eulogy for David as she helped me gently out of the bed.

As time went by, I began to meet people from various walks of life and interestingly enough, I found a great majority of them quite intrigued by the eastern culture and its philosophy. Their curiosity certainly got my attention. Pretty soon, I found myself lecturing on the various aspects of the Indian culture, including the school where I taught. One afternoon, the social studies teacher, Mrs. Ilene Parker invited me to speak to her class about India and I gladly agreed. How else could I illumine those young minds, I thought to myself, if I did not address the forum. It was scheduled to be an hour long affair, of which the last quarter, I was to address questions from the students.

Curiously enough, the situation reversed soon after I got on the platform. I had barely spoken for fifteen minutes when one of the students, I suppose, could no longer hold it to herself, so she blurted out that ubiquitous question that the entire western world craves to know, "that red dot you women wear on your forehead, is that a birthmark or some kine of a paint, what's it really and why d'yoal wear it, is that some kine of a voodoo thing?"

Of course, Ilene had warned me in advance, that should the students expose their ignorance regarding my culture, it must not embarrass, offend or even alarm me. I thought nothing of it at the time. Embarrassed! Offended!! Of course, not. But, alarmed! yes, when I realized the depth of their ignorance. But, it was not the "red dot" question that alarmed me so much as it was the gamut of questions that followed soon after which hit me like a shower of hail-stones on my head, "d'yoal have regular houses and roads like we do or are them all mud houses and dirt roads in your country? No offence, you know, juss curious." And then another one, "how d'yoal prottec yoaself from snakes that hang from trees on the roadside?" And then another, "you know how every now and again we see on TV about all the poverty and everything in your country and I wonder how come yoal don't eat beef, them cows could provide good meat, you know, what I mean?" And another one, "my great grandmother was half Indian, Cherokee, I believe, so, I was wonderin, if that would make us kin?"

In the face of such a blatant dispaly of ignorance, I could not help feeling sorry for the younger generations of this country that remained so embarrassingly ill exposed of the world outside their own. I began to ask questions at the teacher's lounge during lunch break until I found out that one of the reasons being that geography was never offered to the students as mandatory in school. So, I suppose for the lack of real knowledge in the classroom, they remained complacent with bits and pieces of stray information that they could gather on their own from the television — a poor substitute for all the future generations, I thought to myself, what a pity!

Anyway, fortunately enough, that day before I could even open my mouth, (for I do not know to this day where and how I would have even begun to say anything) Arlene promptly came to my rescue. I was relatively new in the States and perhaps therefore my sensitivity towards my country and my culture was still quite intact. Arlene must have quickly sensed it from the sudden rush of colour on my face. She asked for my permission and took over the forum. Neither of us were prepared to receive such questions, but certainly Arlene could be more objective than I ever could. Arlene was considered as one of their own with one big advantage which prompted her to steal the show. As a daughter of an American diplomat, Arlene had lived in India for a number of years and had gone back later to complete her graduate program in Archeology. She travelled quite extensively within the country visiting all the major cities as well as small towns and remote villages. With her first hand knowledge of the country, she carried on brilliantly, responding to every single question quite objectively. So, she backtracked her way starting from the last question first.

"No", she said, looking at the girl at the front row, "we don't believe there's any relation there. Your great grandmother was a native American, whereas Nandini is from India. Two different racial backgrounds from two different continents, no relationship there at all."

"Next, to answer your question about eating beef," Arlene tried to spot the boy just when a hand popped up from the back bench, "yes... you... to answer your question, let me see if I can put it in a proper perspective for you. Cows are considered holy in India and for a very simple reason. Cows milk provide the best form of nourishment for children that most papents can afford, so that's why a cow is considered next to mother and surely you wouldn't want to kill your mother. You would rather go hungry, wouldn't you?"

"Now, as far as protecting oneself from snakes hanging from the trees" Arlene paused for a brief moment and then continued, "I suppose, quite unfortunately from watching certain type of movies and shows on TV, you all have the notion that all of India is one big jungle with snakes hanging from the trees and wild cats roaming around freely and crocodiles swimming in the rivers — far from it. Let me point this out to you first before I go any further, that today we are learning about a country that represents one of the oldest civilizations in the world. India learned to build roads, houses, temples, bath houses, in fact, large towns and cities were built millennia ago, when people in Europe still lived in caves. If you visit any big city in India, and by the way, there are several of those, there are some areas where you'll find lovely bungalows with luscious gardens, beautiful sea beaches and tall sky scrapers and let see... what else... oh! yes, luxurious hotels and large monuments and bridges and of course marvelous palaces and temples that go back thousands of years."

At this point I felt a dire need to share with them a personal experience, so, I excused myself for interrupting and went forth like this, "if you can believe this, I grew up in a city and have been to many of them, but I have yet to see a snake hanging from a tree or any wild animal for that matter anywhere except in the zoo and I'm sure Ms. Parker will attest to that. Needless to say, Ilene unequivocally agreed to it. Last, but not the least, we went back to our first and the ever popular question about the 'red dot', a conspicuous little red dot on the middle of your forehead that can evoke so much curiosity among so many and quite justifiably so.

"Now about the red dot, generally, it comes in the form of either powder or liquid but these days they are made out of plastic which the women ware along with rest of their make up," said Ilene and continued, "now, as far as its significance, traditionally speaking, it indicates that the woman is married."

There I interrupted again and said, "and if I may add to that on a much philosophical level, the red dot symbolises that point where all dualities in life meet, and marriage being one such, where two people not only bodily but also spiritually unite, therefore the red dot signifies its point of unity." Then on a lighter mood, I continued, "in a way it rubber stamps our marital status. Now, if you ask me, what about men? all I can say is, I guess, they prefer to keep it quiet and rather not be reminded of it."

The whole class laughed.

In the meanwhile, I had written several letters to Kamalda filling in with all the details of my personal observation and experience of the people and the places in the new world. I told him how much I enjoyed talking to the Americans, especially with the men. "Their sense of humour is almost ubiquitous," I wrote, "whether he is your dentist or your professor, a fellow passenger, your next door neighbour or your boss, it doesn't matter whether you have met them before or not, or what their social standing might be, they have no qualms about coming up to you and starting a conversation and pretty soon you find yourself rolling with laughter. They have the art of making you feel right at home from the very instant you meet them, which is certainly not the way with Indian men. Now that I have had the opportunity to enjoy the care free, jovial spirit of the Americans, I can see how very pretentious and all too status-conscious our men are by comparison, not to mention the chief executive of the corporate world back home commonly known as bosses, of whom the kindest and the gentlest ones carry themselves around like, 'I am the monarch of all I survey'. On second thought, I wonder if it is due to a lack of self-confidence or a sense of insecurity or is it because they have never been treated kindly themselves as subordinates that makes them all ware that same ugly mask. I guess, I'll never know. But, I only wish they had learned to smile more often, lighten up their disposition, and treat their subordinates with some dignity. That would certainly boost the morale of the people and make the corporate world a bit more humane." As I was candidly putting my thoughts down, I was trying to imagine how Kamalda would react to it. He would have probably said, Oh! come off it, Nandini. I hope you're not throwing that at me, because I'm sure, if you took a survey from all my employees, asking them to describe me with one keyword that starts with any of the letters in the English alphabet, say for instance the letter 'A' or 'F', in both instances, they would have to waiver the very first word that would flash into their mind and quite prudently settle for the second bests that would guarantee them their bread and butter and the words would have to be either 'Admirable' or 'Flawless'. That's our Kamalda.

One other thing I had mentioned in my letter was my saga with David, the cupid in my classroom. I had begged him time and time after to write to me but never heard from him, no, not even once. I felt ignored and hurt until last night when I found out that he had left this world soon after I left for the States. "Why didn't anybody ever tell me that and all these years I kept writing to him and begging him to write to me." I screamed with anger and sorrow and guilt. I felt deceived. I did not know whether I should be angry at my parents for not letting me know or at Kamalda for leaving us like this or maybe at myself for not being there when he was in need. I know I could not have given him his life but at least I could have said goodbye and watch him leave.

"We didn't quite know how to put it to you so we thought we would rather wait till you came home, so that we could be there to comfort you. Soon after you left for the States, he was diagnosed with cancer in the throat." I could feel the remorse in my father's voice.

"He didn't live to see that summer. Your mother and I both know how much you adored him. As you know, I myself had a lot of regard for him, though there were a lot of scandalous tales about him that hovered around in certain circles. But as you also know, I never had the taste nor time for such idle gossips." My father continued. I felt a tremor in his voice that he could not quite control.

"He died in utter poverty. Towards the end, right before he was hospitalized, he lived only on coffee. He drank several cups of coffee a day and you know how much he smoked. But no food. He had no money left in his pocket to buy himself a decent meal. Can you imagine a person of his stature, who was once so highly revered by the elite class of our society for his enormous wealth of intellect and learning should have to end his life like this in dire starvation. Had it not been for a few of his friends, especially Chakraborty, you remember Chakraborty, don't you?"

"Yes, I remember him very well. I used to look up to him as my big brother," I said.

"Had it not been for him our Kamal would have died like a dog."

"Don't say that." My mother choked with emotion.

"That's true," I sensed anger in my father's voice, "unfortunately I found out about him when it was a little too late. When I went to see him he was breathing his last. He was surrounded with heaps and piles of books, magazines and newspapers. The nurse who attended him made a very interesting comment about him. She said that she had never seen a cancer patient in his last days who could single-handedly convert a hospital room into a library."

"What happened to his personal library?" I inquired.

"It's been donated to the M.G. Library. It was his last wish."

Instantly, a name flashed across my mind. M. Patel, the chief librarian of M.G. Library, the oldest and the largest library in the State. Kamalda used to take pride in mentioning his name to me.

M. Patel was one of the very few surviving students of the poet laureate Rabindranath Tagore. Once Kamalda asked me to interview him for a Bengali magazine published in Calcutta which I faithfully did. I recall Kamalda briefing me on my way to the interview.

"Ask him about his student life in Shanti Niketan... his recollections of his Guru... make that your angle and get as much out of him as possible. He's quite an introvert which again is typical of most intellectuals, you know."

I suppose that goes for our Kamalda too. A lingering silence followed. Drowned in sorrow, I spent the rest of the night reading Plato's THE LAST DAYS OF SOCRATES. The only way I could pay my homage to my Guru.

Today, as I leisurely stroll through the country road, I see a shepherd boy sitting atop a hillock playing away a folklore on his bamboo flute. I have heard this tune before, a long time ago. I feel an aura of profound and unperturbed bliss. It is as peaceful as a lullaby. Somewhere, hidden amidst leafy trees, I hear a mourning dove dolefully yearning for a mate. There is something about its call that has always fascinated me. It seems to ooze with melancholy — a melancholy that has been evoked by a thousand years of loneliness. I often wonder if there is a mourning dove in all of us!

Today, as the thought of Mohan keeps coming back, it makes me feel as if it is trying to open a window to a dark room that has been locked for many years. After I left for the States, I imagine he became lonesome and that is when he took to heavy drinking. It was just last Saturday, the day after I landed at Santa Cruz Airport in Bombay when I accidentally ran into Kamini, the Chief Reporter, Mr. Rao's mistress at Juhu. I was thrilled to see her at first, for I wanted to ask her all about Mohan. I couldn't wait to see him. I had not heard from him for a while. His most recent letter had a somber tone to it. He wrote Nandini: "I am delighted to know that you are coming home, though I can't promise to greet you with a handful of rajani gandha, the flower you poetically referred to in one of your earlier letters as one whose fragrance inspires you to unrequiting love. I am afraid these days the flowers in my garden are withering away before they have even had their chance to bloom. I don't somehow find the will or the energy to nurture them as I used to once. Yet, you must know, I'll always wait for you, if not in the best of health, at least in spirit."

He did not wait for me. That made me angry, very angry. He was careless with my affection for him. "How did it happen?" I found myself gasping for breath.

"You know how much he drank!" Kamini uttered those words in a matter of fact tone.

"Yes", I murmured. But I still could not stomach the notion of him dying like everyone else. In the realm of my imaginative mind he was too grand an entity to ever perish, ever. How could I have painted such an invincible portrait of him and not be in the least aware of it! I seemed to find myself at the crossroads between a fantasy that was long buried in the deepest stratum of my conscious and the harsh reality. "He never got married, you know," she added.

"What happened to Mrs. Pani?"

"What about her?" She looked a little puzzled.

"You know..." I kept hoping she would be able to read my mind, after all, she is also a woman.

But before she could say a word, or even if she did, I was not listening because by then my mind had fled to one fateful day in the distant past.

It was the day before I left for the States. The amorphous monsoon clouds took the shape of huge bear like, dark and grim, that had changed the color of the sky from pale blue to a ghastly grey. A storm was fast approaching but I still had to see Mohan, just once, before I took my flight the next day. So I went to the press looking for him. I ran into his colleague and a close friend, Mr. Pani, at the elevator who told me that Mohan was on sick leave. So, I decided to drop in at his place, hoping to find him in his study. Instead, what a surprise! I see Mrs. Pani rushing out of his bedroom holding a book in her hand... Sorrows of Satan by Marie Corelli. "I just came to borrow the book", she stammered nervously as she saw me, as if the flagrant-delicto needed a caveat in her defense. "Excuse me, I should be leaving." She said, busily arranging her long black disheveled hair and then pulling the end of her mauve, silk, crumpled sari from behind her shoulder as she spoke.

"No, please stay." I looked directly at Mrs. Pani whose eyes, I noticed, could not meet mine, "I should be leaving, I had just come to say goodbye to Mohan, but I guess that wasn't necessary." I stopped her as she was about to storm through the door. Just then I heard a voice in the background.

"Nandini, please don't go. I need to talk to you."

Mrs. Pani, like a wet cat, quietly slipped away through the narrow opening of the door.

I stood there, speechless, as if struck by thunder.

"If you must know, nothing happened between us so far. Trust me. But I can't promise you that nothing will ever happen in the future, when you are thousands of miles away." Mohan's voice trembled.

"How can you do this?" I was devastated.

"Do what? She doesn't have to worry about preserving her virginity like all unmarried Indian women."

"But she's married!"

"So!! It's up to her whether she wants to remain faithful to her husband or not."

"But isn't her husband your friend?"

"Not really. He's just one of my subs that has been pestering me for a promotion."

"So, he's using his wife to get a promotion!"

"Maybe so. Anyway, what do I care. I am not in love with her or anything. Besides, why should you care any more?"

"So, is that your excuse?"

"No, but that could be my reason."

Reason! If my leaving him for a career away from home shattered his emotions so much that, that could give him a reason to indulge in an illicit relationship, remained a riddle unsolved in my mind. On hindsight, I tend to have more empathy for Mohan now, than I ever had at the time. In view of the rebound factor which quite often, although unfortunately, is an emotional process from falling out of one relationship and into another, I began to think of him more tenderly. But, what still left me disenchanted was the fact that my Mohan, in all consciousness, could justify himself in an immoral relationship — that he neither had the strength of character, nor the sense of decency to be more discreet about relationships.

That day when I left Mohan's house the storm had already swept through, leaving behind its aftermath, along with me, absolutely crumbled. That night the moon never shone in the sky. The strong monsoon wind howled like a wolf on the other side of the glass window in my attic. The weeping willows in our backyard kept me company all night, for I too had my face buried in my pillow weeping like those willows. How could he do this to me? How could he? I thought I could trust him. Maybe, I was hallucinating or was it real? Should I cancel my trip just to show him how much I care for him? I started having second thoughts. Just then, I thought I heard my father's voice rumble like a thunder, "Nandini, those who are indecisive have second thoughts and only those who are weak-minded are indecisive... not you... you're my daughter... my first born."

The next day at the airport, moments before I boarded the plane, Mohan's chauffeur handed me a sandalwood scented envelope. An hour later when I was up above the clouds flying over the Arabian Sea, my eyes slowly brimmed with tears as I opened the sweet scented envelope and began to read:

My dear Nandini:
As your heart aspires to a bright and beautiful future, you leave me behind with nothing but somber reminiscence. From the day I set my eyes on you, I could never stop loving you. Today as I retrospect, I feel I have a lot to regret for not being able to say that to you, before it was too late. Perhaps, I was a little too pre-

sumptuous about our future together. Little did I know that you had your heart set elsewhere.

About yesterday, I would like to say this much in my defense, that if you cannot judge me with any degree of fairness, then, it is best for both of us that you leave it at that, because I will not have you draw any sort of hasty and biased conclusion. What might have seemed too obvious to you could still be just a matter of perception, and for all the things I have said to you, I must apologize. Please don't take it to heart — that was my only way of getting even with you. You have left me with an open wound in my heart and there is no one I can turn to, no one, believe me.
Your everloving,
Mohan

After reading that letter that day, I felt as if a thorn had been carefully removed from my heart. Finally, a great sense of relief took over me as the pain and the anguish I have been suffering through the night slowly disappeared. For the moment, the letter meant a lot to me, like a child clutching to its pacifier, I held on to it as tightly as I could.

"Nandini... say something," as if I was having a dream, her voice woke me up with a startle. Kamini continued, "you know, since you left, a lot has happened."
"Really, like what?"
"Well!... though, one thing you must know since you left him, he never could fall in love again. He had confided in Rao a long time ago about how strongly he felt about you and how much he missed you, anyway, that's how I came to know about you both from Rao, but you know how some men can be... they'll love someone and yet fool around with someone else." Kamini looked at me in dismay.
"So, tell me, who was this someone else? Don't tell me it was Mrs. Pani." My curiosity was running rampant.

"Soon after you left India, Mr. Pani got promoted as chief sub-editor for the Delhi edition and had to move right away, leaving his wife behind with the understanding that she would follow him as soon as he could rent a flat. You know, how difficult it is to find accommodations in Delhi, just as bad it is in Bombay. So, anyway, by the time Mr. Pani rented a flat," she paused, "it was too late."

"How do you mean... too late? Don't tell me she died!" I was anxious for her to say something... anything... at all.

"I wish she had. Pardon me, if I sound mean, but sorry, that's exactly how I feel." Kamini's cheeks were turning from pale pink to blood red. She kept nodding her head and just couldn't bring herself to say anything. "Well! are you going to say something or not?" I yelled at her impatiently. I just could not take the calm before the storm anymore. "She was carrying Mohan's child!" Kamini had finally uttered the unutterable. The words exploded in my ears like a bomb.

After I had talked to Kamini that day, I wanted to spend some time alone, so I went to the bank of Shivangini where Mohan and I had spent many evenings together watching the sun sink in regal splendor, the sky blush, and Shivangini as always looked bashful with the evening glow of the setting sun. "Doesn't the river look like a bride to you at this time of the day?" Mohan's eyes would glitter in ecstasy. "Yes, just like a bride glowing with passion," I would murmur. But that day as I sat and gazed at the somber Shivangini, for the first time I realized that many waves have come and washed away the sandy shore we walked on. Yet, it could not wash away those invisible footprints that Mohan and I had left behind together a long time ago. Suddenly, I was gripped by an eerie feeling. I thought I heard Kamalda whispering in my ears: "My dear girl, your Mohan was nothing but only a froth in the river of life and so was I, your Kamalda, and so are you and everyone else. With all our aspirations, dreams and convictions, with all our love, passion, pleasure and pain, we are nothing but tiny iridescent bubbles floating in the grand scheme of our universe until one day the air from the bubble slips out and that's when we simply dissipate. So wipe those tears and go on with life. Keep up that charade with a smile as long as the bubble is round and full." I don't know how long I sat there in that pensive mood, but soon I realized, I had quite a way to walk home.

Today, on my way, as I am sauntering through the narrow winding country road, I see rustic women with their sleeping babes in the rucksack returning home after a long, hard day. Weary with the hustle and bustle of life, I too feel like the sleeping babe and want to retire to my cottage nestled at the very end of the country road, when suddenly I heard my name being uttered, the voice sounded familiar, in fact too familiar; yet, I could not believe my ears. How can that be? I said to myself, I must be hallucinating. I turned around and before I could recognize the dark silhouette, I heard my name once again, "Hello! Nandini, don't you recognize me, don't tell me you've forgotten me; I didn't forget you; I never could and never will." I tried to approach the dark silhouette but it was not there, not anymore; it disappeared and so did the voice. I turned around and kept walking forward, while my mind kept hovering over the silhouette I had seen, and the all-too familiar voice that kept ringing in my ears. The large blazing orange bubble in the horizon wobbled, as though, it knew that one day with all its grandeur, it too will dissipate.

GLOSSARY

Adab:	Salute (Urdu)
Agni:	God of Fire
Amavash:	New moon
Amijaan:	Mother (Urdu)
Apsara:	Heavenly courtesan
Attar:	Perfume
Ashram:	Hermitage
Ayurvedic:	Hindu science of medicine
Baagaan Baaree:	Garden house
Banaras:	Hindu pilgrimage
Bhishma:	The noble ancestor of Kuru family in Mahabharat
Chamcha:	Toady
Chandra:	Moon
Devi:	Goddess
Durga Pooja:	Autumnal festival of Goddess Durga
Ekadashi:	Eleventh day of full/new moon
Gajra:	Floral wreath
Ganesha:	God of prosperity
Ganga Jal:	Water of the River Ganges
Ghat:	Wharf
Ghazals:	Ode (Urdu)
Ghee:	Clarified butter
Graam Panchayat:	Village council
Indra:	King of Gods
Khajuravahaka:	Bearer of date palm
Khalajan:	Maternal aunt (Urdu)
Kurta:	Shirt

Lakshmi:	Goddess of Wealth
Mahabharat:	One of the two great epics of India. The other one is Ramayana.
Maharaja:	Emperor
Mahishasur Vadh:	Killing of the Demon Mahishasur
Mangal:	Mars
Nahabat:	Orchestra
Nang-E-Khandan:	A digrace to the family
Paan:	Betel leaf
Pooja:	Worship
Poojari:	Priest
Poonam:	Full moon
Pratima:	Idol
Raag:	Mode of classical music
Raja:	King
Raat ki Raani:	A sweet scented flower that blossoms after dusk. Its literal meaning is Queen of the Night.
Rajani Gandha:	Tube rose
Rishi:	Sage
Rubaeeyat:	Quatrain (Urdu)
Sadhu:	A pious celibate
Sanayasa:	Oath of renunciation
Shahar yaar:	Prince (Urdu)
Shaitan:	Satan
Shama-E-Bazm:	Light that adorns any gathering (Urdu)
Shanti:	Peace
Shehnai:	Bugle like instrument
Shradh:	Obsequial rites
Shiva:	God of Destruction
Soovar:	Pig
Surya:	Sun
Tabla:	Bongo like instrument
Tirthankars:	Jain saints
Varuna:	God of Water
Vishnu:	God of Preservation
Vidhata:	Destiny
Vrat:	A sacred vow
Yagna:	Vedic ritual of an offering to the fire
Yama:	God of Death
Zamindar:	A feudal landlord in British India